# Country of Old Men

# Country of Old Men

## A Novel by Paul Olsen

Holt, Rinehart

and Winston

New York   Chicago

San Francisco

Grateful acknowledgment is made to the Macmillan Co., New York, New
York, the Macmillan Co. of Canada, and Mr. W.B. Yeats for permission
to reprint part of "Sailing to Byzantium" from the *Collected Poems of
W.B. Yeats*, copyright 1928 by the Macmillan Co.; copyright © 1956
by Georgie Yeats.

First Edition

Designer: Ernst Reichl
86509-0216
Printed in the United States of America

Again, for Vivian,

Who sailed with me to Byzantium

That is no country for old men. The young
In one another's arms, birds in the trees,
—Those dying generations—at their song,
The salmon-falls, the mackerel-crowded seas,
Fish, flesh, or fowl, commend all summer long
Whatever is begotten, born, and dies.
Caught in that sensual music all neglect
Monuments of unageing intellect. . . .

*William Butler Yeats*
*"Sailing to Byzantium"*

# Part I

*Those dying generations . . .*

# One

No one in Southfield knew exactly where John Roger Williams had come from. His nasal Yankee voice, with its broad vowels and high-pitched joyless timbre, was unmistakably rooted in New England, his name even more so, and the townspeople guessed that the farthest place of his ancestry lay somewhere within the borders of Maine, though more probably Rhode Island. But no one knew for certain.

He had come to Southfield in 1933, when his son was still suckling; he had come directly down the main street driving one of the first Model-T Fords made, its top excised as if by a gigantic can opener, the jagged edges hammered into a vague roundness, only the driver's seat graced with a remnant of windshield. The other seat had for protection a trapezoidal swatch of plywood fastened to the window frame by bits of string and black friction tape. The rumble seat was slung back and contained, in no particular arrangement, two suitcases and a barrel filled with blankets, sheets, pillow slips, dishes, and several long boards—all filmed with fine travel dust.

The car itself, through swirling traceries of dust, was slashed by gangrenous rust; it lurched and skidded nervously into the circular heart of town, skirting the monument on the square, its noises echoing its queerness, its ugly shapelessness. Then it slowed at the gas station and finally halted, surrendering a thirsty, wheezing shudder. John Roger climbed out and unscrewed the gasoline cap, paying no notice to the few people who had come near, who were staring at the woman sitting motionless behind the piece of plywood. Covered with the same ochrish mist that dusted the Ford, she had bared her breast and was feeding her child; ghostly, subhuman in her chalky mantle, her head was loosely inclined as she watched the infant take the nipple and begin pulsing its lips. It gurgled, and still she watched apathetically, her own lips colorless, almost gray, clean from her licking tongue. Her eyes were black, slitted over whites; her nose thin, with a fragile bone arching from between her eyes to the fork of her nostrils.

The people stared, and soon more came; but they did not approach, were held back by the woman's isolation, the audacity of her feeding, her icy manipulation, with two fingers, of the breast in the child's mouth. Self-conscious, fascinated, they could not turn away; and John Roger they hardly noticed, until his clipped Yankee voice broke the air quietly, yet shook them like a hand placed cunningly on their pocketbooks.

"I want one gallon," he said.

The attendant, a boy, gazed awestruck at the woman, then turned away and rubbed a hand over the back of his neck.

"I want one gallon," John Roger repeated, and again repeated.

The boy removed the gasoline hose from its socket, cranked the pump handle furiously, and plunged the nozzle into the mouth of the tank, while John Roger carefully watched the whirling click of the meter. Almost immediately a man ran from the small office-shack, shouting, "You got more than a gallon rung up already." And the boy jerked the hose from the tank, sloshing a stream of gasoline from a fender to the ground.

"I won't pay for but one gallon," John Roger said.

"Didn't you see that gauge going?"

"I wasn't looking," John Roger said.

The man spat viciously at the pump, snatched the hose from the boy's hands, kicked him in the behind, then turned to John Roger, raking his fingernails across his stubbled jowls. "Can you go a gallon and seven-eighths?"

"I asked for one gallon," John Roger said, hunching his shoulders, and leaned forward a little distance from the car.

"That's true," the man said, and bent toward the evaporating puddle iridescing on the ground; the blotch on the fender, already dried, showed rivers of rust. "Must of lost a good two gallons," he said, then looked up at the woman in the last moment of feeding, the child's insatiable gums squeezing, sucking, throbbing against the swollen breast. His eyes still on her body, he asked, "You come far?"

"Yes"—screwing the gasoline cap back in place. "You might say far. How much for the gas?"

The man took his eyes from the woman. "You can't go the one and seven-eighths? 'Least meet me halfway?"

"I said no."

"Eighteen cents. One gallon."

Paying him, John Roger said, "I want to talk to you," then turning to the woman, "You stay here," as if she could, child and car, wander off somewhere carrying the whole migrant mystery securely in her arms.

She did not look up at him; she began to button her blouse.

John Roger walked slowly to the shack and entered it, the man beside him. "Is there work around here?"

"There is and there ain't." He blinked. "Times ain't exactly the best, you know."

"When there is work, where is it?"

"Mostly on the tobacco farms. You must of seen them on the

way in—covered with nets." He sat on a backless chair and scratched his face again. "Of course, they tell about a tool-and-die works going to set up in Bluefield—you must of seen that too, fifteen miles east. But I don't see as anything's going to come out of it; they just sit around and hope. Times is . . ."

"Are they hiring for the tobacco?"

"Off and on. Now ain't a bad time; picking's coming up. I was even thinking of it myself, that's why I asked if you could go the gallon and seven . . ."

"Where do I go?"

"There's a five-thirty truck stops right out in front every morning. Just get on it if you can find the room. You get there, wait on line like everybody else."

"Much obliged," John Roger said, and walked through the door.

The man called after him, "Say, you ever farmed tobacco before?"

"I guess any man can pick a leaf," John Roger answered, not looking back, not even turning his head toward his shoulder. He asked the boy, who had sulked behind the pump, "Which way is Route 12 going south?"

The boy pointed; John Roger nodded, and strode past the Ford out across the square as though pacing it off, and went into the drug store. He sat at the fountain, drank a lemon phosphate, then left a nickel and walked back to the car. And all that time the woman had been sitting under the hot morning sun, the baby quiet and bundled in a piece of blanket. The people had mostly gone away; it was only the car now that attracted anyone since the feeding. John Roger ground the engine and started off along Route 12 south.

"Four miles, according to Henry," he said to no one, and exactly four miles later he stopped the car and gazed up at the house which stood, or leaned, on a small hill sixty or seventy feet off the road. "Just like Henry left word it would be," he said, thinking: *All planked up and dirty, shingles dropping off like scabs. But Henry was right. It's here, standing, and that's something for Henry.*

Staring ahead, a hand shading his eyes, he had forgotten that Henry was dead.

He climbed the gentle incline of the hill and approached the house; as if jarred by his steps on the scalded weed-strangled earth, a rotted drainpipe teetered, broke away from the roof, and clattered against an eave.

Watching the drainpipe's progress, he said, "Maybe it ain't worth four hundred dollars."

He went up the creaking porch steps and thudded his fist against a post; it was more solid than he had expected, and he tested it again, feeling the raw grain of the wood, all color blasted out. Then he took a key from his pocket and, after straining and prying at the old demolished lock, threw open the door; sour, morbid air pushed out at him and he peered in tentatively, his nose wrinkled by a tincture of excrement. Far off something flapped and squeaked.

"Bats," he said, then stepped back and leaned over the porch rail. "All right," he called, "get on out of there. There's more work here than you ever done in your life."

Slowly the woman opened the door and swung out onto the road; even more slowly, hugging the child against her, she walked heavy-footed, reluctantly up the hill.

John Roger clapped his hands twice. "Come on. You ain't dead yet."

# 2

Only Cass Nowell, a town councilman, who had neither seen the woman nor the Ford, went out to the old house to call on John Roger. Had he watched the unconcerned feeding of the child, had he examined for himself the tin-can car, he probably would not have made the special trip on Sunday; he would simply have waited until he met John Roger by chance. Mostly because the queer nomadic family could not blithely steal a house, move into it without drawing attention, not in Southfield; and, too, because the house would appear molded to them like flesh stretched over bone, they had a landed, inherited right to it perhaps not through actual ownership as much as physical resemblance. And more, Cass had his own problems; he wanted to stay at home where they began, progressed, were about to end.

But without seeing anything at all, having only been told at the gas station of the arrival, a detail or two, he drove out on Route 12 to check the deed.

He passed the Ford as he walked up the hill, glancing at it as if it were an ironic mirage; heard the sharp reports of a hammer striking metal and wood; saw, as he climbed the porch steps, the child swaying silently to and fro in a hammock torn and knotted from old sheets. The hammock, strung at eye level between two posts, bobbed spasmodically under the kicks and thrashing of the child's legs, then calmed again.

Cass knocked, the hammering ceased, and in a moment John Roger swung open the door, sheathing the hammer in a loop of his overalls. Cass held out his hand, but John Roger shifted his eyes from it, raising them to a point somewhere at Cass's left shoulder, ignoring the hand as if he had not seen it. He said, "What is it?"

"My name is Nowell, from the town council. Part of my job is to check deeds of newcomers to Southfield. I know it's not a proper kind of welcome, but . . ."

Leaving him alone on the porch, John Roger went back inside the house and returned immediately with the deed. He held it out by one parchment corner, saying, while Cass read it, "My cousin Henry willed it to me—in writing."

"It's yours," Cass said, watching John Roger refold it with exquisite care and slip it into a pocket. "Fine," listening now to the thumping inside the house. "I hope you don't mind me disturbing you, but we don't get strangers in town very often." Adding, refusing to relinquish the point he had not had time to make, "My job is to see that everything is proper. I want you to understand that—no offense meant, it's just the custom here." He wanted to smile, to say, "Welcome to Southfield," but he looked into the long dour face and dropped his half-raised hand to his side.

"You saw the deed," John Roger said, patting his pocket. "I guess that's enough said about it."

"Yes." Cass listened again to the thumping, suddenly punctuated by the child's methodical demanding cry, listening as if the sounds were mysterious, particularly attracted by the child. "Fixing it up," he said absently, "after all these years," and knew he was saying it only because he was possessed of the remnant of an obligation to extend a welcome.

Then he looked back at John Roger, who was staring at the child with a malevolent grimace, then raw hate. Snapping his head away from the hammock, John Roger said, "I would like to fix it up if I could get the time."

Cass shook his head, all thought of welcome gone, yet gazing up at the second floor where two windows dully reflected the sun off swirls of drying soap.

John Roger removed the hammer from the loop and pointed toward the roof. "I would like to nail up the drainpipe." Then he turned and vanished into the house, closing the door behind him.

Suddenly Cass flushed, knew he had turned color by the heavy heat rimming his ears; he had been left there alone like a prying fool. Ruefully he spat and walked down the hill to his car, perplexed and angered by his perplexity. Why, he wondered, had he stood on the porch gaping; stood there, unwanted, refusing to leave? Perhaps the noise, the actual sight of the house being prepared again for life, and the frozen, bitter stare of the man at the child.

Driving back to upstreet Southfield, squinting with the early evening wind in his face, he tried to fit John Roger to a type: strong, taciturn, and arrogant, when he was able to produce the deed, show some incontrovertible proof; but probably squeamish, shrinking, afraid if the law found him wrong. Strength was bred of either right or faith. John Roger did not seem possessed of faith; if wrong, he would crumple, would this minute—if he had had no deed—be fleeing in the opposite direction to God knows where.

As always, when he felt the annoyance of a foolish judgment,

17

Cass bit his lip and softly swore aloud; but a man could not prevent his thoughts, not the ones that broke through his tiredness or defenses.

He pulled into the gasoline station and pressed his horn. The old man came out of the shack, propped a foot on the running board, and leaned his head partly through the window.

"Your description could stand one of your fifty-cent grease jobs," Cass said. "I think you might have cataracts, George."

"Cataracts? What cataracts?"

"Why didn't you tell me what he was like?"

"Who's that?"

"Williams—out at the old house."

George craned his corded, sunburned neck deeper into the car, blinking, saying, "Well, you didn't ask me. Anyway, I did say they was kind of odd."

"What's the woman like?"

George withdrew his head, scratched his cheek, and said, "To tell the truth, we was watching her feed her kid."

"So?"

"I mean that's why I didn't get a good look at her face, is all."

Grinning, Cass said, "I hope you didn't get excited, George."

"Well, I ain't old enough to be above it yet." He scratched again. "She's a cold one. I seen my wife, God rest her soul, feed four kids—sometimes when she was even washing the dishes. But I never seen her not care, if you know what I mean."

"I don't know."

"You will soon, I guess. I mean not that your missus won't care, but you'll know the difference."

"Go ahead."

"This woman just like that whipped out her tit like she didn't give a living damn for nobody. Then she put it away, slow, real slow—the whole thing showed. You couldn't help but look, but you couldn't feel anything about it. She just buttoned it up like it wasn't hers." He nodded. "You'll know the difference all right."

"They seem poor."

"Well, he asked after work."

"Tobacco."

George nodded, saying, "Any man can pick a leaf, he says," nodding again as Cass started the engine, waved, and drove into Washington Street. Parking in front of his house, he saw a neighbor's wife standing on his porch, then coming down to meet him, her skirt whirling as she ran, her face split in a broad smile.

"This is the happy day, Cass," she said. "The doctor says it's time."

He vaulted the porch steps and entered the house.

Sitting on the davenport in the front room, his fingers intertwined and pressing his knuckles white; his eyes tracing the blurred squarish flowers of the linoleum, Cass had already become used to, absorbed, the strange odor, the cloying sweet-sick fog that he thought must be part of the process of birth. Or perhaps merely something the doctor had poured from a bottle, perhaps his own fear made palpable. He rose and began to pace, randomly at first, then carefully, implanting his heels on each flower.

Both he and his wife were forty-two, but he had not even considered the age when she had told him almost a year before; it was a gratuitous fact, relevant to nothing. Then his sister Katie had written; it was impractical, absurd; middle age was no time to conceive a child, let alone rear one. And it was dangerous, women could not carry well past forty; they could not bear up under it; sometimes their minds warped, snapped like twigs. She, being a woman (no matter childless, unmarried) knew. He answered her; he was proud, happy. And as for the danger, it was not as if Martha had miscarried a number of times; it was simply that in fourteen years of marriage nothing had happened. There was no danger.

Yet he heard it from others, all complicitly clairvoyant with Katie; heard it incessantly until he himself began to worry, then fear, then question. The doctor tried to reassure him: a woman giving birth after forty was hardly an oddity. But the tenth month came and still the child was not delivered, and he began to think of deformities. Again, reassurance: too long past nine months was not strictly normal, yet the exact time was impossible to determine, at best it was always a guess. And now, almost the eleventh month.

His hands were hotly moist and a small constellation of sweat broke out across his upper lip; he heard the beginnings of a cry, thought for a moment that the child had been born, but it was only Martha gasping shrilly in a quick spasm of pain—timeless, he knew, for her.

He sat again and impotently cursed John Roger; he should not have gone out to the house; he should have been here from the beginning instead of abandoning her to a neighbor's wife. He cursed John Roger again, pounding his fist into a cushion which had somehow found its way into his lap, wondering suddenly about the limits of his fear and how he had come to be here, how it had all come to pass.


By 1919, he had managed to lay aside some money through his service in the AEF; he served, but he had not expected to become Southfield's hero. He was one of three men who left the town for France—and the only one to return. The town council voted approval for the erection of a soldier's monument in the square (later, everyone called it *his* monument; he had a forfeited right to it), and at the unveiling he delivered a speech in full uniform, his blouse decorated with three American medals and the Croix de guerre. They all said that he was splendid and handsome and brave, and on the power of the performance he received a bank loan of several hundred dollars, added it to his savings, and set about expanding his father's hardware store, a business intractably tottering toward bankruptcy, mismanaged by the old man even to the day of his death in late 1918.

Cass, home after a short postwar stay in Paris, had wanted to sell the business; for a parentless bachelor (his mother had died somewhere beyond his remembrance) a small-town store seemed idiotically confining, an unnecessary handicap, a trap. He wanted to travel; in Paris he had recognized the power of his mind; he began to read as if he had never before seen a book; he relinquished his ex-sergeant's façade of toughness and allowed himself to absorb instead of direct. So he returned to Southfield only to sell the store and settle debts. But perhaps against the background of the town (hamlet, really, almost a crossroads), with its circle of stores, its simple uncluttered purpose of pure quiet existence, his intellectuality appeared inessential, pretentious. There was no Louvre, no Champs Elysées, no sidewalk cafés, not one man who had ever tasted or heard of Pernod, only Southfield; and here he knew what he was. He stayed, without illusion, and ran the store.

While he attempted to force his business into some logical mold of profit (he had not fully realized the extent of his father's incompetence), he noticed Martha Jarachowski, a farm worker's daughter, almost by accident. She merely appeared. During the summer, he would sit alone in the store, a book on his knees, looking not at the book but over it at a produce-clearing barn across the road, watching Martha drop down from the back of a wagon several times a week, often dragging bulging burlap sacks or carrying armloads of bound tobacco leaves. He began to anticipate her, waiting for the wagon; he was puzzled; he told himself that he had seen more beautiful women in Paris.

He told himself also that there was really nothing to see; she was always dressed in formless pants and man's shirt, a blue kerchief bound about her head, all thickened and rutted with earth from the fields. And her house, like all the rest of the farmers'; he could see it by closing his eyes and remembering: gray planks, pungent with bad cooking, sweat, and the stench of feet and mildewed clothing. Yet it did not matter, she was irresistible; her face, streaked and powdered with earth but gayly intelligent, perhaps illusively so; her random-packed hair nervous to unfurl from the kerchief; her walk, despite the sexlessness of the denim pants, absurdly feminine, almost wanton. And perhaps that was why he came to desire her so desperately, so powerfully that twice he refused to watch her, refused to see the strength of her womanness, not truly obvious unless it was sought for, hardly perceptible even, but a strength sharpened by her clothing, her man's work, a strength she was helpless to conceal. Something true, he felt, true and natural and alive; not like his porcelain intellectuality, which flourished in the dream of a city like Paris but paled in the concreteness of a practicality called Southfield.

And after a July of patient spying and inexplicable hesitance, he opened the door of his store, strode across the road, and confronted her; he stood firmly before her and met her eyes; and now his power sprang forth, a feeling that his maleness was equal, more than equal, to her femininity.

"My name is Cass Nowell," he said. "Will you go to the nickelette in Bluefield with me tonight?"

She almost smiled, just a parting of the lips, her face upraised and inquisitive; she answered, without pause, "I will ask my father," in a voice heavily accented, deep, euphonic, which supported his trust in her womanhood. And a voice which also betrayed the neglect of English in her house, their castigation (although immigrants) of the New Englanders who had built Southfield, came to it straight across the state of Massachusetts from the Cape, Boston, and before from the kings of England. And yet she was American, and must remain so, Cass felt, if they would let her.

"Will you ask him now?"

Without answering, she left him and went into the barn, returning almost immediately, saying, "My father says no."

"Then when can you go?"

"I don't know"—shrugging her shoulders.

"Well, do you want to go?"

She looked up at him, her eyes crinkled at the corners with faint ridiculing amusement, playfully chastizing him, as if his question could possess any meaning in the face of her father's refusal. "I am Martha Jarachowski," she said, and walked away from him to the barn.

At the door stood a man, no doubt her father, tall as Cass, powerful in hard middle age, awkward force in every gesture. He took Martha's arm and led her through the door.

All the next week Cass asked her the same question, and each time she dutifully retreated into the barn, always emerging from the door's great square of darkness with a refusal; yet she did not

22

seem thwarted, unhappy, only quietly amused. Then one afternoon he crossed the road, passed her, walked into the damp musty
half-light, and found her father. "I want to take your daughter
to the nickelette."

Jarachowski hardened his face into expressionlessness, dug both
fists into the sockets of his hips, and moved his feet a few inches
apart, simply saying, "No."

Doubling his own fists, Cass said again, "I said I want to take
your daughter out."

Jarachowski caught Cass's stare, met it, held it, and without
moving, shouted, "Mart'a."

She came inside and they chattered in Polish for several minutes, he gesticulating, she calm; then, casting a final appraising
glance at Cass, he turned and went out into the sunlight.

"Well?" Cass said. "I'm damned sick and tired of this."

"He said yes."

But they did not go to Bluefield that night; instead they climbed
straight above Southfield to the summit of Arrowhead Mountain,
where King Philip's cave was now accessible by a man-made path
with even the man-made touch of a sign: ELEV. 634 FT.: more,
carved initials, hearts and arrows. And inside the cave they talked
in the light of Cass's kerosene lamp, discovering that they were
both twenty-eight, laughing—heartily though with vague embarrassment at the subject itself—that neither was yet married.

After an afternoon of troubled apprehension, Cass found that
his desire for her had softened, relaxed; now she was a woman in
woman's clothes and he was comforted that all things were molli-
fied, palliated in context. He listened, absorbed in her impossible
dreams, impossible wants; but somehow for her, thinking, envisioning, conjecturing made all things attainable. She sat on a
cross-logged bench, also initial-scarred, her legs drawn up on the
seat, her arms girdling her knees, gazing down at the beads of
light which flickered through wind-blown trees like reflectors in
the tracery of a spiderweb. Her profile, pensive and almost
haughty, undulated in the lamplight, as if her face had lost the
dimensions of its features, melting softly back and forth from

the darkness like the golden head of a portrait, indirectly then directly lighted.

As she spoke, releasing what might have been years of pure unexpressed thought, her learning clarified itself through her lack of words, her feelings through the poetry of inexpressible emotions. What she believed of the world, thought it could be—not what she knew of it, read of it—stupefied him, mocked him.

Eventually she fell silent and he said, "Did you want to go with me—that first day?"

"Oh, yes."

She smiled and he knew why she had never offered him a crutch, a bridge to her father's acceptance; she wanted to be fought for, taken; perhaps it was her way of being sure. Or the remnant of a fairy tale. Suddenly she threw back her head and laughed deep within her throat.

"What is it?"

"Oh, no, I can't say it to you."

"Please."

She tightened her lips against another spontaneous laugh and leaned her chin on her arm.

"Tell me," he said.

"I had a bath for you tonight," and even in the colorless light, which spread, dying, into the crags of the cave, he saw her face grow darker, her teeth plunge into her lower lip. She turned her head. "I am ashamed."

It was then that he first kissed her; and later, after a silent hour of dreaming down at the steadily vanishing lights, he took her home, letting her slip, with a last touch of their fingers, into her father's house.

In October Cass proposed; she did not smile this time, simply kept silent; and he went to see her father. When they were sitting alone in the kitchen, facing each other across the plank table, Cass watched the massive, unresponsive peasant face straining hard to think, to weigh the balances. He had his house, Cass said, his business; he could provide; he was Catholic.

Her father, no longer deliberating, rose and shook his head. "No."

Cass, leaning into a broad patch of light, trying to penetrate Jarachowski's mask of indifference, said, "Why? Tell me why?"

"You are not Polish."

"Give me a reason, not an excuse."

"You are not Polish, I said to you."

"I won't take that."

"I said to you, now go."

"There is no reason, is there? Except your stupid, ignorant pride. You'd go to hell for your pride; you'd take Martha there for it."

With almost a twitch Jarachowski reached across the table and hammered Cass's mouth with his fist. Cass's head snapped back, but he kept his chair; he fought desperately against unconsciousness, as the blood spewed out from his gums and broke through his cracked lips. He looked down at the multiplying drops on his shirt, felt the fragment of a tooth jangling against his tongue. In agony, he stared up at Jarachowski, spat squarely onto the table, raised his fist, and brought it down on the clot of blood and spit. A cup and saucer bolted to the floor; a spoon spun several times in the air; the table split down the center and buckled inward.

Through a milky film, his head crushed and disjointed, he watched Jarachowski trace the ragged crack with his black scarred fingertips.

"Now why?" Cass said, thinking that he might faint from the pain of the two words.

Jarachowski muttered softly and sunk back into his chair, suddenly small, helpless, defeat shrinking his sad eyes and mouth. "Go," he said, "marry her."

Then Cass took his handkerchief and stanched the blood, leaving the house without a word.

Cass and Martha were married in St. Stanislaus Kostka Catholic Church, where in deference to Martha's family the pledge was read in Polish; they spent a week in New York, then a month in France, where he showed her Paris, walking her along still-remembered streets, retelling and inventing stories to perpetuate her wonder. They returned to Southfield deep in a love they believed perfect, childishly miserable at even a half-hour's separation.

In 1929, he was chosen for the town council; and when the depression struck, he clung to his store and survived through the crumbling of the paper mills in Bluefield, the burning by strikers of the small rug mill, the laying to waste of nearly half the tobacco land.

He thought no more of children; children would not be born to them and no one could explain it, not the doctor to him nor the priest to Martha. He grew even closer to her, and lying next to her at night, his hand secure and tenderly possessive on her hip or thigh, he felt that with all the palpable misery of life his punishment for so much love and peace was physical barrenness; not felt, philosophized; he did not really feel that at all.

He rose from the davenport again, quickly, trembling at the slap, the gurgle, the cry and its abrupt halt; he waited an eternity until the doctor came from their room, treading softly, almost tiptoeing across the floor. "A girl," he said somberly, his eyes dull, focused inwardly. "Beautiful—a miracle of a girl."

"Martha?"

"One of the most beautiful girls I've ever seen—maybe eight pounds."

And then somehow he knew it, the end: Martha was dead. He could see it in the doctor's unpupiled eyes, the professional trick of looking toward, yet not at, someone as the pronouncement of death was for a time avoided; the practised evasion that made it always so brutal, useless, insane. He knew. He knew but asked, "Dead?"

Only a nod.

"Bring me the baby."

"It might be too soon."

"Bring me the baby. Please."

And when she was brought, tousled shapelessly in a wad of blankets, he peered at the creased scarlet face and choked, stammered, "Martha. Dead?"

"I'll get the priest."

Alone, he stood with the baby in his arms and knew that she

must be called Martha too, another Martha; his eyes darted from the folded face to the floor until his vision was muddled by the linoleum flowers. Blinking, he saw a tear fall against the child's cheek, animating the flesh for an instant. Then he carried her into the bedroom and looked at his wife's face glinting remotely from the frozen sweat of her death agony, her eyes not completely closed, yet not open.

The child was warm in his arms and hate struck him, then died of its own quick fury; he hugged her close to the protection of his body, bent to the dead Martha and kissed her cold dry mouth.

# 3

On Sunday the small procession—hearse, two cars—crept up Route 12 in an ache of slowness toward the cemetery, which lay five miles from upstreet Southfield. John Roger, standing on his porch, hammer in hand, watched the moving threnody inch past the house, the hearse itself setting a maddeningly snail's pace of grief, so slow that John Roger could read the bronze plate in the window: SIMON FORBES. And Simon Forbes sat erect behind the wheel, a white handkerchief folded around his neck. Cass Nowell, hypnotized, immobile, drove the first car, both hands cemented to the wheel, his arms locked at the elbows; what appeared to be a priest sat next to him—at least he was dressed in black and his bent head might have covered his collar. A woman sat in the back.

The car behind held four people, all numb-featured, their bodies stiff either from sorrow or the unaccustomed collars and ties and black shawls: broad, squat faces, huge-boned, shiny with sweat. John Roger recognized one of them, a Polack he had seen his first day in the tobacco fields.

As Cass's car seemed to pause, suspended, in front of the house, John Roger removed a nail from between his lips, and with four sharp blows drove it into a loose floorboard. Only Cass reacted, slowly, unsurely; he turned his head toward the house and stared without perception, then dully fixed his attention back to the wheel.

The hammering had also stirred the child; the hammock bobbed, its motion activating John Roger. Sneering, he jumped from the steps, walked a short way down the hill, turned, then surveyed his work: the house seemed if not straight then at least intact, unpainted but clean and inhabited—Cousin Henry's gift. Cousin Henry had owned the old house although he had never lived in it nor even seen it; it bowed under thirty-five years of desertion, and no one in Southfield could remember when it last echoed with living voices. But it was Henry's parents who had lived in it and who had left it to their son—which son was now himself dead after a life of parsimonious shop-keeping in a Rhode Island town. Despising and avoiding all taint of charity, he had, as John Roger told Cass, willed him the house; but on condition that he pay four hundred dollars to Cousin Hope, the widow. Henry, who had always wanted to leave a will (it had been said that the thought of it excited him, that it made the finality of death nearly attractive) had bequeathed whatever property he collected to all his relatives, to be claimed only if they reimbursed Hope—a variation (again it had been said) that he must have enjoyed.

John Roger agreed to the terms; gambled as an alternative to what he was convinced would end in a jail term: he had beaten a priest about the head with a flat board after an argument concerning marriage and religious responsibility. The priest, having turned the other cheek and finding the board there also, fled down the street, and in the rectory wrote his bishop; he believed that a few months in jail could only profit John Roger, not merely as punishment for the physical fact of assault and battery but because he had deprived his wife of her religion and refused to rear his infant son in the Catholic Church.

It was during the interim in the correspondence, pending the bishop's answer, that John Roger belatedly accepted the provisions of Henry's will. He gave Cousin Hope a twenty-five-cent deposit (struck dumb, she accepted it), packed what little he had in a suitcase, and bought the Ford from a junk dealer. Then he left for Massachusetts.

Five months before, he had married Esther Snow, a girl ten

years younger than his thirty-six; at the time he worked in a factory that manufactured thermometers, and he sat hour after hour scratching the metal ends of the tubes against a fluted board to level the mercury, then consulted a chart which listed twenty-one steps for complete and effective testing. He whirled the thermometers in a centrifugal-force machine, scratched them several more times, snapped them with a painful jerk of his wrist, spun them once again, then soaked them in water of varying temperatures. And one day he did what he had continuously wanted to do, was compelled to do: he threw a bundle into the street below, watching the thermometers splinter and sparkle away on the pavement. After he was fired, he tried house painting, failed again; and when he struck the priest, he had not worked in weeks; he was whaling the board against religion, against bosses, against even himself; he was still flailing it through the air long after the priest had disappeared around a corner.

The priest had come about Esther. Parentless, she had been raised by an aunt, who educated and trained her as a Catholic, sending her to a parochial school, standing by her as she received communion and was confirmed. She could not attend much high school (her aunt's income was by then a small pension), so she worked at a marrow machine in a knitting mill and seemed content. She went to Mass each Sunday, was apparently devout, never dressed or spoke immodestly; she seemed secure and resigned in what she had learned from her aunt and the nuns. And the aunt, genuinely regretting Esther's lack of education, took consolation in the obvious fact that she was a good girl, and religious, and would someday make a suitable man a pure and competent, if perhaps docile, wife.

But the years passed and suddenly Esther became pregnant; she named John Roger, not because of malice or fear, but because in her own way she considered him responsible, considered him so because she had permitted him to end her virginity quietly and without hesitance only because she could not help herself; she wanted and loved him. In her own way. And when accused, he said in her presence, "I wasn't the only man who fooled with her," believing it because women did not give themselves unless they were whores. She did not answer, and staring at her until she lowered her eyes, he said, "A whore is one thing, but a lying whore is something else again."

Yet he married her; he had no alternative. Her aunt's reputation as a reverent and charitable woman slowly accumulated the odds against him. The chief of police took him one night to the rectory and he sat while the priest paced and lectured, and as the drone of the monologue rose in anger, hissed with recrimination, he knew that he was doomed, and surrendered. They told him that he could not leave town; the police watched him; and an hour before the wedding he was locked in jail where he dressed in his newly-ironed only suit.

They were married in the sacristy, not at the altar, because John Roger confirmed his atheism (if he had ever doubted his beliefs or lack of them, he said, he was sure then). And when he was told to sign a paper swearing that his child would be brought up a Catholic, he refused. The chief of police tried to force him with two sharp slaps in the face, but he said, "Do that again and there won't be any wedding even if you kill me." Near hysteria now, the aunt screamed to forget the paper; she would swear for him, just get Esther married. And in the sacristy, as the priest read the words and three times reminded him to say *I do,* John Roger looked through the open colored-glass window, watching two self-appointed vigilantes laughing lewdly as they lounged against a tree smoking and holding baseball bats, not even guns, turning the whole miserable day into a practical joke.

After the wedding John Roger left his one room above the grocery store and moved to the aunt's house, and both he and Esther went to work the next morning. Several weeks later he destroyed the thermometers; Esther began to swell; and when Matthew was born, the hospital bill was paid from the aunt's savings. Then a month later the priest came, berated John Roger for preventing Esther's attendance at Mass in the teeth of her aunt's protests, and said that he was determined to baptize the child. But John Roger said that he had been badgered and bullied enough, beyond the limits of his endurance; he had accepted the marriage under threats of violence; now, come what may, he would not allow the baptism, would not allow Esther to see a church, let alone attend one, would never as long as he drew breath permit God to be mentioned in the house. And before the priest had barely an opportunity to speak, John Roger struck him with the board, struck him twice in the face; and he rolled down the porch steps, regained his feet with the resilience of a rubber ball, finally running hysterically, his nose bleeding, the collar torn from his neck. And later wrote his bishop.

Then John Roger quieted, discarded the board, walked to Cousin Hope's house, and accepted the terms of the bequest. He sold everything he owned; took what belonged to Esther and sold that too. He threw the aunt into a chair and stood over her, irascible, menacing; called her a miserable thief, threatening to kill her and set fire to her house and the church and seek out the priest and kill him too. She gave him fifty dollars from a secret lard can. He now had slightly over two hundred dollars; he returned to Cousin Hope with it, added it to the twenty-five cents, and arranged for monthly installments on the balance. Then he bought the Ford for eighteen dollars, packed Esther and Matthew into it, and drove away.

The aunt sat still on the porch watching them go down the street, and when the backfiring had ceased, becoming only a memory, she lowered her head and wept. The next day she confessed to the priest, saying, "No, I don't want either of them back. I don't ever want to see them again. They are dead anyway. If it's a sin, I'll never stop sinning. I'll go to hell. I don't care."

And the priest said, "Amen."


The cortege returned, the hearse speeding well ahead, its mission paid for, done. John Roger sat on the bottom step of the porch, his chin in his hands, his eyes on Cass's car; Cass sat slumped over the wheel, looking almost through the spokes, his face flat and yellow. Over his shoulder, illusorily perched, was the priest's head, as he bent forward, talking, his collar visible now. A woman dipped her nose into a handkerchief.

The Poles passed, the same blank faces; the only activity was a man struggling to prevent a woman clawing at her face and hair. Then it was all gone, and in a moment the road settled into hard visibility through a mist of dust.

The child coughed, began to cry. Looking away from the road, John Roger shouted, "Get out here and shut him up."

And when Esther appeared he said, staring off, "Take him away—sweet Jesus, just take him away."

# 4

Simon Forbes sat in the drug store drinking a Coke, planning his brief report for the town council, anticipating its reaction; he hadn't much to say and he was already late, but he needed time to unravel the proper words from the possibilities, time to extend a simple no into something less hopeless; but it was not working, no was no. He shifted his weight on the stool, thinking, a tall man whose once spare body was slowly running to fat, whose face was still firm save for the flesh under his eyes and jaw, which drooped in shallow, wide slats.

People who didn't know him well thought him physically slow, but the care and deliberate ease of his movements were merely a conservation of energy; he could catch flies in midair; could catch, before it reached his knees, any object that fell from his hands. He smoked pipes with holes drilled through their stems to accommodate a curved, protruding eyetooth. And although he did not sweat excessively, he constantly wiped and dabbed at his face with one of three or four handkerchiefs he carried in various pockets.

He was a lonely man, lonely and respected and a bit feared; feared irrationally, because he was Southfield's undertaker, had been since 1923, and had come to achieve the beginnings of a symbolic stature. He had a profession; he was a town councilman; he spoke softly and well, with a vestige of the South in his voice— all these were solid, acceptable. But the superstitious avoided him when possible (only the superstitious; the truly religious ignored him because he attended no church); old women were seen to cross themselves when he passed, not maliciously as if he were a devil, just protectively. And for the others, Simon was simply the undertaker; for practical reasons no one wanted to be his client, not in any sense of the word.

Harry Chase, the druggist, audibly worked his mortar and pestle behind a partition, sending a rasping buffer against the hot, still evening, crushing solidity to dust, causing Simon to remember Martha Nowell's funeral, to say "Ashes to ashes"— embarrassing himself. He swabbed his throat with a paper napkin, dropping it on a heap of crushed and shredded remnants, pushing them all away with his wrist. Then finishing his Coke, he lighted a pipe, hearing the familiar hiss whistle through the hole in the stem, dropped a nickel on the counter, and went off to the town hall.

Strange, he thought; he was walking, verbalizing silently, because the Great Atlantic & Pacific Tea Company store had gone out of business—or had anyway left Southfield. Most everyone had traded there, especially since the Depression, but the proxy management could not meet overhead with profit.

Which left Kazu Smolenski's Warsaw Market; he had never realistically competed with the Great Atlantic, except that he gave credit; he held on grimly, hoping, praying that his customers would return, even pay his higher prices. But Kazu recognized the dream and began preparing for his inevitable ruin. Yet the miracle happened; the hope was rewarded; the Great Atlantic closed down and he possessed even more than he had ever expected: a monopoly.

And then it appeared that the profit he had been dreaming of suddenly meant nothing; his years of waiting warped him, and he plotted an odd revenge. He retaliated against the people who had stayed away, who had cursed him for his high prices, who had slipped by the front door with furtive eyes and drawn breath, slipped by to save a few pennies in the impersonal food machine across the square. He raised prices; he hounded his debtors; he took to smoking long green cigars and wearing bow ties. And the people just hung about, watching, cursing, swearing that he would never see a nickel of their money. But they had no choice,

**33**

and once inside the store they were trapped, facing Kazu Smolenski, who stood imperious and outwardly serene behind his counter, smirking, blowing clouds of acrid smoke at their faces, impaling them on vicious Polish puns.

As Simon interpreted it, Kazu Smolenski snapped—because he continued to raise prices until in time no one could afford even flour or groats; he cared nothing for sales; he was content to sit all day in the accumulating must and rot and, through his greasy window, spy on the people who tentatively approached the store. He watched them pause to count their change, watched them cast agonized glances at the provisions hanging on hooks five feet from them, encased and protected by plate glass, hanging prime and untouchable—and he let them rot off the hooks in plain sight. And, he told Simon, he would continue to let them rot.

Simon entered the auditorium in the town hall and walked up front to the council table; he sat next to Cass's empty place and looked at the six or seven men sitting in a row of folding chairs: a farmer or two, several storekeepers, and Willy Kling, a half-vagrant. They returned Simon's gaze expectantly and he diverted his eyes to the green felt of the table; they did expect something, he thought, but there was nothing to give. The sheriff, sitting at the end of the table, toying with a gavel, cleared his throat and said, "I guess we can start. What did he say, Simon?"

"It's no use. I couldn't budge him. He'll go out of business before he'll lower prices. His wife told me he's just about ruined them." He ran a handkerchief under his chin, then motioned helplessly with his smoked-out pipe before sliding it into his pocket. "That's the way it is."

"What do you suggest?" the sheriff asked.

"There's nothing to suggest. No one can make him do anything. He's gone crazy, out of his head. There's no reasoning with him—so we're stuck."

"To tell the truth," the sheriff said, "we didn't think anything would come of it." Pointing to the man at Simon's left, "George said he had a last-chance idea."

"Like Simon says," George began, "you can't get anywhere

with a crazy man. Now here's the thing. Ever since Kazu got beat up by that brother-in-law of his, he backs down from a fight. There's nothing he's more scared of than a fist in his face. So long as he keeps doing what he's doing in that store we got no choice but to grab him and show him what for."

"What do you want to do, George," Simon said, "lynch him?"

"I never said that. I never even said beat him up—'least not at first. But if he don't listen to a warning, I can't see no other way out. I say beat him up if need be, but maybe it won't come to that."

"No," Simon said, but a few of the men shouted against him. "No," he outshouted, quieting them. "Leave him alone; he's got troubles enough. Past talking to a man, there's nothing you can do."

"You said yourself you can't talk to a lunatic."

"That's right. Maybe you can't scare a lunatic either."

"You got to see our position," George said. "Hardly anybody's got a car to go buy food in Bluefield. I know that better than anybody. I sell maybe a gallon a week. We got to buy here; we're broke. You ain't got that problem, Simon—people die all the time; you got a dollar in your pocket."

"There's nothing to do. Besides, the sheriff won't let you beat him up."

"Well, look, Simon. I don't like this any more than you do, but I'm going to look the other way just this once. What George says is true; we need that damn store."

"Use my hearse. Get your food orders together and I'll take them into Bluefield."

"That's not the point. Why, that would make us a ghost town, like some place in Alaska."

"Then it looks as though you just want a mob to beat him up."

"There won't be any mob. What we'll do is send somebody over to the store and let him know that a couple dozen of the men are thinking of a little violence. I think that will do it; maybe he'll see the light. Like George says, he's not too brave."

Simon didn't answer; he looked away.

The sheriff said, "I guess you've got to go back there, Simon."

"Me? Why me? I won't do it."

"You're the senior member here."

"Cass is. I don't figure in this at all."

"Now, Simon. Cass has trouble."

"All right, I forgot. But you won't even wait until he gets over his trouble, because you know he won't do it either."

"It's got to be done now," George said, slapping the table. "There's children got to eat."

"You said I had no stake in it; I've got a dollar. That's my logical out, my excuse."

"No it's not," the sheriff said. "You're the elder here; you know the rules. We've got to do this right."

"Right? There's nothing right about it."

"Simon. Please."

Simon sighed, mopped his face, then threw up his hands. "All right, I'll talk to him again. My way."

"The hell you will," Willy Kling shouted.

"Now, Willy, you shut up," the sheriff said. "This doesn't concern you."

"I live here, don't I?"

"I should have kicked you out the minute I saw you."

"I say I live here," Willy said, screwing up his diminutive body like an angry cat, his arms folded across his chest. For as long as anyone had known him, he had always protested—against everything, as a matter of course.

Simon knew him, had avoided him since the day he had swept out the funeral chapel and stolen a wedding ring from a corpse. Now he was a part-time sharecropper, still cunning, even more shiftless, irksome with his little man's perfect marriage of superiority and persecution. No one ever liked him; they often hated him; he invaded card games, cheated children out of pennies; had to be, through some maniacal drive, the loudest, the drunkest—and always failed. Sometimes in the fields he was punished; they would pick him up and toss him from hand to hand. But they could not get rid of him.

Yet once the Depression came, the men no longer cared, and let him grouse with them on the square, even listened to him

36

curse the politicians and moneygrubbers with second-hand weapons picked up by eavesdropping on gossip. Getting rid of him was hollow now; throwing him through the air was hardly funny. All they had was purposelessness, and they admitted him into its company.

So, Simon thought, they should have expected his protest; and now, as some project of action, no matter idiotic, stirred their idleness, galvanized them as far as possible, they tried to silence him. But he shouted, jigged his feet, rattled his chair on the floor, saying, "I know how to make that Kazu listen; I know how to scare him as good as anybody."

Suddenly, mercifully, they laughed, a kind of nervous therapy.

But he raved, waving his arms, cursing the men and Simon, especially Simon who had caught him robbing the corpse and had kicked him in the buttocks and out the door. He leveled his finger at Simon. "I bet he ain't strong enough to scare anybody. Maybe he ain't strong at all." And puffing out his pitiable chest, "I'm stronger."

"What's strength got to do with it?" the sheriff asked.

"You want to scare him, don't you?"

"You're not equipped for scaring, or talking either. Now why don't you go on home?"

"I got a right to be here; I got a right to show I'm stronger."

The sheriff paused, then, "All right, if you have to be convinced, we'll have a test. If you prove you're stronger than Simon, the job's yours."

Simon closed his eyes, swabbing the lids, saying, "Now you've done it. You've surely done it."

"He can hit me first," Willy said. "Right in the mouth. Then it's my turn. Longest one down loses."

"No," the sheriff said. "You know damn well if Simon didn't pull his punch he'd kill you. Anyway, Simon wouldn't hit anybody, and maybe you know that too." And before Willy had the chance to protest again, "You can hand wrestle. All right, Simon?"

"Damn, no. It's not all right. I wouldn't touch him, you lunatic."

"Then you'll wrestle with me; I'm as strong as Simon. Take it or leave it."

"How in hell do you get so sidetracked?" Simon mumbled.

"It'll only take a minute. I just want to get it over with."

But it was lost now, Simon thought; this was worse, because what the sheriff could not see, or had not grown to understand, was the absolute quality of Willy's stubbornness, his refusal to simply lose; he was a man who always manipulated the best two out of three into the best three out of five, and so on up the line to infinity—until he won by boring his opponent, or infuriating him, to death. Or tears.

So Willy and the sheriff sat opposite each other, elbows on the table, hands locked; the sheriff won with no show of effort, won again, won still again. Finally the sheriff said, "All right, it's settled," but Willy screeched, "We didn't set no limit. We didn't."

The men began to mutter, shuffling their feet; one of the farmers called out, "Two out of three—enough's enough."

"You go to hell," Willy snarled, still clutching the sheriff's hand, trying impossibly to bend the arm; the pores of his face almost burst blood; his fingers were white, trembling.

And then Simon stood and pounded the table. "Stop, damn it. Both of you. Before I watch this any more I'll split all the money on my next funeral, if there's any money to split. I'll feed everybody. But just stop this—I feel like an ape." To the sheriff: "You lost; he beat you the minute you agreed to this. Let him go and do what he damn well pleases."

"Now, look, Simon, we're looking for somebody to save the town; we need a man. Why, Kazu will laugh at Willy," jerking his hand finally out of Willy's straining grasp.

"No he won't. Willy will get him in a corner and talk until both their brains rattle in tune. Willy will follow him around like a dog until he gives everybody a free month's groceries just for a minute of peace." He turned to Willy. "Go right over to the store and say you're saving the town. Go ahead, Willy, do what the sheriff wants—be a man; save us all. You'll be a hero." And to the sheriff: "You see? Anyway, he's your man for a thing like this. He fits the whole idea. He belongs."

Then Simon left the hall, drying his palms on a handkerchief, wishing that he had left long before. Somehow, no matter how strong his effort, his quest for immunity, he inextricably involved himself in what he called the joke, sometimes the hideous joke, of living where other men lived. He flushed in his foolishness, pained and ineluctably caught up, shuffled along in the disorderly, illogical lives of others. No, not only others; himself as well, illogical as any.

He walked down Washington Street to Cass Nowell's house and knocked lightly at the door; a glow was diffused through drawn shades, but there was no answer and he did not knock again: realizing his mistake, knowing that Cass's grief must have its solitude to struggle; boundless, illimitable time to confront God with the logic of His destruction. This is what Cass was doing, he knew it, knew him well enough to judge; his love for Martha was too unquestioned, too great to bow in weeping, passive acceptance. So he was struggling; but there could be no winner, only a result.

Simon turned from the house and walked back through the night.

# 5

The knock was faint, yet Cass heard it like a dreamer who is not quite certain whether a sound or motion is the dream itself or an encroachment upon it; and if it were real, it had nothing to do with him; he let it cease of its own accord. He was crying; he could not face whoever was there; he could not be that brave.

Bravery—it had come to him, buoyed him throughout the day in the unreality of an all but insufferably false male egoism: driving to the cemetery with Katie and Father Franosz, standing by the grave in a retching fantasy of Latin monotone and maculating coffin, driving back to the railroad station and depositing Katie on the 4:27 to Hartford. He had succeeded in at least tricking her, who long ago had rooted herself in religious inevitability, but not Martha's family—a wider knowledge held them, and him, together; and they shared it. But it excluded

Katie; she was immune from this mutual, easy recognition of grief; she could not detect it in a wayward movement of a hand or a cast of an eye, immunized by her belief in an impersonal suffering, formulized by a conformity of raised handkerchiefs and the clichés of condolence.

So not seeing this she had chattered beyond endurance: about his obligation to remarry because of the child (Might it not be better to name her something else? He would forget sooner), to give her into the needed care of a woman's tenderness. He wanted to scream that his wife was dead, just that, without qualification, merely the statement: she was dead.

Katie: "You mustn't have illusions about bringing up a child. Indeed, Cass, you mustn't have illusions about anything. Just trust God, and someday all this . . ."

And saying to himself: *To hell with God.*

Back from the station he drew the shades and sat in the dimness, and when dusk became night and dimness darkness, he snapped on a lamp in the fear of his loneliness, and stared at the naked bulb until diaphanous swirls of light rolled past his eyes like hoops. Then he rose and went to their room.

He opened a drawer or two and leafed through her clothing, sliding his fingers against the cloth, the familiarity of an edge of lace, a handkerchief with a tatted monogram, the slowly unraveling elbow of a sweater. Looking away from the rose-scented relics at objects: a small stuffed rabbit with a caricature expression; a hairbrush, its silver handle tarnished and scratched, its bristles clinging magnetically to a long strand of hair; a pair of worn slippers, one with a pompom, the other without, peering at him from under the bed; a nightgown draped on the bedside chair.

He lay on the bed, wondering what life would be, was even now, without her. With counterfeit calm he reasoned that what had happened was not unique; it was part of a plan; a process of realignment was needed, merely that: a realization that he must consider only his daughter now, that love could not in fact exist between the living and the dead. The problem was to cast out,

40

slowly and laboriously if need be, the intimacy they had both dreamed of, then created and jealously guarded.

Except that they had ravened it: the familiarity had not lapsed to habit and the intimacy had been born of their own intense desire, an intimacy that not only destroyed secrets but, he felt, laid bare every subtlety between man and woman. They had come together with a brutal delicacy, a forceful groaning rush into an embrace of peculiar tenderness, which became at times maddeningly incomplete because more satisfaction, more love, seemed beyond any power of invention.

Wildness in their bed: a seeking and burrowing into each other's sex that tied tongues, froze words. Lying naked and ful-filled, legs locked, sensation still plucking at their tiredness, sated and euphoric with orgasm—and yet, no, it was not that simple; there was the mind, the thoughts, and the full knowledge of having spoken and understood through their bodies, a deep gentle communion while loving furiously, as if that love were forbidden, nearly sinful. Perhaps they had never needed to marry; merely a coming together, a meeting of consummation that rendered marriage gratuitous. And perhaps it had all happened, continued to happen, because they came together virgins; he had never taken a woman, not even in France or in Army towns, con-cealing his fear in the looseness of his religious feelings, knowing it. Or, too, because their desire sprang from a fear that, having always touched love with their fingertips, they would never grasp it with a hand, holding. Taking from each other because, for them, the taking was late, because it might end too quickly.

It did. Now their years together seemed not a fertile, com-forting memory but an obscene cruelty, which had not at all prepared him for deprivation. The days were blank mockery; he could never translate them into a compressed, essential nostalgia, could never say: *I look back on those times as the happiest of my life.* Because it was also impossible to resurrect the dead. Memory, emending and manipulating and shading reality, breathed scenes which had never truly occurred; it floated the cream of life to the surface of anxiety and fear, the richness lingering there, coating, immunizing, even though it might only be the spoor of one ephemeral moment. He did not want that; more, it was not what he needed, but might come to accept. He wanted it as it was.

And he must live with the child. (Where was she now? He could not remember; he did not care.) He must always look at her and wonder what prophecy she concealed, what touch of God's will had created her, timing her birth on a freakish balance of life and death which stopped for a single instant on the head of a pin. The cause, simultaneously, of joy and misery; the paradox of God: the joy that was no joy; the statement of God: the misery that was perpetual.

As never before he must believe in God; he believed in happiness and now, unhypocritically, in sorrow. And he must believe that God had given Martha an aweful happiness, a happiness which invalidated everything that he himself had given her on earth, in their bed, their touch.

Yet was he to sing "Glory to God" because she was called? To hope for his own quick end, his dissolution into dust so that he could be with her? Spend the remainder of his life weighing every minute action on a scale perched between heaven and hell? Exist in perpetual terror of damnation because if damned he would never see her again? No, he could not live that way; no man could. And yet what choice had he? With his whole being, a synthesis of flesh and thought, he craved for a single touch of her, even in heaven, where touch was not needed or desired or obtainable.

He snatched her nightgown from the bedside chair and buried his face in it, muffling his cries of hysterical emptiness, consciously driving himself to insanity, forgetfulness, forcing his tears and moans, kissing and fondling the marble smoothness of the cloth which had once encased and caressed her breasts and thighs and the vague triangle of rick dark hair. And suddenly he threw the gown aside and lay on his back, shamed by his courting of grief, as if he were acting it out for some pitying, sympathetic onlooker. Perhaps her, so she could see him and know.

Pressing the top of his forehead against the headboard, he

42

stared directly above him at the crucifix over the bed, at the base sprigged with leafy shreds from a past Palm Sunday, made broader by the line of his vision: the outstretched arms of the cross, the Christus invisible because of the tiny holy-water font which supported the nailed feet.

"Must I tell in confession what we have done?"

"Don't be silly, Martha. It's part of loving."

"I didn't know anyone did that. I thought it was just . . ."

"Having intercourse? I did too—once."

"I love you; I want what we did. Always do beautiful things to me. Always."

The base of the crucifix broader now, black and shadowed and pressing downward, hurtful to his eyes.

"The doctor said the tests show nothing. There's no reason why you can't have a baby."

"Then something is wrong with our life."

"You believe in God's will. Believe it now."

"Yes, His punishment."

"Punishment for what? What have we done?"

"Loved each other too much."

"Is that such a sin?"

"Yes, selfishness. To be married means to have children."

"Martha, do you really care if we never have a baby?"

"I . . ."

"Do you really care? I don't, even if it's a sin to say so. I have you."

"No, my darling, I don't care. I don't."

How often had they lain here together without thought of the crucifix, unashamed before it, yet without consciousness of it. It had gazed down at them with its leaning head and punctured body seeing all, watching, cold and wooden and silent.

"I am happier now, I really am. I look at myself in the mirror and feel my belly and I think, this is what a woman is."

"You've always been a woman."

"You don't understand; you're just a man."

"Yes. You have a secret now. Your first secret."

"Not a secret, only a feeling you can never have."

"I love you all the same—in spite of your secret."
"I have never been happier. Is that such a secret?"
"No, I can see it in your face."
"We will name him after you."
"I don't like my name. Now come to bed."
"Should I? Is it all right?"
"Yes. Yes."

God had tricked him, took her with a divine effortlessness, and with the taking had twisted his life, and would perhaps destroy him with the same insignificant tremor. For an instant he burned to tear the crucifix from the wall and splinter it in his hands—impossible. He did not understand God, and he strangled on the inscrutability, rebelled against that unfathomable omniscience. Questioning: Why weren't the infallible and impenetrable strokes of God delivered in impenetrable manifestations, in cold problems of philosophic logic? Why in understandable human terms, in unbearable suffering? Why was the destruction always clear—but not the vaguest shadow of the destroyer? Or perhaps God was just another insanity.

He did not want to believe, fought against belief; yet he did believe. But now he could not love; it was too great a demand; and God must expect exactly that if He issued tragedy so humanly palpable. He was not a saint; he could not bear, fight, contest his sorrow, not when he could only submit, accept. He had not always believed firmly; but he had not needed this proof. With or without God, life was senseless.

He left the bed and went out to the bathroom. Opening the medicine cabinet he removed a bottle of iodine and uncorked it, bringing it up to his face, carefully inhaling the bitter, ugly fumes. One drink: a burn, a convulsion, pain that would not matter, pain to cause laughter by its pitiable attempt to hurt. He held the bottle, gazing down at his trembling hand already streaked brown-red; and then the bottle fell to the floor and shattered, puddling the close-set white tiles, eating into the grout.

Closing his eyes, he lowered himself to the edge of the bathtub, crying, "I can't help but believe in You. I'll take any punishment, but now give me the answers."

44

He would search for them. His life had no meaning, but he was doomed to it; he would simply go on living with his new Martha and hope, perhaps finding the answers in her, perhaps finding nothing. He would wait and see, living.

# 6

Simon thought: *Yes, the struggle,* removing his coat, still damp from the afternoon and evening's work. The struggle, the wrestling, the battle, the great war ending in stalemate; the conflict that no one wins, just resolves, thinks he resolves.

Locking the front door, he sidled familiarly through the darkness past the desk, a bronze casket that no one would ever buy even if gold were struck in the square, past the black-draped and cushioned wooden horses on which tenanted coffins lay in view, the horses fronted by a wide prie-dieu, then into his living rooms in the back.

He switched on a weak table lamp, loosened his tie, poured out a small whiskey, and sank into a deep chair of faded brown leather, scrofulous at the seams of the arms. Easing out of his shoes he propped his feet on a hassock and dipped his tongue into the calming whiskey, thinking again of the struggle and Cass's sudden involvement in it, a condition new to him. The confrontation of God, of belief, perhaps for the first time—yet inevitable. *Be careful,* he quietly, remotely warned, because two results were possible; it could accomplish two things: galvanize or enervate, catalyze hate or love, strengthen or weaken. Or acceptance: of God or nothing. It happened that way, he knew, because he had been there years before and had oddly survived, possibly because he wanted to, felt he must, possibly because he was like most other men: resilient instead of insane. What differentiated man from animal was not merely the mind but the devious uses of it: the multiplicity of escapes man found available, the ways out, the sudden realization that it was harder to be an animal and merely exist than to search for that way out, that alternative, the ability to reverse direction and become new, somehow new.

He leaned his head back, his hand warm on the glass, his eyes closed, the emotional response to his own life long gone, transformed to mental explication, reasoning, tranquil contemplation, touched not with doubt but with a light frost of knowledge and an almost objective bemusement. Because he had once had the same alternatives and, taking one, had found it not an alternative at all—merely an inevitability.

In Northern towns Simon (called Lucky then) became a conversation piece, as if he were a fossil unearthed in a heap of unlikely ruins by a group of disillusioned archeologists.

He had come from the South, wandered through the Midwest for several years, and pushing always northward found himself in Fallsville, Massachusetts, faced suddenly, impressed for the first time, with an immigrant displacement and fear of strangeness. He was by chosen profession a preacher, a preacher without a sect who defied organized churches simply by treating their existence with indifference. He had seen and met countless preachers and ministers dressed in funereal black; and when he had tried to emulate them, he discovered that instead of appearing somber or imbued with dignity he became, because of his thin spidery body and knobby Adam's apple, a huge migratory bird, almost a vulture. Yet he found his two necessities, his essentials, to be a black frock coat and a flat wide-brimmed hat; for the rest he settled on whatever trousers he could get and a shirt contemptuously open at the throat.

His mother had died of pneumonia shortly after his birth; his only remembrance and identification of her was a small oval tintype which he carried in his watch pocket. During his childhood, he first constructed outlines of her, then filled them with images until she evolved to flesh and blood, truly tangible in his mind; he attributed to her all the sweetness, loveliness, and grace that he knew she must have possessed.

By fifteen he knew the undertaker's profession as well as his father—except his fear of death grew limitless, his agony at the preparation of a corpse became so powerful that he prayed incessantly, slept fitfully, nauseated at the prospect of a day's work. He would stare in horror at even a simple wicker basket, an empty coffin; he had fits of vomiting and a kind of partial amnesia, and one day he collapsed.

While he was recovering at the house of a paternal cousin in the fall of 1907, his father made his annual trip to Atlanta, where he fell down a flight of steps and died within an hour or two after his arrival at the hospital. The cousin kept Simon, used his horror of death as a basis of teaching the glory of salvation, inculcated in him a devout and profound fear of God. The cousin had once been a Baptist, but because she had been crippled since early womanhood had not attended a service in over thirty years; so to compensate, her Bible-reading was strenuous and perpetual; and she believed with the passion of a martyr in witnessing for Christ. What she understood and eclectically philosophized through personal interpretation and application, she poured into Simon's mind, until he could parrot entire passages, although he was disturbingly unsure of their meaning.

A traveling preacher arrived at the town one day, driving his team through the streets, beating the bottom of a washtub, and the cousin urged Simon to attend the prayer meeting. While there he hardly heard a word, but what fascinated him was the preacher's hypnotic ability to wrench the crowd's interest to his own design; his power, like a great actor's, to hold his audience spellbound, mesmerized, and the ease with which he caused the people to sway and moan and twitch, miraculously shriving them with a snap of his fingers. And at the end of the meeting, after choral shouts of Hallelujah, he watched the preacher's hat passing from hand to hand, being filled to overflowing with coins dropped by eager, clutching, privileged hands.

Returning home, he remembered none of the preacher's admonitions, none of his threats of molten perdition, only envisioning money slopping over the inverted brim of a flat black hat. To him, the transition from spirit to coin was neither illogical nor sacrilegious: the money was a disciple's due, a reward for spreading God's word to the unenlightened—and Simon was attracted by the whole process. So he took his Bible and left the cousin, and at first worked his way farther South.

He met more preachers, and found most of them frauds and petty thieves, liars and confidence men, and he despised the ones who claimed to heal the sick. Yet they were successful; he was not. Realizing finally, after continually, often disastrously, failing to fill his hat, that the quintessence of a preacher was the gift of projecting his sermon on the sinful souls of his listeners, he sought help from experience. His wisest instructor was an old man from Arkansas, who called himself a Unitarian, then a Baptist, then a Witness for the Precious Tabernacle, until he ran out of names. He let Simon sleep in his wagon; he taught him the proper intonations, the proper posture; taught him to improvise, to cut short antagonistic questions; taught him to be appalled, visibly disgusted by ignorance; to color his speech and laconic tone with a proselytizing furor and flame. Also, Simon would need a miracle tool: something he could use to prove visually the power of God through his medium, the preacher of His word. The old man's tool was a finger ring in which was set a cheap, two-colored stone mounted on a raised wire: one side was whitish-blue, the other red, and when creating a vision of hell he twirled the stone on its wire axis revealing a satanic, deep crimson gleam, and the people swore stars were visible; they could see them shooting from the ring like sparks in the glare of a torch-light. Simon learned the substance of his preacher's life from the old man.

One night Simon woke suddenly, the old man leaning over him, touching him, fumbling with the buttons on his underwear; jerking aside, striking out, he watched the preacher slump away to his own pallet as if he were sleepwalking. He watched him for a long while, fearful of sleep, and for a week remained almost continually awake, staring at the rise and fall of the preacher's chest, watching him open his eyes for minutes at a time, then close them with a snap. Simon could no longer bear it; he left his teacher, heading alone into Texas.

After twelve or thirteen years of wandering along the twisted roads of his life, it came to Simon, suddenly and sadly in a Florida saloon, that his belief in God was threadbare; he was losing his faith. Perhaps, as he analyzed it, he had never firmly possessed it, had mechanized or drunk it into submission. Later, in his hotel room, he stood before a mirror and preached to his reflection, watching his brows knit, his lips twist, and the bobbing of his Adam's apple. His rueful, disillusioned eyes looked at themselves and turned away; yet he continued to speak, chanting, intoning, calling on God to reveal the light to an invisible throng of people, their conglomerate souls now filtering away and focusing in communion with the sorrowful face in the mirror.

Finally he lay on his bed, fully clothed, and watched for his old teacher to come quietly in the middle of the night and attempt to touch his body. He waited silently and expectantly, but the old man did not come; instead he dreamed that he stood elevated amid a crowd of cheering people.

And so he eventually came to Fallsville, parked on the main street, and propped a sign on his car:

PRAYER MEETING TOMORROW NIGHT
WITNESS FOR CHRIST AND BE SAVED!
7:30 RIGHT HERE
THE REV. SIMON FORBES

Then, as the beginnings of a crowd gathered, he stood before the car and held up his hands, saying: "And the Lord said: Suffer little children to come unto me, and damned be he who denieth his son my blessing," knowing that no one would discover the emendation of the line; they never did. "Hell burns bright with black fires"; also knowing that paradox was the best weapon: new, frightening, mystifying. "Hell waits for every man, the Lord Jesus waits for nobody."

Waving his arms, he cleared a wide circle in front of him and, taking a pair of dice from his pocket, said: "See here—see what happens when you take up with the devil," rolling the dice on the ground, turning up a two. "You crap out," he said solemnly. He rolled the dice again and again, and still the two appeared.

*49*

Then he scooped them up and said, "The great Lord Jesus, show us thy almighty ways and let us see thy glory and breathe the evil from our souls." And this time, as the dice came to a halt from his fingertips, they showed a seven. "Thank thee, O Lord"; and he bowed his head.

Almost by sleight of hand he passed his hat into the crowd, his eyes betraying none of the knowledge assimilated during his voyage North: the farther he traveled through Pennsylvania, then New England, the less impressed were the people, the less money was dropped into his hat. It was the puritanical streak, he felt, an inbred Eastern hardness that caused the people to weave their souls so tightly with emotionless steel that it became the bulk of their life's fabric, the core of their righteousness.

His head still lowered, his eyes followed the progress of the hat as it went from hand to hand; many people edged away, and he waited, externally serene, until the collection was returned: almost nothing. "Amen," he said, placed his Bible inside the hat, then looked at the people again, watching the rest of them file away in broken ranks. Silently, he accused them again of emptiness.

He took a room in the boarding house and once inside knew that the end of his road lay within sight. He would not hire a hall; and halls, even back rooms, were what Easterners required; but that was not part of the game; it violated the rules. Here, his meetings in the open were failures; he was compelled by the nature and temperament of the people to surround his work with an air of material respectability; Easterners demanded four walls and a pulpit, a place in which to hear the reverberations of his preaching strike the comforting cushion of walls, become buried there, and lose its intensity; what they wished to hear, they wished to hear muffled, softened. And inside a room he felt caged, neatly trapped like an animal in a zoo that frightens people but whose imprisoning bars make them aware of security, supply them with the permission to scorn.

From his room he looked through the window at his old car, the back seat a receptacle for several suitcases and an empty bird cage. A woman inspired, unable to offer money, had given him her most beloved possession, a parrot. At first he refused it, told her not to worry about the money; but she insisted, and to calm her hysteria he had taken it. For miles he drove with the parrot screeching in his ear, and to fight a growing temptation to eat it, stopped by the side of the road and freed it; it flapped away and he watched it longingly. And then, from nowhere, a tramp appeared and caught it, running with it into the woods.

He turned from the window and lay on the bed, drawing a pint of whiskey from his coat, drinking, then propping the bottle on his chest. Draining some more into his mouth, he recorked the bottle and cradled it in the crook of his arm. Gazing up at the ceiling, he saw his life projected there, his fate etched and blistered into cracked plaster; the close-patterned wallpaper, unchanged in a score of years, echoed the stagnation of his soul.

Thinking—he was not even a good preacher; and again the vision of the old man, his arms outstretched, appeared in his mind's eye. He had said: "Lucky, God is like an old white horse that everybody sees chewing grass by the side of the road. Now they all see it, but ain't sure they want it because you can't hardly trust a horse that's off by himself. You got to sell God, got to sell Him like He was some kind of goods. Why, if there was a For Sale Cheap sign hanging off that horse's neck and a man was sitting alongside of him with a cash register, people would pop their veins for a chance to buy. But don't never lose faith in that horse or you can't never sell him."

Well, he was losing it, more all the time, by inches; and it was no use saying that it was the will of God.

He drank and ran his fingers along the bottle, his eyes still on the ceiling, watching the dusk light gray it, erasing the cracks, first small then large; he felt as if he were lying in a coffin, the lid lowering on him with excruciating slowness.

Thinking longingly of the South: Georgia, Texas, Arkansas, Carolina—where people lacked, had always lacked, the answers; where even their infrequent thrills of personal goodness seemed a complacent sin of sloth. Saved, salvation: They all wanted it even if they were deaf, dumb, blind, and could commit no sin at all, not even the thinking kind. Never knowing if the good they did was accepted and approved by God, they came to the preacher weak-boned with the need for purgation, perhaps even for the guilt they felt in their own happiness; unaware of their hates, their rankling bigotry, even their hatred of Negroes which they condoned, for which they exonerated themselves by invoking the word of God. There, perhaps, was their guilt: never knowing what they were, just being so. They were wrong so deeply, so past consciousness that they could not face themselves, much less understand one thin line of their existence. They could not be happy; they could only be, and that was hard enough.

But no one was happy, not here in the East, where they locked and keyed their women; he knew; he could tell from years of moving and looking. They changed wherever he went: easy-to-take dirty farm girls, spinstered at nineteen, who smelled of corroded hay and manure when they lay down on their backs; frightening city girls with *Stay Away* not *Come Ahead*, as you would expect, engraved on them in paint and bulging breasts; simple ones, daughters of Mennonites, Amanites, epicene, a lost race; and now the grayness of New England girls, their hearts and souls flayed by desire, needing love, swelling like a tumor with the need of it, showing it in their faces.

He turned on his side and pressed his hands into his groin; his right leg began to throb and he reached down and massaged the scar, pronounced even through his trousers. He had had her then: grimy and smelly like swamp water, but he had had her, willing, breathing bad breath in rattling gasps; and then the door swung open and the man's spread legs were two immense black towers; and she contracted like a wasted ball of cotton. Half-naked, he took flight and felt the rifle's sear on his leg, but miraculously continued to run until his car carried him past danger and out again into the vast nowhere of open desolate country.

And it was desolate in Fallsville; he was desperate for some logical action. Certainly, he knew, he would go no farther East. But where? He had no answer.

He knew even less the next night, when he returned to his

room after the prayer meeting and washed his face of the slime of rotten eggs and tomatoes, washing it all away along with his tears, sobbing over the sink. He looked up at the mirror, his face so like a corpse that he knew his fear of death had dissipated at the same rate as himself, his faith. And then he understood that the people were not simply empty but that they had cracked him open and looked inside, seeing what he could not, a finality. He reeled back on the bed, his soul floating free from its prison, circumnavigating the cracks and corners of the room, returning finally to the bed, to the body. He stared up into the thick milky haze of the ceiling, his eyes tracing the age-old gashes as they crackled into spidery lightning; and he could not move; he could only receive the prophecy in dumbness, in pain. He did not believe in God; he had lost all faith, and the loss was everywhere to be seen.

Then he sat up and dug his fingers into his cheeks; his eyes contracted, trying to penetrate the dimness of the room where chairs and the table and the lamp stood exactly where they always had, stood fracturing dreams, crushing life with a brutal unwanted reality. It was the end.

But peace came after sleep, and even if he did not believe, he would live like a man, by at least the law of God. He had a profession; and if he could remember it, he would try to live by it. The fear gone, only the sober dregs of knowledge left, he would be an undertaker again, return home.

Except that somehow he could not return, despite his roots, his need of them; he could not accept the South; it could not accept him; so he took his savings and drove through Massachusetts until he came to Southfield, where the undertaker was old, heirless, and willing to sell. And he remained there, in Massachusetts, where the struggle had ended, where his old life died—stalemated.

The old life must stay dead, he thought, half-dozing in the armchair, as dead as Martha Nowell. He widened his eyes, wondering why he had used her as the example; he had cared for her, felt something in her presence that he always felt obliged to repress; cared for her perhaps too much. He knew her because of Cass, because Cass was the only man in Southfield who knew of that old life, who would never reveal his knowledge. Simon had told him, at least part of it, because no matter the difference of their beliefs, they were friends; and because he needed to tell.

The front door rattled violently, the glass pane clanging like a flat bell. He rose, went out into the chapel, switched on the light, and threw back the latch. The sheriff brushed by him and walked to the middle of the room, as if he intended to stride straight through the building and out the back, then whirled, breathless.

"You see what you did?"

"What are you talking about?"

"That goddamn Willy went over and took a shot at Kazu. Missed him, lucky for all of us." He pointed his finger. "And you know why it happened? Because you quit on us."

"That's one more stupid idea you can forget. All of you put that foolishness in his head, not me. I told you he was made for it. So he missed him. That's one thing at least. Thank the Lord for small blessings."

"Yes. Peppered up the whole wall with a twelve-gauge. The kick knocked him through a window, glass and all."

"Where did he get a gun?"

"God knows. Stole it, probably. George and me were sitting out on the square so we heard the shot pretty clear. At first we thought it was a backfire, but then we heard the glass break, and Willy comes running toward us as scared as hell. He didn't even remember where he left the gun. You didn't hear anything?"

"I was half-asleep in the back. Where is he now?"

"George is driving him out of town—far away, I hope the hell."

"You kicked him out of town? You didn't arrest him?"

"Do you think I'm crazy? He'd tell everybody what happened at the hall tonight. I just told him he had his pick—beat it or ten years."

"Looks like your brainstorm cost us a citizen."

"I still say it's your fault, Simon."

54

"You got your wish, didn't you? Kazu's scared, so don't complain."

"Suppose he presses charges?"

"Against who?"

"Maybe all of us."

"I'll back up your insanity plea."

"I said, maybe all of us. That's why you've got to go over to the store and smooth things down."

"Me. Again. How long are you going to hide behind that tin badge you never even wear?"

"Now look, Simon. I got three more months in office left and I don't want to lose what I built up. How would it be if I went over there to talk him out of a lawsuit?"

"Logical, just logical. But no one here seems up to it. I'll smooth things down, I really will."

He pulled his coat from the clothes tree, jarred past the sheriff, and walked outside, skirting the square, toward the Warsaw Market where five or six people stood trying to see through the store window. Simon pushed through them and went inside; Kazu Smolenski sat, almost fanned out, on a milk box, his wife and Harry Chase, still in his druggist's spotted white smock, standing over him, fluttering vials under his nose. Seeing Simon, the woman skipped backward, then crossed herself, shrilling, "He's not dead; he's not dead."

"Well," Simon said, "he might be before long." Then to Kazu, "Now, you goddamned old fool, you see what somebody just did? Tried to kill you, blow your brains out—and I doubt if you have enough brains to make a polka dot on the wall." Jerking his thumb at the woman, "Do you want her killed too? Because you're so stupid and stubborn? If you keep this up they'll not only kill you, they'll be shooting themselves in the street over your rotten meat. You've had your revenge; you almost got overcharged for it. The fight's over. Now do business like a man and feed some of these people."

"Please, Kazu," his wife said, and when he did not respond, still immobile, she looked at Simon. "He will. I swear on God he will."

Simon walked back into the street, and as he passed the monument saw the sheriff waiting by the door of the chapel, the glow of his cigarette flaring, dimming. *So they got me to do it after all,* he thought. *Exactly what they wanted right from the start.* Smiling: *A burlesque show: The Follies of Southfield. Like everybody, I court them, belong to them, commit them in spite of myself. Laughing and crying, they're both the same. Only the face looks different.*

At the door he said, "He's suing you."

"Me? Suing?"

"Don't look so stricken, Ralph. You can go over to the store in the morning and buy your gumdrops. Good night, Ralph," mopping his forehead. "Sleep in peace."

# 7

Near midnight, as he drove around the square, John Roger could no longer contain his sickness. He had felt good leaving Bluefield, when he first began to drink the bootleg rotgut; after a few pulls at the bottle he realized that whatever he was pouring into his stomach was changing its character: it was not blended; the ingredients had separated; and after the first swallow of something like alcohol, the mess had become deadly, oily, with the consistency and smell of hair tonic. Bitterly (it had cost him two dollars, one pint), he flung the bottle out of the car and held his breath.

Now he gagged on the sourness in his throat, fought the mulching of his stomach. Nothing worked. He parked near the Warsaw Market, leaped out of the car, leaned his head over a ditch, and vomited. The effort weakened him. He dropped to one knee; his head hung, staring down into the blackness of the ditch. To his left a glitter, reflecting the moon, caught his eye. He watched it for a few minutes, then moved two or three feet and reached down, his searching hand first touching what felt like cold stones, then sliding smoothly over a shaft of metal. He drew out a twelve-gauge shotgun, raised his eyebrows, and instinctively looked quickly up and down the road, then behind him. He reached into the ditch again, and after groping found two shells.

Forgetting his sickness, even the two-dollar loss, he pocketed the shells, dropped the shotgun onto the seat of the car, and slid behind the wheel. He drove off, thinking: *Maybe I ought to watch that gun. Maybe it's a rattlesnake in disguise.*

But he thought of hunting and skeet-shooting, although he had never done either, driving faster back to the house.

# Two

The old house, a faded temple, a testament, had been built with a kind of pretentious space-wasting old-etching architecture favored by aspirants to gentility and bric-a-brac charm: vulgar with ornateness, spired, weathervaned, cupola'd, porch-posted with ionic or doric or cherubic bases, quick to chip, gash, break, decay. And for the servants (probably none, but the imitation was faithful) a winding hidden stairway leading from the rear of the huge kitchen pantry to a trapdoored upstairs room, now Matthew's room.

As he grew older, he often crept down through the labyrinthine passageway, down the dust-choked circular steps, pausing, his ear to the crack in the pantry door, then eyes fastened to the keyhole or to the solitary streak of light, spear-sharp, which struck the top of his forehead and set his hair ablaze. Trembling, chicken-skinned, he crept back up the steps and pushed open the trap-door; letting it gently back into place, he tiptoed to bed and ruffled the covers over his head, thrilled by the nothing he had seen, heard. The trapdoor, the passageway, was the delight of his childhood, housing the secrets of kings and castles, of witches, vampires, the myriad shapes and shades in human form which never lurked for him to see.

And, older still, he cast off the fantasies and descended the steps no longer in anticipation of dreaminess, peering deliberately through the pantry door. Sometimes he saw John Roger leafing automatically through a newspaper or paring his toenails with a banana knife or even drinking, his head gliding low, lower to the table. And his mother working at the stove or sink (still in its pump-handled, scabbed-zinc archaism); he scrutinized her, noticing the clumsy movements of her hands and arms as she lifted or ironed or folded or opened cupboard doors. From his secret vantage point he felt like an omniscient spy, always with the spy's morbid fear and embraced self-torturing satisfaction of discovery; he watched Esther bend and marveled at the immensity of her bosom, although he did not quite realize its function and regarded it as merely an over-ripe appendage of no earthly use but to pronounce itself, a kind of hindrance to the chest.

Other observations: a certain prettiness at the eyes and nose, none at the mouth or ears or hair; she moved with a large limpid sway which reminded him of a cat he had once seen, stretched with its own heaviness, about to issue a litter. Perhaps her breasts did this, because she was hardly fat, hardly even plump. Naturally thick-waisted, her torso was softly squarish, her legs spindly, the ankles not thick but as wide around as the calves. Her head, with its vague, odd attractiveness, was tiny, the size of a small melon. Her hands seemed sheer bone, with wrists like marble through the flesh; hopelessly fragile, no matter red and grainy.

He watched, but held no opinion of her, did not interpret her actions; she was there. He observed her as he might observe anything familiar to him: a cow, Arrowhead Mountain, the road, the porch rail, relating them to nothing, without evaluation. Once he discovered what she was, could think, verbalize it—a woman, his mother—he lost curiosity and interest. Because it was his father he came to watch, wanted to decipher; John Roger was indefinable, opaque, boundless, as unfathomable as the secret passageway had once been. He studied John Roger; and, watching him, he felt at times a terror of deafness because he never heard speech through the door.

He feared his father, never knowing how or when he would offend him; it depended completely on the man's mood alone. And John Roger's punishments also puzzled Matthew; he had been struck only once, palmed in the cheek; otherwise he was locked in his room, the muffled voice outside the door saying: "If I see you or hear you I might kill you."

John Roger's unreliability, his vacillation was the pivot of Matthew's confusion, causing him to be wary of most people and a great deal of what they said. He found himself in a world both ambiguous and whimsically concrete; he teetered between dreams and life, and at six or seven developed a precocious stoicism, plumbed not from even any serious child's thought but from the necessity of self-preservation. He came to believe only what he wished; developed the habit, infuriating to everyone he knew, of denying an obvious truth if the acceptance of it threatened him in any way. He longed for something, yet longed for nothing; he dreamed and thought, and wondered which was the reality—the dream or the waking. And one day he knew.

Because when he was twelve and worked parttime in the fields on Saturdays, worming along the ground on the burlap mat strapped to his seat, pruning, tending the shoots, he heard boys and men talking of things that seemed peculiar to a working life, blatant refinements of naïve scraps picked up at school. They joked about women, and when they saw him listening, laughed and leered about a girl named Jane Nartiewicz, who could, and often did "take on eleven in one night." The similes blinked his eyes: she was a piece of tail, a snatch; she had tremenjous knockers, buns, headlights; you took one look at her walking down the street and said, "If she don't, nobody does."

And after women, they remembered that tomorrow was Sunday and usually spoke of church and confession, and a few of the boys routinely taunted Matthew about religion.

"Is it true you ain't got any religion?"

"I guess so."

"Hey, Matty says he ain't got any religion."

"Now you stop kidding us, Matty, or we'll grab off your pants."

"Come to think of it, I never seen him in church."

"Maybe he's Protestant. Are you Protestant, Matty?"

"Maybe he's one of them Jewboys—like Punchus Pylate."

"I'm not anything."

And at the end of the routine, as usual, they could not understand him any more than they had at the beginning; they called him a spook and sometimes remembered his house and his recluse mother, and someone could invariably tell the story of the rattrap Model-T and how he suckled at his mother's breast in front of the whole town. And even though only ten or twelve people had seen it, and some probably dead, everyone in Southfield claimed to have been there on the spot; and the incident had by now come to be so genuinely folkloric that they would all have rather had their tongues uprooted than admit they had not witnessed it, seen local history in the making. So they spitefully repeated the story in his presence, frilling it, annoyed that he "wasn't anything." Matthew shrugged his shoulders.

There were two churches in upstreet Southfield, the Polish Catholic and the Presbyterian, and Esther was forbidden both. True to his word, John Roger obliterated the mention of God in the house; he refused to admit the priest or minister when they had called. He worked on in the tobacco fields and sent money each month to Cousin Hope until the house was his free and clear. Several nights a week he drove the Ford, fenderless now, to Bluefield, where he got drunk and went to a brothel. Esther he never touched, and Matthew was left entirely in her awkward care; he was unimportant to John Roger, superfluous, until he was old enough to work a few hours a week in the fields.

One day he said to Matthew, "I spent a lot of money on you.

You're going to get it all back for me. When I think it comes out even I don't much care what you do. You can go or stay as you please, so long as you don't get underfoot. But fair's fair, and I want what I put into you. And don't be afraid I will cheat you because I never cheated anybody in my life. I only want what's rightfully mine. I guess you got to live, so I'll give you something out of your pay. I never kept any books, but I know what I'm due."

And he looked down at Matthew with little concern, thought for a moment, then said, "I don't know as I'm your real father. I don't believe I am, and I never go against myself. That's why I must get paid back."

But afraid he had spoken more than necessary, he left the house and drove to Bluefield, Matthew watching the car bounce down the road, then going to his mother, telling her what John Roger had said.

"Don't pay no attention to what he says. You're his boy. I know you are, and if you don't believe it look in a mirror."

"He told me I wasn't, that he felt I wasn't. He said he never goes against himself."

"No, he never goes against himself. He don't have to. He goes against everybody else." Pausing, nodding her head, then "Yes, against everybody else."

# 2

After driving several blocks up the wide main street of Bluefield —a city, compared with Southfield—John Roger parked the Ford and walked to the saloon (lounge, the sign read). Inside the familiar burnished half-light and the mist of old whiskey and stale beer he sat at the bar, said hello to the bartender, and ordered a rye; sipping, nursing it until someone he knew came along, who would talk, grow expansive and garrulous—and buy for the privilege of talking, revealing in womanless sanctity a slop of confidential, never-to-be-repeated troubles.

He sat, waiting, thinking that by some sort of magic they had all been born that way, the talkers: they would talk themselves dry on their deathbeds. And suddenly cursed himself for his carelessness, his quick, uncontrolled drinking, because the bartender stood in front of him and by his presence forced another rye on him. This time he let it sit untouched, the glass biting into the syrupy circle of the last drink.

In ten minutes he began to squirm on the stool, checking the clock above the bar, glancing over his shoulder at the door, worrying that he might sit alone all night; and he knew it meant just that, sitting there willingly and deliberately, because once immersed in the airless smell of drink, caressed by the short blazing sips, he would never want to leave. But not alone, not again; a man could take a certain measure of loneliness, and he had taken it. Now it was no longer a matter of drinking free, he felt that already, after only a drink and a half; it was not even a matter of talking, since what they bought him drinks for was listening; it was a simple pure need to see, feel someone on the stool next to him.

Forgetting again, he raised the whiskey to his lips and snapped his head back, the glass molded to his teeth, and the bartender dirfted toward him again. Eying him, John Roger thought: *Can't you at least let me set down the glass?* But he said nothing and felt that he would even listen to the bartender, except that the bartender never talked, only poured and squeezed rags and made change—an ox, like the Polacks in the fields. He blankly watched the glass refilled, the bottle placed back on the shelf; he concentrated on the glass, determined this time to outlast the bartender, again panged with deprivation, self-denial. Intent, he did not notice what he had been waiting for, the man sitting next to him, leaning his elbows on the bar.

"What have you got in there, John?"

"What? Nothing. Just thinking, I guess."

"I figured maybe you found a cockroach in there."

John Roger smiled tightly, shaping his lips with effort, forcing the mirthless upturn of his mouth. "That's a good one," he said, starting to append the man's name, but freezing, the smile gone;

he could not think of the name, wondering if he had ever known it.

The man knuckled the bar. Nodding, the bartender poured him a drink, then retreated to a stool where he lapped at a short beer and crackled a newspaper, holding it high to catch the light. The juke box began to play, responded to by the only others in the bar, a boy and girl huddled hand-holding over a corner table, both obviously under age.

"Always like to drink to something first crack out of the box," the man said. "You name it, John."

"No, you go ahead," raising his half-empty glass.

"The end of the war, how's that?"

John Roger drank, knowing only that the war was being fought somewhere at least out of Massachusetts; knowing, too, that it meant siphoning gas out of A-stickered cars; B's were unpredictable, C's useless. He supposed America was winning.

"It sure looks like we got them on the run now, don't it?" the man said. "The Germans are about dead—the bastards."

"Sure looks like it."

Where had they met? Here? In Southfield? Not the bar in Southfield, nor the roadhouse; he could not drink in peace for the stares. John Roger watched him order two whiskies, then push a five-dollar bill into the slop well, tapping it with a clean, pudgy forefinger. He didn't work in the fields. He said, "John, you got anybody in it?"

"What's that?"

Ignoring him, the man reached to his back pocket, grunting, struggling out with a wallet; he opened it and uncoiled an accordion folder of celluloid-sheathed photographs. "My boy," he said, jabbing the same pudgy finger at a skinny corporal with a splotched face—either all his or a discoloration of the celluloid.

John Roger tried to make out the name on a social security card partially covered by the man's thumb. Hoping the thumb would move, he pointed to the boy's sleeve. "Say, what's that?"

"T-Five stripes, for Jesus' sake. The boy's a specialist, knows what he's doing with a truck."

"Yes. Must be the light in here."

"I ever show you my wife?"

"Not as I can remember."

"I was sure I did." And vaguely annoyed, John Roger thought: *Then why did you ask me? Why in hell?* Saying, "She's a good-looker, all right," distastefully running a glance over a yellowed sour face planted askew with small button eyes and shapeless nose, and below the layered chin a huge random bosom gracelessly draped with a flowered bodice. He had never seen her. He said, "Sure, I remember now."

"You know something? This picture don't show her off right."

"Don't it? I guess they never do."

"No, it don't. Clara's ugly as sin. Lots of sins."

Not answering, John Roger finished his drink, watching the wallet groaningly returned to the pocket. The man drank quickly, catching up.

"She's all right though," he said. "Got what's called a good nature. The kids always got along fine with her. You got a picture of yours?"

"No. I don't carry any."

The man motioned to the bartender, ruffling his small pile of bills. "Does your kid respect her? That's the main thing nowadays—kids are all going to hell."

"I got no kids."

The man knitted his eyebrows. "I swear you said you had a kid. If I'm not mistaken, I think you brought it up last winter."

"Well, my wife has a boy. She was married before."

"I guess that ain't the same thing."

"No."

Tossing off his drink, the man ordered again, raising his glass, saying, "Well, one for the road, John."

"Ain't it a little early?"

"Promised the missus. Besides, work tomorrow."

They drank, the man lightly pummeling John Roger's shoulder and, picking up his change without paying, said good night and left.

John Roger watched the bartender slip a dollar out from under his nose. After a swipe of the rag, he said, "Again?"

"Yes," John Roger said, "and don't leave either. I'd like to see you get through that goddamn newspaper." He drained the glass and flicked his fingernail against the bar, saying, "Go ahead. And you might as well buy yourself a beer since you think I can afford it," adding as the bartender filled his own miniature glass from the tap. "Well, Jakey, what's this war like? What's your paper say?"

"We're running them out of the islands."

"Germans. I never could stand them."

"On the islands? There's no Germans on any islands. Only Japs."

"Well, what the hell's the difference? They're fighting, ain't they?"

"Thanks," the bartender said, carrying his beer back to the stool.

John Roger gulped the whiskey. "How about another one?"

Turning, his face passive, uncaring, insultingly expressionless, the bartender refilled the glass.

"Don't this place ever buy back, Jakey?"

"Not whiskey, chief."

"That's all the difference in the world." Drinking, burning deep inside. Tilting his head back, he gazed up a calendar, a brightly-colored drawing of a girl leaning from the waist at a forty-five degree angle, bursting at the seams with the fullness of her flesh. Tall, ridiculously pink, straw hair tumbling out of a Stetson, dressed in a short vest which uncovered the upsloped bottoms of her breasts; excruciatingly, painfully tight shorts welded to her behind, showing half of it; long arched legs ending in abbreviated cowboy boots like sexually-rooted plants—she stood astride a hobby horse, just above the legend: *I want my horsie.*

The colors fuzzed, blurred; he blinked, forcing his eyes into focus, using them to stroke the breasts, the legs, removing the shorts, sinking deep into the innocent yet powerfully lascivious arch smile. Licking his lips, he said to the bartender, "Let me have a bottle of rye."

"Can't do that. This ain't a package store."

"Two bucks for a cigar says it is."

66

Paying, he tucked the paper-wrapped bottle into his armpit and left the bar, stiffening himself as he passed the couple kissing at the corner table. He walked up a side street, a gradually inclining hill; crossing under a street light his knees unclamped and he lurched, almost dropping the bottle. Shaking the blur from his eyes, he twisted the paper bag securely around the neck of the bottle and started off again, finally turning into an alley, climbing a flight of noisy wooden steps at the side of a barber-shop. He rapped at a glass pane; curtains parted and a woman's face appeared, nodding in recognition. She slid the curtains together, opened the door, and let him in.

The heavy air collapsed him with keen drunkenness, inflating his head, causing him to lock his legs against falling. The woman paid him no attention, merely nodded again and led him through a too-bright kitchen and then along a hall hung, between swaths of blistered wallpaper, with colored reproductions of movie stars clipped from magazines and rotogravure sections of Sunday newspapers. She opened a door and he walked ahead of her into a room cramped with a bed, chair, lamp, and sink.

"Anybody special?" she said.

"So long as it's a woman. I guess you can bring me that."

After she left, he unscrewed the cap from the bottle, found a glass on the sink, and poured it half full. He could hardly see in the ochre glow from the lamp, and tried to turn on the ceiling light, but the switch flicked up and down uselessly. He sat on the bed and drank, the first mouthful edged with vicious nausea, the second calm, unfelt.

A girl or woman entered—it was hard to tell in the light—said something indistinguishable, and immediately removed her blouse, hanging it on a hook behind the door.

"Take it easy," he said. "I got money. Have a drink."

She sat beside him, leaning on an elbow into the light where he could see her clearly, smiling. She was dark, plump, her hair hanging in short wisps on her powder-plastered forehead; her breasts, rising from the ridge of her black brassière, tremulous, overripe; she looked like a hundred others, nothing, not a shadow of the girl on the calender. *Shit,* he thought, *they never are.*

He touched her wrist, drawing his index finger heavily along her forearm, trying to summon up a dreg of tenderness, feeling. Then he took his hand away, saying, "Maybe you better take off your skirt."

She did, squirming exaggeratedly out of it with rolling hips, walking the few steps to the hook; her behind bulged slightly from black pants; her thighs rippled not with fat but with a pliable currying softness. She returned to the bed, taking the glass he offered, himself drinking from the bottle until he dribbled on his chin.

"Thanks," she said. "There you go." Then, after drinking, "Kind of early tonight, no?"

"You a Polack? You talk funny?"

"Not me. Don't you like Polacks?"

"See them all day—hundreds." He belched. "They work for me."

"That so?"

"Yes. I got a tobacco farm."

"Boy, you must make a fortune, Lucky Strike Green Goes to War—like that."

"Yes. A fortune." He drank again, sloshing his shirt. Then, wiping his mouth with the back of his hand, "I only come in here because you got a nice room. It ain't bad to take it easy in. Don't need no women, got all I want, free. Polacks, Wops, everybody. Even a Chink if I wanted."

"Sure."

He squinted, seeing her undulating, weaving, although she sat still. He said, "Go ahead, take off the whole shitload," watching, over the upraised bottle, a stocking peeling from what vaguely resembled a leg, two smears of black wafting toward the hook on the door. He lay back, feeling her work at his belt buckle.

"How about a little help?" she said.

"What's that?"

"Damn it, John, come on."

He pushed her hands away and dragged himself to a sitting

**68**

position; he could barely undo the buckle, the metal eluding his fingers, and finally he got his pants down and rolled over and couldn't see a thing. . . .

He found himself sitting in the chair, his eyes wavering into clarity, seeing her buttoning her blouse, a cigarette dangling almost vertically from her lips, the smoke blooming upward, forcing her to blink. Seeing him, she said, "I got you buttoned up. You know what you did? You passed out on me as soon as you put it to me." She sighed. "I guess I do that to fellows."

But he could not remember, simply knew that nothing had happened; he twisted his lips, his body inoperative yet his mind momentarily clear; he blinked.

She came toward him. "Five, honey. That'll do it."

"No. Never paid for it 'til I came here. Had all the women in the world, any time. Goddamn, no."

"Please, John. Now be good this time."

"You think I'd ever come in a shithole like this if everything didn't go against me? I never needed anybody like you."

"Now, John, you always said you liked me."

"Don't even know who the hell you are. . . . Yes I do. You're the one that stinks. Get the hell away."

"Honey, I got to have that five."

"I said get away."

"I need it," touching his shoulder.

He bolted up and struck her backhanded; the blow was mis-aimed, knuckling off her right shoulder, yet it drove her sprawling to the bed. Standing over her, the breath of her screams full in his face, he struck out again, this time squarely on the side of the head. She shrieked and bellowed like the breakage of thunder, a great primitive instrument; and he raised his arm but stumbled and staggered on his heels back against the wall. The woman who had let him in came into the room with a man, the man not even stopping, fluidly seizing John Roger's arm, pinning, twisting, jammed the wrist up to the shoulder blade.

The screaming stopped, the howls now words, gargling. "Dirty son-of-a-bitch won't pay. I said I didn't want him again, I told you what he does. He's crazy; he could of killed me." She kneaded her cheek, simpering, beginning to cry. "I quit. Frig this place, I just quit."

John Roger set his teeth against the pain, wanting to bellow, choking on his tongue.

The woman pulled a small wad of bills from his pocket and shuffled them, counting.

"Leave the shit a dollar," the man said.

When she had stuffed a bill back into John Roger's shirt pocket, the man pushed him ahead through the door, still twisting the arm, along the hall, kneeing him in the buttocks down the flight of stairs, whipping the arm, whirling him into a wall. Then John Roger almost heard the roar in his stomach, the splashing of the entrails as the fist drilled and turned just above the belt, and as he doubled forward felt the flat of a hand against his head, pushing, and he threw his arms out as he fell to the ground.

He lay there for a time, sick, afraid to move, then rose disjointedly, bracing himself against the wall, gasping, getting truly sick. He sat on a trash can until his stomach eased; then, with a fierce effort, groped in the darkness until he found what suited him, a piece of broomstick. He heaved it weakly up at the door, but it fell short, clattering and bouncing on the stair landing. Giving up, he limped out of the alley and, needing to bend at the waist, tried to remember where he had parked the Ford.

But wherever it was, he could not find it; his mind softened. He staggered down a hill, recalling that he had climbed one, and came out on the main street; sitting on the curb he gazed intently up the street, eventually picking out the winking sign of the bar. He rose and walked toward it, then suddenly reversed his course, remembering, he was sure, that he had parked in the opposite direction. Walking on, he steadied himself against lurching, peering into side streets until he saw it, humped like a cracked beetle, rusty and repulsive under a street light.

On the way back from Bluefield he drifted from lane to lane and almost ran into a ditch, finally skidding dangerously around the Southfield square, swerving widely onto Route 12. He cursed furiously; what had happened during the night knifing clearly through his drunken fog. Humiliated, he raged into the night and lashed his foot against the bottom of the door, pounding the steering wheel with his fist.

"Oh, sweet Jesus, what they done to me," he roared, his eyes bobbing over the broken white line dancing in the arc of a single headlight; thinking now of the nameless man in the bar, the whore, the blow in the stomach—the meld of thoughts churning from brain to heart to belly, pumping sick bile up again to his mouth.

"This is my punishment," he shouted, and once he had said it grew outraged beyond constraint because he was admitting the power of someone, something capable of punishing; admitting that he warranted punishment, saying yes to the existence of— but he would not think that; no such thing existed. He could prove it now, by driving, foot pressed deep into the accelerator, straight into the tallest, thickest tree; no, he did not need to prove it; but if one day he did, it was that easy, a short turn of the wheel. There was nothing; there had to be nothing; he had had a fantasy, wallowed in his sickness and pain and outrage. No more.

At the house he parked halfway up the hill, walked the rest of the way to the side door, pushed through it, and, stumbling around in the dark, finally went up the stairs. A long rod of light stretched up the wall opposite Esther's room; he almost went on down the hall, then paused by her partly-open door, looking in-side. She was kneeling, a rosary woven through her fingers; he trembled, hating, thinking that she knew not to let him find her praying, but that she had not heard him enter the house, she was that absorbed, retreating further into what he must prevent. He kicked open the door, menacing as she jerked her head up; she could do nothing, only stare, the color gone from her face, her shoulders twitching. Yet somehow she rose and leaned, half fell, against the wall, her eyes expanding whitely over the dark crescents of her cheeks. And as he advanced, she could not run, hide, even scream; but with a humming whine she thrust the tiny crucifix of the rosary out in front of her as if its power could drive him away.

He paused, then stepped forward again, entranced by the crucifix, thoughtlessly flailing out at her. And as she clenched her arm up to hide her face, she involuntarily whipped the rosary across his mouth, the crucifix and beads snapping off the weak chain, sparkling away like buckshot.

When he removed his hands from his lips, his palms were seamed with blood, yet he felt no pain; his body was still numb from whiskey, and now his mind disintegrated under a slashing of emotions, as if her blow had been the final drink before oblivion. He saw her cowering against the wall and he knew that before the oblivion came, he must strike out; but not at her; it was not she whom he must destroy.

He went toward her and, with the energy of every tendon, muscle, nerve drove his fist into the wall near her head; drew back and swung again, hearing, seeing the plaster shatter and cave in; drew back again, but stopped at her shriek. He stood, his head low to his chest, obliquely watching her, his hand gloved red, dripping. The crucifix lay glinting at his feet, one arm buried in a crack between the floorboards.

Then he left the room, unaware of his movements, not seeing Matthew standing in the hall, merely groping unconsciously toward his room. But he did not reach it; there was no breath for a moment, no thought or memory, only darkness and a tinge of rubbery feeling in his head as it thumped against the floor.

# 3

After early Mass, Cass took the short walk from his house into town, immune from the late-morning heat in a pale gray suit and straw hat with a blue-and-red band. Emerging from Washington Street, heading for Simon's, he saw Matthew Williams sitting alone on the bench which fronted the monument, sitting with his elbows on his knees, staring at the ground, shuffling loose dirt into ridges with his feet.

As always, when he passed the square, Cass looked up at the monument with a kind of planned inadvertency, almost a compulsion, a tic that raised his eyes; after twenty-five years of neglect the bronze statue had turned a powdery, unhealthy green; the soldier stood, his knees slightly bent, prepared to throw a hand grenade at an invisible enemy, his face shot through with grim idealism, as if his solitary grenade could rectify the crimes of the world. Up close, from bird-droppings and the chip of a wildly-thrown rock, the mouth seemed disfigured by an idiot protrusion of the tongue. Archaism hung over it like a cloak, like an abandoned spider web no longer a nest. And below sat Matthew, alone, a hint of sorrow and pessimism in the slouch of his shoulders and the idle scrapings of his feet.

Cass almost continued on to Simon's, then suddenly crossed to the square; for a moment he stood over Matthew unnoticed, the boy caught up in the desultory, aimless ridging of the dirt, now constructing four low walls around a nervous ant.

"Hello, Matthew."

Matthew rose and clasped his hands behind his back. "Hello, Mr. Nowell."

Cass ruffled Matthew's hair and smiled. "I saw you sitting here all alone, so I thought I'd drop over and pass the time of day. Why aren't you playing with your friends?"

"I guess they all went to church."

"And you don't go, do you?"

Matthew looked at him quizzically, his head cocked.

"It's a small town," Cass said. "No one really has any privacy," circling Matthew's shoulder with his arm and, sitting on the bench, gently easing Matthew down beside him. "Have you ever been in church, Matthew?"

"No, sir."

Cass nodded, taking his hand from Matthew's shoulder and draping it on the backrest of the bench. "I suppose you're just not churchgoers, right?"

"No, sir. I'm not anything."

Cass nodded again—the rumors of this family, the gossip, snatches of overheard conversations beginning to crystallize, to fit into a pattern of truth.

"You see, my father . . ."

"Yes, I know about that. I just didn't know how deep it ran. Your mother—what is she?"

"She's a Catholic, she told me. She prays a lot."

He looked at Matthew carefully, not knowing this, a secret

73

that had somehow been permitted to exist. He folded his hands in his lap, speaking, but turning his eyes toward Arrowhead Mountain, the black mouth of King Philip's cave sharply defined in the clear morning, towering directly, almost protectively, above the square.

"Doesn't she want you to go to church, son?"

"She never told me to. My father says I can't be anything."

Cass paused a moment, thinking, wondering if he should ask a question—one almost completely self-directed, created of his own rankling curiosity. He needed to know; he asked. "Do you feel Catholic, Matthew? Do you ever have a need to go to church?"

"I don't know what you mean, Mr. Nowell."

"I mean, you know you're Catholic. Do you ever pass by the church and think: Maybe I should go inside?" realizing now the futility of the question, the senselessness of asking a boy, especially this boy, who could not feel the deprivation of what he had never possessed.

"I guess not," Matthew said. "My father told me to stay away from church. He says it's a bad place."

Cass twisted his lips, stifling a retort, an attack; instead, controlling himself, he half-whispered, "Do you believe that?"

Matthew shrugged his shoulders, then grinned coldly. "No, I guess not. He says lots of things."

"Do you know my daughter, Matthew?"

"Sure, I seen her lots of times around your store. Doesn't she go to school?"

"She goes to parochial school in Bluefield, Catholic school. What I mean to say is, do I look like a man who'd let my daughter go to Catholic school and church if they were bad places?"

The answer did not come automatically. Surprised, Cass watched Matthew scan his face, scrutinizing, as though even a polite comment depended on an appraisal.

"No, I guess not. Maybe church is just bad for my father."

Cass looked toward the mountain again, perplexed and annoyingly disappointed by the small failure of his brittle logic; annoyed further by what he interpreted as either Matthew's in-

74

telligence or his vague patronizing irony. Yet he was only twelve, a little older than Martha; of how much irony was he capable?

"Matthew, you know that someday you have to go to church, don't you? You're bound to a law; your mother must have told you that."

"No, sir, she never did."

"Well, you must. You are bound," halting abruptly, hoping that his impatience had not been detected. "I mean, do you want to go to church?"

"Maybe. What's it like?"

And again, a touch of puzzlement; he could not decide if the question were inquisitive or merely conciliatory. He said, "It's very beautiful," suddenly finding that any description, outside his philosophical one, failed, meant nothing to him. Yet, "The priest tells stories about Jesus and the saints. There are pictures and statues and singing." Finally he had to say it. "And being there gives you peace and a reason for living. You feel close to God, a part of His wisdom, closer if you receive communion." But it was not working; he'd failed; for the boy it was illegible rubric, he could see it as soon as he could no longer talk of the pictures and statues. "Do you think you'd like to go?"

"I would like to see it. All the kids go."

"Do you have a friend to take you?"

"No, I guess not."

"Then you can go with Martha and me. How about next Sunday?"

"I don't know." He began shuffling dirt again.

"Why not ask your mother to let you?"

Matthew grinned strangely, as if correlating the movement of his lips to the effort of thinking; not really a grin at all. "I'll ask her."

"Maybe she'd like to come along."

"No, I know she won't."

"No matter. Then let's meet outside the church next Sunday at ten to nine. St. Stanislaus."

"I'll try."

Cass rose, squeezed Matthew's shoulder, and said good-bye.

He watched the boy run off toward Route 12 and pause by the juncture to hitchhike, squatting, waiting for a car. Cass turned and crossed the street to the funeral chapel; he tapped at the shade-drawn door, and in a moment Simon let him in and preceeded him to the back.

"I was just talking to Matthew Williams," Cass said.

"The boy?"

"Yes. He frightens me a little. He's clever, too clever. Sometimes, when he looks at you, his eyes are like an old man's."

"He seems to shift for himself a lot. I suppose he has to be smart, living in that house with his old man. From what I hear, it's bad."

"Did you know his mother is Catholic?"

"No. The boy tell you?"

Cass nodded; Simon grunted and settled into his armchair.

"His father passes himself off as an atheist," Simon said. "I suppose you know about that."

"Yes, I thought that might be it. He put the priest out once. I don't much like to listen to the gossip in the store."

"Personally, I wonder if it's really true. He's running scared—you can see it in his eyes. When he scratches his head there's violence in his fingers. Fear, too."

"Well, whatever he is, I'm taking the boy to church next Sunday if his mother lets him go. I think she'll have to."

"You have reasons?"

"He's a Catholic."

"I don't think she'll have much say in the matter. But if he does go, what then?"

"We'll find out, Simon. Someone has got to show him what he is. When I saw him all alone, I just wanted to give him a friendly word. And then he told me and I had to ask him—I asked him before I even thought about it. I could see a whole life of rejection in his face, and I couldn't bear it."

"You know what's just liable to happen if his old man finds out? He'll probably whale the hell out of him. You might be playing missionary with the wrong people."

"I'm not playing anything. I did what has to be done."

76

"Yes, I understand that. You feel you have to; you're obligated to. I can't agree with you and I can't argue with you. Only I'd hate to see that boy beat to a pulp."

"I don't like to think of that either, but if it has to be that way, if it's necessary . . ."

"You're not that hard. Don't pretend you are; the shoe doesn't fit."

"Then if it happens, maybe he'll realize what he is, maybe nothing will ever keep him from God again. He'll fight."

"You talk like a fool. He's a baby, like your daughter. You see her every day. What's she got to fight with? What's he? Do you want to force some kind of martyrdom on him when he doesn't even know which side is up? You're involving him in grown-up business. I'm tempted to ask you what your angle is, if you've got some kind of demon on your back."

"You don't see my point."

"Sure I do, it's all black and white. The only thing that kid can do is take a beating, be choked off like a little bug, maybe get so scared he'll puke up whenever he sees a church. Go slow, Cass."

"Hold back?"

"Yes."

"As you say, I have an obligation."

"I see that, but you're up against a stone wall. The boy's too young. You can't do anything constructive. Face it, will you?"

"You don't understand. If you believed, you'd understand."

"Then you know you're wrong. Whenever you throw that up to me, you know it."

Cass watched him light his pipe, heard the wheeze, the curls of smoke obscuring his face.

"Not wrong, Simon. I'm hopeful. I think everything will be all right."

"Yes. His mother might say no. Hasn't she lived with that fool's sickness long enough to know him, know what he might do? The man hates God, Cass. I've seen him spit when he passes a church. A hater like that can tear down half the world before a stray brick kills him. Why not listen to the gossip in the store?

Ask anybody in town; ask the farmers what he's like. They've seen him in bad times and they've seen him in good times—and he's never changed. Drive out past the house and take a good look at the woman. She's been beaten down so long she's nearly invisible. Then start talking about your obligation."

"I'm sorry for all that. The boy deserves better."

"Exactly. He's young; he has plenty of time to let God find him. In his situation it's got to be that way."

"No. If he's left alone he may never have the chance. I know it will turn out all right."

"Yes. As I said before, she might say no."

"She can't."

"My friend, you *do* have a demon," sucking on his pipe, letting the smoke billow up from his mouth in dense, aromatic clouds.

# 4

"Mr. Nowell wants me to go to church with him next Sunday. Should I?"

She sat still at the kitchen table, her hand cradling a chipped, earless cup, her eyes suddenly filmed. "Who's Mr. Nowell?"

"He owns the hardware store."

"What church, son?"

"Catholic."

"Why did he ask you?"

"I don't know. He said I was bound to it. Am I bound to it?"

She bent her head, her eyes searching among the coffee dregs in the bottom of the cup. "Do you want to go?" she said.

"Is it all right?"

"Yes, you go ahead."

"What about Pa?"

You didn't ask *him*, did you? You asked me."

"Yes."

"Just don't bother telling him. If he finds out later it won't matter; it'll be done." And then, with more passion than he had

78

ever heard in her voice, "I want you to go. And when you're there, pray for me. You'll find out how."

# 5

They sat in a pew close to the altar rail, absorbed in a heavy, abnormally long June heat which became denser, airless, wet as the Mass progressed, breathing graduated to a harsh labor: Cass, Martha to his left, Matthew. And Matthew, the head-wagging stares of the people now forgotten, watched the curious, rigidly-patterned glide of the priest from one side of the altar to the other, pausing with supple serenity at the center facing the small gold-leafed enclosure that Cass had said contained the sacrament, the communion, the body and blood of Jesus.

He let his attention leave the priest and drift freely about the church: the statues, on either side of the altar, of a young man holding a miniature church in the crook of his left arm, of a pretty young woman cradling a child, her breast overlaid with a flaming, exposed heart, radiating. In back of the rail, two banks of squat candles, red and blue in glasses, not like the pair of white tapers on the altar.

The pitched roof was thickly buttressed with beams extending halfway down the gold-fringed purplish walls, the walls themselves intersected by curtained wooden booths and long arched windows of tinted glass—pictures of saints crowned with halos, shining bright and happy with the sun floating in through them, the donors' names etched in black at their feet, mostly in long tongue-mocking Polish. He gazed, especially curious, at the small bas-relief plaques on the walls, fourteen of them, each a different scene with the same cast of characters; and the one near the end, the bearded man, Jesus, hanging from a cross in a tortuous twist of plaster.

At times his examination was interrupted by people moving in ragged unison: standing, kneeling on narrow padded boards, sitting. He followed them, cued by their preparatory shuffling. When the priest went to the pulpit and read in English from a book, they stood; when he closed the book and talked naturally, they sat. He listened to the priest say that the war was almost ended (he knew that from school), only the atheistic Japanese left now; and that prayer had accomplished it; God was about to triumph. Everyone seemed happy, and the way it was said, with almost a shout, with the priest's arms outstretched, he expected singing, but there was none (only, Cass had said, at something called High Mass). And they were called on to say a special silent prayer; he, remembering what his mother had said, sliding to his knees with the rest of them, trying, groping, finally saying to himself: *I pray for Ma.* Then the priest crossed himself (as he had seen his mother do, but not as slowly or formally as the priest) and returned to the altar. Some men began to stretch long-handled straw baskets into the pews, Cass leaning over and giving Matthew and Martha each a dime; he dropping it into the well of coins and bills passed under his nose. And soon the metal shirring of bells and the people kneeling; the priest opened a tiny house (holding his breath, waiting to see flesh and blood) and drew out a golden cup, turning and—again the bells, three times—holding a piece of white roundness, elevating it with both hands above his eyes. He bent over the altar again and people began leaving the pews, filing along the aisles toward the rail, all kneeling and touching their breasts at the three new tinkles of the bells; the priest holding the golden cup before him in his left hand, the other hand raising a smaller white circle, placing it then into the mouth of the boy who served him. And the boy following him as he descended the altar steps and came to the rail, offering the circles to the open mouths of the people, who remained there for a second or two before making way for someone else immediately filling the vacated place; offering the circles with strange nervous movements of the fingers while the boy bobbed a gold plate under chins.

And suddenly he saw Martha and Cass at the rail (glancing at their empty seats as if pinching himself out of a dream), both kneeling there together, he tall and pious, she with a toss of her head that trembled her short brown hair. She lifted her face, a small tongue breaking through the lips to take the host,

flicking it inside the privacy of her mouth like the almost unseen movement of a tiny animal, her hands stiffly steepled. And
then, heads bowed, eyes reduced to humble slits, they returned to
the pew and knelt, their faces buried in their palms.

When the hands were drawn away, she looked at him with the
awareness of his watching her, smiled complacently and somehow complicitly, and he remembered what Cass had said: *Closer
to God in communion* (then this was communion); but she
seemed no different. He found himself staring at her, flushed,
then swiveled his head away, back to the altar.

With a snap, the priest locked the house, the boy crossing
behind him, carrying a huge book on a wooden shelf, almost
tripping as he climbed the steps.

Matthew looked down at the missal in his hands, one page
Latin, the other English, given to him by Cass—and which he
had closed after a minute of confusion—the imitation leather
cover now limp and shimmering with moisture. He closed his
eyes, itchy with the sweat prickling down his spine to the hollow
at the small of his back, the clammy clotting in his armpits; and
when he opened his eyes, Cass's met his, Cass smiling warmly,
encouragingly.

Then stirred by the scrambling movement of the bodies he
had not anticipated, he hurried forward to his knees and listened,
while the priest prayed aloud and the people answered, an in-
articulate droning of timbres. They stood, and the priest left the
altar holding something veiled in green cloth, followed by the
boy. It was over; the people milled together in quiet disorder,
sidling into the aisles, some going to the banks of colored candles,
the rest crossing themselves from a marble bowl of water.

Outside in the sun, painfully bright but, despite its heat,
cooler than the church, Cass said, "Well, Matthew, that was all
right, wasn't it?"

He answered, politely, not feeling it, "Yes, sir."

"How about coming home with us for breakfast?"

"I already ate."

"Bacon and eggs," Martha said.

"I really have to go home," Matthew said, and looked down

at the ground, the dusty tops of his shoes. He felt Cass's hand on his shoulder.

"What about next week?"

"Well, I'll have to find out, Mr. Nowell."

"You do that," removing his hand.

"Good-bye," Matthew said; stood in confusion for a moment, then turned and trotted off.

"Why didn't you tell me he was coming?" Martha asked.

"Because I really didn't know if he would. Why? Did you mind?"

"No."

"You don't know him, do you?"

"I guess. He lives out in the haunted house."

"It's not really haunted, you know."

"Maybe it is and maybe it isn't." She tossed her head and looked back in the direction Matthew had gone. "What's the matter with his mother and father?"

"It's a long story, honey." He took her hand and they walked along the road toward the square, her small mouth puckered quizzically, her eyebrows curled, almost meeting.

"Well, what is the matter?" she insisted. "Are they crazy or what? I mean, that's what the kids say. Doesn't he have a suit to go to church in?"

"No, I suppose he hasn't."

"Are they crazy?"

He was tempted to say yes to end it. He found it obscene, too abstruse to tell her that at least the father had no faith. It might worry her, nag at her own unthreatened, unquestioned belief. He said "His mother is Catholic, but his father isn't."

"Then why didn't his mother come?"

"Well, his father has some strange ideas. For one reason or another he might not want her to."

"I guess he doesn't believe in God, does he? Lots of people don't."

"Where did you learn that?"

"Oh, Mrs. Majewski is always talking about her son. You know, she talks a lot, especially when she washes the floors. She calls him names. Once she was so mad at him, she almost broke one of our good cups."

He nodded.

Martha said, "Boy—*people!*"

So she had grown past another stage that had eluded him, broken through another thin protective shell that he had attempted to reinforce and seal. He missed it all again; she grew too quickly; he could not keep up. Yet he had laid a solid ground; he must not worry about her: strong, like her mother, saying *people!* as if already at her age she knew full well what enormities they could perpetrate, saying it in a voice tinctured by resigned disgust.

Entering the house, he said, "You the cook today?"

"Yes, sir. A pair over easy," disappearing into the kitchen.

Now he was sure that the morning had gone well, that no demon possessed him; Martha was living proof. Of course, Matthew had not responded with any particular animation, but in time he would; there were things he must learn, knowledge he must acquire.

Smiling, whistling, he felt happy and vindicated, and reached for the Sunday paper. Not knowing the subtlety of what had happened, giving no mind to the obvious fact that Matthew and Martha had sat together, that he had watched her, inhaled her little girl's chaste perfume. And someday would come to want her.

# 6

He clattered through the door and into the kitchen, his entrance cutting short their meal, causing them to look up warily, uneasily, tensing by habit into a useless preparedness; he stood facing them for fully half a minute, then said to Matthew, "Where were you this morning?"

Matthew, not answering, lowered a piece of bread to his plate, training his eyes on it, waiting.

"Tell me or I'll tell you."

Still Matthew said nothing. John Roger seized his arm and jerked him from the chair, spinning him like a top until he came to rest, his wrist pinned by one huge clutching hand.

"You were in church, in that goddamn church. You were seen." Turning to Esther, "Was this your doing? You better tell me now."

"She didn't know about it," Matthew said. "I swear. I wanted to go."

John Roger dug the fingers of his other hand into Esther's shoulder, angered even more by her blank eyes set staring as if the pain he was giving her went unfelt. He dug deeper.

"He don't fool me, missus, not him. You can just sit there; I'll fix you later." Releasing her, he lifted Matthew off the floor, holding him by his biceps. "Who took you?"

"Nobody. I went by myself."

Shaking Matthew now, pushing him back and forth like a concertina, he said, "If you don't tell me it means she put you up to it."

Crying, his voice rattling, stammering under the breath-crushing movement, Matthew sobbed, "It was Mr. Nowell, Mr. Nowell . . ."

"Him," John Roger muttered, then put Matthew on the floor, dragged him through the kitchen and up the stairs to his room; he dropped Matthew at the foot of the bed, began to remove his belt, then rebuckled it and slid Matthew's out of its trouser loops, finally tying his hands to the bedpost.

"I warned you," he said. "Now see what you get."

Then he left the house and drove furiously upstreet, skidding the square and turning right into Washington Street, brake-screeching up Cass Nowell's driveway. He vaulted the steps to the porch and hammered at the door; and when it opened, Martha looked up at him, her face tilted inquisitively, a newspaper comic section unfurling from her hand.

"You tell your father Mr. Williams is here."

And, when Cass appeared, stepping out onto the porch, shutting the door behind him, John Roger said, "Just who the hell do you think you are?"

"What do you want?"

84

"You know goddamn fucking well what I want. You took that boy to church behind my back, against me. Keep your nose out of my life, you hear?"

"The boy needs church, Williams; he's becoming an outcast and he's beginning to realize it. He doesn't even have a friend. Someone had better do something for him before he's lost."

"Shit."

"I happen to believe church is the house of God," his voice pitching. "I hope Matthew comes to believe it too."

"It ain't my fault you can't think straight. Just keep your beliefs, or whatever the hell they are, away from me."

"I say someone has to look out for him. You won't; it's no secret. I did what I know is right."

"You ain't going to get to heaven by going against me. I guess maybe you think you can."

"You'd better go home."

"Let me tell you, if you ever do that again I'll knock the hell out of you."

Gripping the porch rail, his knuckles white and bulging, Cass said, "No, let me tell you. You've denied Matthew his God-given right. He was born a Catholic and must always be a Catholic."

"Who told you that?"

"And you're afraid he'll find love and acceptance in the church, everything you can't or won't give him. Afraid he'll find everything and show you up because you can't find a thing. You should see yourself; you know what I'm saying, all right. You can't find God in your stupidity and you know it—and it's killing you. Someone told me you were running scared. I didn't know how much."

"You shut up."

"It was his right to go to Mass," unable to stop, pressing. "He made the decision to go with his own free will and you can't stop him. Don't think I'd bother to go against you—I took Matthew and was proud to. Maybe someday he'll undo what you've forced on him. That's all I'm going to say."

"Shit. You're just like that God of yours, always sneaking up on people from behind."

"That's enough about God from your mouth."

"Yes, that's just the way you people are. You hide behind God and do everything in His name, and get away with it too. You got all the answers, and that makes people like me turds. Well, listen, mister, I don't give a damn for God and that means you stay away from that boy or one night I'll come by here and kill you—you and that daughter of yours."

"Get the hell off my porch."

"You and your daughter both. The priest and the nun."

Cass hit him then, swung into his face and knocked him backwards down the steps. He lay there a moment, watching Cass move toward him; and he reached out for something, a weapon, and when his hand had found a stone, his fingers almost on it, he wrenched his arm away in blind agony as Cass tramped onto his wrist, grinding it under a heel. He rolled away toward the house and rose to his knees, seeing Cass stalk him again; and this time he charged forward, butting, his head caving into the softness of a stomach, hearing the grunt, yet progressing no farther, trembling under the electric paralysis in his head and shoulders as Cass's fist battered down on his neck. He clutched at Cass's groin, holding it, but the knee in his face jerked him up and drove him back against the house, his head beating against the clapboards, his own groin catching fire, and then his face bubbling into a rain barrel, stuck there as if in concrete, choking, feeling his head pulled free by the hair into the air, gulping for air, then back into the water, out again. It was strange now, desensitized and curious, he fell but did not remember falling, just being dragged to his feet, then staring into a face whose lips were drawn back over the teeth. Dangling in a void of almost-arrested motion he saw the fist inching toward him, huge and shapeless, and there was even a moment of total cessation before it found him between the eyes, exactly at the bridge of his nose.

Matthew crouched on the floor, squirming under the cutting belt, his wrists numb and his arms aching, wrenched and seared in their sockets. He should have known, he thought; he had been warned. He had often seen his father in violence, but never understood the precise reasons, not the reason for this. But it was all

86

clear now; it went back to the time he had asked John Roger about church and God, and John Roger glared at him, the pulses in his temples tumescent and blue, his rough beard no mask for the sudden crimson of his face.

He had said, "I'm a fair man," his voice quivering, hauntingly nasal, "and you don't know no better, so I'll leave it go this time. Just you think of the worst thing in the world, the worst thing that could happen to you. That's what church is. . . . There ain't any God, so it would be stupid to talk about that." He had seemed to strangle on the word, the name, wiping his mouth with his sleeve as if to expunge a foul taste. "Just don't you ever bring it up again. Don't ever give it another thought, hear?"

Matthew had said yes, not knowing that he was lying (not knowing truly what he was violating when he also said yes to Cass). But now he understood: church was not the worst thing in the world; it was just hot, crowded, stale with old smells. And Martha sitting beside him. The worst thing in the world was his father, to do this, for reasons that perhaps existed, but were not right.

Esther entered the room, untied him, then sat on the bed, faceless, her back to the light from the window.

"Maybe you shouldn't ought to," he said, rubbing his wrists, kneading them with his knuckles.

"You can't stay there. Go out and play. Go ahead, son."

"I'm scared he'll do something to you if he finds me gone."

"Are you really scared for me?" She paused, then tremulous, "That makes me happy."

"I hate him. I wish he was dead."

"It don't do any good to say that. I know. I know how you feel and I don't know what else you can say. But not that. It don't do any good."

"I hate him."

"It's the way he is, that's why he's suffering."

"Suffering?"

"Yes, dying inside. You just don't see it now; you're too small. He wouldn't let you get baptized, nor me to even pray. But he lives with us; he don't run off because something in his head won't let him. Oh, yes. Dying. And he's running out of things to hate because he won't be able to hate me much longer and then all his hate will turn on him, not just part of it. That's why you shouldn't hate nothing. Promise me to never hate."

"Promise," he said. Then, "Should I go back to church again?"

"If you want to I suppose you should."

"Do you want me to?"

She said nothing for a time, her breathing harsh, unrhythmic; saying finally, "I want you to go away from here as soon as you're big enough. That's all. But I can't talk about God or church no more, Matthew. I just can't. Now go outside and get some sunshine. Go ahead."

When John Roger returned to the house near dusk, she saw his demolished face and knew that not only had he lost, but that he would never win again, anything, would probably never make the effort; it left her with no feeling. He slumped into a kitchen chair, gasping, each breath punctuated by thick bubbling, his shirt filthy with rust-red, blackish blood, all his features gorged and shiny with a sickly greenish cast. Blood flowed quietly from his nose in a thin squirming line.

"That's broken," she said.

Nothing.

"Stick your head in the sink."

His look, she knew, was intended as malevolent, but his face permitted no expression.

"Come on," she said.

He rose, clutching his stomach, hobbling toward the sink, then stopped and, facing her, raised his hand.

"Are you really strong enough?" she said. "Will it do you any good?" She remembered what she had told Matthew about hating. And despite herself, although she had never seen him, she vaguely loved Cass Nowell.

John Roger lowered his arm and groaned his head into the sink; and she burned the cold water down on his neck.

Simon: "That was one thing neither of us counted on. You didn't much act like a man of peace, did you?"

"I carried it too far. I couldn't stop; maybe I even enjoyed it. I kept thinking: he's a devil, a devil."

"Well, if he is, you at least made Southfield safe for Christianity."

But Cass did not smile, react in any way; he sat, listless, his eyes riveted on the restless gleam of the old bronze coffin, still unsold and moved in back now, the reflected spears of metallic fire playing throughout its serrated design.

"As soon as it was over I wanted to say I was sorry. I wanted to beg forgiveness."

"But you didn't. A man doesn't."

"No. It's too easy and too hard to ask forgiveness when you smash something. Like spanking a child, saying, 'This hurts me more than it hurts you.' Rubbing salt in. No, I couldn't, not when I saw the blood pouring out of his face. I didn't do anything; I just let him lie there. My neighbor helped him—God knows what he thinks of me now. He must feel he's been living next door to a maniac all these years."

"Rubbing salt in? What else?"

Cass took his eyes from the coffin, looking at Simon now. "I suppose I was glad I did it. In a way I still am. I wish I could feel more regret."

"You don't regret it because you think he deserved it."

"From me? What am I? No, it's hard to understand why I did it. I don't think God had anything to do with it. The whole thing was inside me, twisting me, even though I stood there lecturing. Actually lecturing. God, I just don't know." He closed his eyes and breathed deeply. "You were right; he's probably home beating the boy right now."

"From what you say, I don't think he has too much left."

"When I looked down at him I got nauseated. That's when I

knew I needed his forgiveness, but I couldn't bring myself to it. I still can't."

"Forget it, because you'll probably hit him again if you see him. You'll just start it all over again."

"Yes, I know that too. I'm not superstitious, but I keep seeing the devil in him. He said he'd kill me, but he couldn't stop at that; he had to say it about Martha." He bowed his head, rubbing his eyelids with the fingertips of one hand, then running the hand across his cheek, blinking. "He defeated me, you know. I smashed him up, but he won."

"How so?"

"The boy, for one. Something went wrong there. And I've only made his father worse; I'm not kidding myself into thinking that I beat sense into him. Even when I was hitting him, I knew nothing was right, nothing I'd done all day was right."

"For God's sake, forget it. It's done."

"There's more. All that time hitting him, drowning him, Martha was watching from a window. She saw me for the first time, the way I must really be—more violent than Williams, more violent than a hundred of him. Just pounding until I had nothing left to hit but air. I can't remember the last time I had a fight, but yesterday it seemed as natural as breathing or eating. And I know I enjoyed it—oh, Christ, I enjoyed it. And she saw it all. I think I must have felt her watching me. I looked up at the window and there she was with her face pressed against it. She was terrified and sick, her eyes were popping out of her head. We stared at each other longer than two people can. It was me who looked away."

"Yes, it was a hell of a thing for her to see. All you can do is hope she forgets it."

"She won't. Strangers, maybe, but I'm her father, Simon—the hypocrite. All my stories of her mother's gentleness are lies now; I know she doesn't believe them any more because I was the one who told her. She's afraid now, for the first time in her life. She'll see violence in everything I do, I know it."

"You know, you know. For God's sake—"

He waved Simon quiet, saying, "And it was my fault, that's

the worst part of it. I have no excuse; I started it and she probably saw that too. I'm telling you, I don't understand what happened to me. I could have kept my mouth shut; I could have let it pass, let him talk himself out and blocked my ears. There's no reason why I took him so seriously, a fool like that. But you see, I couldn't do any of those things. I never knew I couldn't. And she saw me."

"I say she'll forget. She's a child and things like this wear off. Try talking it out with her. You can convince her."

"You can force a child to listen, Simon, but you can't force her to be convinced. I know, I'm a father. You can't convince . . ." Stopping in shame, remembering painfully that Simon had said exactly that, looking now at Simon to discover the triumphant cast of his face. But he saw nothing and gagged on his bitterness; because, of course, Simon would feel no triumph, not even express an allusive nod. Somehow he had veered off in a frightening direction, his confusion had momentarily wrenched him out of knowledge, even full sanity. "Everything's a mess," he said.

"Calm down, will you please? This is no tragedy, only a fool mistake."

"Isn't it? Isn't all this stupidity a kind of tragedy?"

"What? What we do to ourselves, how we screw each other up? No, not tragic, just a big mistake. Think they're both the same and you're dead. Look, you once told me that two thousand years ago up on Calvary the greatest single tragedy took place and that all the troubles of all people added together mean nothing compared to it."

"Yes, it's true. I still believe that."

"Then why are you torturing yourself? Not because your troubles don't matter."

"No, of course not. Because they matter too much. They shouldn't matter too much."

"They have to."

"When I saw Martha's face in the window I wanted to die. What can I do about that?"

"Look," leaning slightly out of the armchair, "they say God's only limitation is that he can't create a weight heavier than He can lift. The same thing goes for a man. Unless you're out of your head, all problems have answers somewhere."

"Even if you involve other people in them?"

"Maybe. At least for you. All I know is that we have to live in this crazy world that maybe God gave us. That's one strike right off the bat. Even if people are made in the likeness of God, they're not like Him. They're wild and strange and you have to treat them as they are, not what they might be. Things happen that you can never be responsible for, nor take on the responsibility for. You're your brother's keeper only when he wants you to be. Otherwise, there's no law over it." Leaning back again: "That's the only reason I had for objecting when you wanted to take that boy to church. Square pegs in round holes don't work. Everybody has a pattern to his life, no matter how crazy it seems, how wrong. Take people out of that pattern and you might lose them, because you never really know if that pattern is wrong; you can only believe it is. Damn, Cass—I've read the Bible a thousand times; I got an old greasy Shakespeare and a Lord Byron in my drawer; and every one of the people in those books is different. They have to be or what would you read them for? The whole world would be just a lot of stupid dumb faces and everybody would do the same thing at the same time and they'd all even belch in tune. You're alive, can't you see that? People belong to places and things and a lot of miseries and happinesses; they don't run around free. You have to be careful with them or you just might hurt them. That's all I meant, that's it." He sighed and blotted his upper lip, drawing the handkerchief under his chin, then crushing it into a ball between his fingers.

"I hurt the boy, is that it? And Martha?"

"You'll never know. If you did, they'll heal. God knows, everything heals."

"Yes, but I knew something had gone wrong in church. The boy looked bored; he didn't feel anything I wanted him to feel. It's the thing I told you before—the whole day was ruined. I'm just wrong."

"Maybe not wrong. Reckless, too quick is all."

"It's the same thing." He paused, raking his lower lip with his teeth, saying finally, "I can't force the boy, not now. But I do believe that God's law is a single law, Simon. Maybe the circumstances . . ." Trailing off, tangled for a moment in his words, thinking that the law did, must overlay every pattern like a fine screen on a matrix. Just not knowing how.

"Then you've quit on the boy?"

"Yes, now. I think it's wrong to, but someday he'll be old enough to understand."

"But you won't quit on him for good."

"I don't know. I can't say that."

And watching him, Simon thought: *Could it be that there's something in all this that you don't see? That past the rule, beyond the duty is the question of your own salvation? That there is something in the law of God that troubles you because you can't explain it?* Cass was using Matthew, had used him, perhaps not wrongly or even knowingly, but used him nevertheless: to impale an intangible, to shore up, clinch, even vindicate his own belief.

He slid from the core of their talk, yet not entirely out of its bounds, saying tangentially, "Maybe the law has divisions. A lot of people would call me a liar or worse because I say I saw straight once I lost God. For the first time in my life I could move like a free man. You never called me a liar, you believed me."

"Because you said you pretended."

"Yes, at the end. And giving up the lie freed me."

"What I can't see is how you can have a morality. Where does it come from? Why should anyone be moral without belief?"

"Because I'm scared of evil. And there's God's law again. It's a good one; I live by it because I want to. But I say it doesn't go in a straight line." Pausing, then, "That was no question to ask, Cass."

Cass shook his head wearily, looking down at the corded backs of his hands, the split, raw knuckles, mumbling, "I know. It was dumb."

Simon saw the sadness in him and suddenly, although Cass's expression remained unchanged, although he said nothing, the sadness was unbearable. And, as always, whenever revealing a part of his old life to Cass, he felt as if he were tearing a piece of himself away. He said, "But I know everybody would ask it, would call me a lying cheat. It's one of the reasons I never went back South, because nobody, nothing would ever believe me or accept me. I had to stay here, where it all happened, where people didn't know me to mock me. Where they'd leave me in peace. I felt I went through enough."

"Sometimes," Cass said slowly, "sometimes I wonder how we can be friends."

"Do you really wonder that?"

"Yes."

Simon smiled. They fell silent, and after several minutes Cass rose and tried to shake looseness into his joints.

"It's been a bad day, Simon. No better than yesterday."

"Yes, I suppose it has."

"I think I'll take a walk up the mountain," pausing, adding, "Do you want to come?"

"No, you go on. I'm tired."

Simon let him out, then returned to the armchair and poured himself a half glass of whiskey. Thinking: His thoughts involved God again and he knew that before his life was done, he would wrench out all the parts of himself and lay them before Cass for assessment, perhaps for a kind of judgment. But not yet, he had not told everything even though the gulf between them was now perfectly bridgeable; because he was afraid, exactly that, to tell it all. (Only smiling when Cass had said, "Sometimes I wonder how we can be friends," smiling frostily because he himself often wondered too, wondered if anything would sever the links.) Thinking: Leave it this way until it was no longer possible to keep from telling him all the reasons why he had never gone back South.

Because before the last great humiliation of the prayer meeting in Fallsville, he lay for hours on the boarding-house bed, suffering under decisions to make, plans to formulate, desperate for a course of action. Certainly, he knew, he would go no farther North or East; Fallsville seemed to him a pivotal point on his

94

mental map of the country; an inch more toward the Atlantic Ocean and even the freak's drawing power might vanish; he might be jailed, beaten, run out of some town on a rail. His first impulse was to return, retrace his steps, find hamlets and whistle-stops he had never before visited; but he had seen, smelled, touched so much of the South that he could hardly bear the thought of traversing it again; and there were many, too many places where a pound of buckshot would welcome him, places he had regretfully failed to note somewhere for future reference, future self-preservation.

Yet it seemed as if he had to return; his roots took moisture there, roots of communication, of understanding; there, at least in certain parts (he could not remember these either), he was more than a man; he was a prophet, a cleanser of the soul, a shriver, a human magnet of the Godhead who could preach to unashamed people, could set ablaze enough awe and fear to convert sinners. All that a key to his rediscovery of God.

Money was unimportant now, piteously laughable; just saving one soul would be the answer, his grip on a slipping, crumbling faith. And so, before he had learned otherwise, he thought he must leave Fallsville, must never again set foot in a strange land.

Along the streets he moved, and they watched him, brought their children spyingly to curtained windows, pointed fingers at him. He was bent like an old man when he walked, stoop-shouldered and shuffling, a beetle with the split tails of his coat and its worn, almost sat-through glaze, iridescing blue-green in the sun. The backs of his thighs shining too, stiff and pressed flat by dirt, threading cuffs inches above his old shoes; his hat, a broad-brimmed fantasy, shadowed his perpetually squinting eyes and bony features; his lips were rancid with tobacco, caressed each second by his darting tongue. Like a bird, he seemed to crane his neck under a wing, then scurry it out over a weak shoulder. Hearing someone say: "Why, look at him. He's a young man!"

No, he could not tell this to Cass, nor even the countless ac-cusations against him, the false charges that he prowled about school yards to seduce children, not even his trips to brothels.

Let it be just that he had been a preacher of sorts and ceased to believe; it was almost inconsequential.

Yet he knew that a time would come when it must all be told, when he must gamble by necessity, when both were bent under the ache of their own emptiness and crushing need for love, when their passions and longings and failures had nothing in the world palpable to touch. Then he would again tear something from himself, offer it, and perhaps be refused.

# Three

When she was buried, it was only the second time in thirteen years that Esther had gone past the road at the foot of the house; John Roger had forbidden her to go farther than the crude fence he had built from stray logs and boards. But it was not true, as gossip claimed, that people drove out to the house on Sundays to watch her walking about inside the shapeless circumference; they let her alone, avoiding her, wanting to believe that she was mad and dangerous, saying so, eventually calling her simply "crazy," without the real connotation of insanity, simply crazy. Though once someone had said she must be a leper; then she had smallpox; all agreeing that no pregnant woman should ever risk a glance at her for fear the child would be born with six fingers or two heads or born still.

But after the Depression, new prosperity buried Esther in oblivion; she was unable, by witches' deeds or wails in the night, to create and foster a mysterious legend; few even remembered her feeding Matthew at her breast; but once remembering, savored it. She finally drifted into that commonplace craziness which means different or odd or inexplicable, and they rarely spoke of her; she was unworthy even as a curiosity, living or dead.

Only once had she tried to escape, when Matthew was still an infant, and John Roger crushed her as he would a bug between his toes. On Sundays she would sit quietly near her bedroom window, and if the wind were right, listen to the church bells; she left the house when the feeling overpowered her, running, fleeing down the road. But he overtook her, caught her back, locked her in her room, and cursed her for a whore through the door; cursed her that way, with the door between them, afraid he would beat her, kill her if they faced each other, bellowing, "You don't need any God. You were the judge when you did this to me; you are the God here."

Then he went downstairs and lay on the cool floor with his arms across his eyes.

She had never told him about the pain in her body until it was past telling of, until he himself was afraid; he had never seen a face so close to living death, had never before heard her gasping behind her door; he stood uncomprehending as the doctor told him. And he watched the process of death for a year, and finally her screams, stifled into whines and grinding teeth, were planting seeds of insanity in his mind, and he committed her to the hospital in Bluefield.

(Lying back sunken against the pillow, waiting for the ambulance, alone in the dim lamplight with Matthew, her empty body flattened beneath the blanket, without contours as if it were not there, only a ruffling up of cloth; her face, when he squinted and diffused the light, skeletal, a tissue of translucence pulled tight by the knots of her cheekbones, mouth lipless like another wrinkle, eyes like two great globes of shattered charcoal, her hair neatly plaited and ribboned, too heavy for her head.

"You won't die?" he sobbed.

"Die?" A tremble of the wrinkle, an almost imperceptible upturn of the lips, a smile? Some inchoate remnant of secret knowledge betrayed.

"Mamma?"

"Listen. Here," drawing his head close with strengthless bone tapers, "you make your life what you want of it. No, that's too late." Thinly breathing, "Don't hate. Leave here." A quick fierce convulsion of the mouth. "I love you. I'm allowed that." Then a relapse into nothing, breathing barely maintained, a flutter of the blanket like a soft wind through a mound of brittle leaves. The droning halt of the ambulance outside. He left the bed, hiding in his room, his soul intense with her dying.)

The cancer in her uterus destroyed her without either Matthew or John Roger at the hospital. There were no more bills to pay (John Roger had signed a paper allowing her to be used for some experimental therapy, but he would not, somehow could not, permit an autopsy), except for the funeral.

He went with Simon Forbes to claim the body and rode in back of the station wagon, shivering in the cold, listening to her rustle and thump about in the wicker basket. And later, in the cemetery, just he and Matthew and Simon, and the gravediggers slipping off the sham carved coffin and sliding the dazzling pine box into the hole, dug so rectangularly and formally that it seemed the essence of all order, the final simplicity of the chaos of death. There was not even a flower to place against the hump of freshly-turned earth striated with snow; they had not even done that, leaving before the grave was filled.

"Here's the certificate," Simon said. "She had a priest."

Silently, John Roger took it and folded it away, casting a final look at the shoveling men.

After the cemetery he and Matthew ate some cheese and bread, and he looked across the table, saying, not really asking, "You ain't sad, are you."

"I guess not."

"There's no cause for it." Then, "You won't miss her?"

"I guess not."

And he stared at Matthew's moving jaws, machinelike, rhythmic; and he was awed slightly (not knowing that Matthew would miss Esther, just refused to show it, refused to reveal himself as he pushed the bread and cheese against the suppressed sobs, the great, invisible, choking welt that had risen almost to his mouth; trying also to reveal no hate, the hate burning enough to kill) thinking that the boy was cold, hard, unfeeling, wondering if they might after all be father and son.

Sunday, timeless days later, sitting drugged with drink at the window, he saw Cass Nowell drive past toward the cemetery, a wreath of flowers propped up against the back seat, reflexively bringing his hand up to the crook of his broken nose.

"Bastard," he whispered, and when the car had disappeared, rose and shouted, "Goddamn it, I'm hungry. Esther, goddamn it, Esther."

Then remembering and staggering weakly to the bed, watching a kind of mirage: Matthew standing motionless in the doorway.

# Part II

*The young*

*In one another's arms . . .*

# *Four*

Almost nineteen years in the old house, older now and deadly with rot, had brought John Roger no peace or contentment or hope. The oldness itself drugged him with a sleep of scattered and broken images wrenched from the furrows of his memory, imprisoned him in mounds of decay and stagnation, mocked him with sounds of cracking wood and crumbling shingles. Yet he clung to it; it protected him; he owned the deed.

He had not come or gone since Esther's death, could not understand the coincidence of her burial and the simultaneous stoppage of time. For a few months, sporadically and with little appetite, he had driven to Bluefield for whores, but his need of them finally broke down along with the Ford. He retched with hate at the sight of them—their laughs, grimaces, smells, skin, and especially their open, waiting hands. Perhaps his hate and the death of the Ford was coincidence too; he had considered that for a time.

But he had not stopped drinking; he had merely stopped getting drunk in any pleasurable way. It would not come. He drank ceaselessly, joylessly, without pain but without anything else to replace it. He had, for the flicker of an instant, tried to battle his retreat to oblivion; when she died, he told himself that it was all as it must be, repeated and reaffirmed his hatred of God, of her, of his own name, which had made him this way, until the thoughts beat against his brain, until he needed whiskey to cloud his name—and her, and God.

Time was dead; he had not been able to measure it while sharecropping, nor while Matthew grew tall, nor by forgetting one morning to leave his bed, nor by never again working, nor even in cursing the whores who ground him to pieces with their cavernous machines. He simply drank.

He lay wherever he fell; each night an epileptic seizure in which sleep appeared, taunted, but never controlled. And he thought more often about Matthew, and came to believe that calling him son—just that—might open a back door to salvation. His hatred had gone, crept away, like a beaten animal, with everything else; but he would not admit it.


Near the front of the house a car was parked at the foot of the hill, parked, after several false starts, by Billy Chase. Biting his lip, he gauged Martha Nowell's state of mind, then swallowed drily and looked at the house. It was silvered by the full September moon, gaunt and bleached like bone, and they sat watching it for almost five minutes before Billy plumbed his courage and draped his arm across the back of Martha's seat, snaking it forward until it touched her shoulder. She leaned away as imperceptibly as his arm had moved, but she shattered the contact as surely and abruptly as if she had suddenly left the car.

"Ah come on," he said.

"No. Now take me home or I'll slap your face." She hadn't really objected to his arm; in a way she had enjoyed it, as she had enjoyed the only two boys who had asked her to dance at the party. She had magically wished her lack of popularity into a half-believed illusion that she has highly and properly discriminating, denying the advances of boys when, in fact, they were not interested in her. Perhaps, she decided, she was too grown-up—which in a sense was true. She was pretty enough, a bit round in the face; but at seventeen there was already an aura of placidity about her, as if she were married or committed to someone or at least possessed of some detached poise, which relegated her to the periphery of her troupe of loud gangling friends.

She said again; "I really will slap you."

He faked a grin, and remembering some phrase he had heard on television, said, "I wish you would, but you'd break your hand."

"Act your age," she said; and saying it, she mournfully realized that it was stodgy and stupid, and it angered her. But when he groped for her hand and mistakenly fingered her thigh, her anger deepened, switched direction, and she elbowed him viciously in the ribs, intending to hurt, to cripple him if she could, saying, "That's enough. Enough, enough. Now take me home or I'll tell your grandfather."

"Well, why," he began, but his voice cracked, and after a moment of silence he said, "why did you say I could drive you home? Why didn't you just go with the rest of the creeps?"

"They didn't ask me," she shouted, hating him for prying the admission from her.

"Yeah. Sure. Well, I bet if I just got back from Korea with a bunch of medals you'd be all over me."

"Why don't you go to Korea?" When he grunted and seemed to settle back into the seat, she said, "Take me home, Billy. I'm not fooling. Take me home or I'll blow the horn."

He lunged to his right and tried to kiss her, and as she fought him off, a deep rage swirled tears into her eyes. Blinking, she caught sight of the house and saw a shadow fanning across the porch, then the protrusion of what seemed a face, ashen pale in the moonlight. She stiffened and screamed.

He bolted up, driven away by the moribund tightness of her body; he stared at her, then at the house.

"He's out on the porch," she whimpered.

Her fright galvanized him; at the same time he tried to turn the ignition key and switch on the lights, fumbled, cut his finger on something, then cursed at his terrified response to her pleading: "He's coming." He sucked in his breath, held it, turned the key, found the accelerator, and drove off; and despite his confusion he had the presence of mind to show off his superchargers, roaring and whistling like demons.

Roared and whistled like demons, but John Roger did not hear them; as was happening lately, he seemed to find himself in different parts of the house not knowing how he had gotten to them, drugged, almost somnambulistic. Now he had stumbled out to the porch, curled into the broken rocker, and prepared to enter midnight as he had for years: rocking arhythmically on the flattened runners, the splintered wicker needling his back, his hand clasping the neck of a bottle, his eyes not seeing yet contemplating the never-washed drinking glass, the rush of darkened woods across the road, the low breadloafed mountains miles beyond.

He gazed up at the moon, rocking, caressing the bottle, then closed his eyes and saw a tombstone engraved with small carved words poisoned by oily green moss:

HERE LIES JOHN ROGER WILLIAMS WHO DID NOT HATE EVERYBODY

And he thought that after fifty-five years that was all he could say for himself; it was all he had done. Fifty-five years—he stared, surprised; time existed after all; he could judge it. He had just done it.

# 2

On Saturday night they sat on the long bench in the square, Billy Chase and Frank Dombrowski, talking about the Korean war and girls in no particular order, Matthew sitting some distance away from them, listening as he usually did, not really engaging himself.

During a long silence, Matthew craned his head toward the monument; lately, whenever it caught his attention, he considered enlisting.

Then Billy Chase said, "I bet you guys wish you were me last night."

*I'm not much,* Matthew thought, *but I wouldn't go that far.*

"Get in?" Frank asked.

After another pause, during which the furrows of his brow worked like an accordion, Billy finally said, "No, but I could of. She was all hot to trot, excepting she got scared."

"Sure," Frank said.

"You never been out with her; you don't know one thing about it. I'm telling you I could, and next time I goddamn sure will. She all but asked me."

"Yeah. So what stopped her?"

"Well . . ." He turned to Matthew who was still contemplating the monument. "Look, Matty, I don't want to get you mad. Hell, I mean she just stopped."

"Tell," Matthew said.

"Well, actually—actually your father came out of the house— 'least that's what she said. I guess he just scared her."

"He couldn't scare anybody," Matthew said.

"That was a dumb place to park," Frank said, "right in front of a house."

"Anyway, who are you talking about?" Matthew asked.

"Martha Nowell."

Somehow Matthew could only think of her as a little girl, a child, who had sat near him in church. He had seen her grow, had spoken to her from time to time, had even dreamed of her once; but she was still the little girl, the memory of a far-off Sunday morning; and he could not understand how she belonged in Billy's car, parked in the darkness of his father's drunken night.

"You're a liar," he said.

"I'm not, honest to God. She's hot as hell."

"No," Matthew insisted. "No, you could never get near her."

"It's just because I can't prove it."

"You couldn't even give her a feel," Frank said.

The image wrenched Matthew; Martha was suddenly grown; and he saw her now as she was: somehow old-fashioned, not the most beautiful girl in Southfield, with odd, vaguely darkish crescents below her eyes, her skirt always too long. He could not picture the voluntary leaning of her breasts into anyone's hands.

He meant to sound indifferent, surprised by the irritation in his voice, "You're full of shit."

"I'm not."

"If you went over to her house right now and asked for a date, she'd kick you the hell out."

"I don't want to take your money."

"I wasn't thinking of a bet, but it's all right with me."

Billy rose and half-turned, fixing his eyes on the red and blue globes hanging in the window of the drug store. He dug his hands into his pockets, rattled his change, then shrugged his shoulders, saying, "Nuts."

"You're still full of shit," Matthew said, this time angrily; and he knew that because of his insistence they would silently accuse him of jealousy. Silently, because they feared him.

"Well, I bet you wouldn't," Billy said.

"How much?"

Billy jangled his change again, then sat heavily on the bench.

"Two dollars?" Matthew asked.

"Frank? You want a dollar of it?"

"No, because he will."

"Goddamn," Billy mumbled. "All right, two bucks." They each gave Frank two dollars, and he solemnly said, "Bet's official."

Without a word Matthew set off for Washington Street, thinking that he was doing this foolish thing only because the challenge had suddenly seized him, compelled him as it did at times, swelling his body with a tension that only pure movement could release. Also, he had nothing to lose but the two dollars. Thinking of the complex, unfathomable reasons that drove him to swim in the half-frozen river, to box (and knock senseless) a local academy champion, to drive Billy's car for a half-mile blindfolded. Most terrifying, most sickening was going to Jane Nartiewicz's house to find her not a whore at all but a retarded drooler with dead saucer-eyes and the patched print shift of a twelve-year-old;

he left her feeling as if he were dirt in the road. Nevertheless, he would do it again.

But what he was doing now—it was different, past foolishness. The challenge strangled him; he broke stride for a moment, wondering if he had been jealous after all. And suddenly he doubted if he could carry it off; he was not about to confront an icy river or a blind car. She could simply say no, perhaps even laugh, defeat him without the chance to fight back. She would have to want to accept. He could not force her; he had no control; and her consent could only mean that she liked him, which, he felt, was like asking for the moon.

His stomach turned, taunting and angering him, and now he could see her plainly, amazed that he possessed such a sharp image of her, confused by it. She did not have the kind of beauty that intimidated him, but she was still too beautiful for him. Her face was somewhat Polish, but the features were not broad or heavy—except for the eyes with their strange dark bases. Her hair was plain brown and she allowed it to fall where it pleased below her shoulders. And over the past year the two or three times he had sat next to her in a classroom, she had smelled good, simply good. She could go out with, love anyone she chose (perhaps her beauty *did* shake him); she might even be out now. His stomach had settled, but he hoped she was not home; he rang her bell and hoped.

Cass Nowell opened the door, swinging it in wide and expansively, flooding the porch with light; he squinted at Matthew although he could not have failed to recognize him. He said, "Matthew? Hello, Matthew."

"Mr. Nowell." He nodded. "I don't want to bother you, but could I see Martha for a minute? I forgot to tell her something at school."

"I don't see why not," Cass said, letting him in. He cupped his hands around his mouth and called toward the stairs, "Martha," waiting for her almost inaudible answer. Then he led Matthew into the living room, motioned him to a chair, and when they were both seated, said, "I haven't seen much of you, Matthew."

"Oh," steepling his fingers, pressing his palms together, "I've been sort of busy. I did mean to stop by the store," he lied—"for a flashlight."

"Anytime," Cass said pleasantly. "I've got them by the case."

They fell silent. Watching Cass's set face, Matthew almost squirmed, wanting to ask him the price of fishing tackle, of a wrench, of anything—just to keep even the most idiotic conversation flowing; because if they continued to stare at each other he would begin to sweat under the heat of the appraisal that Cass was making no effort to conceal. He was about to make some comment about lawnmowers when Cass said, "It's been a long time since we've talked, hasn't it?"

"Yes it has," remembering now, surprised that he had forgotten Cass had been with them in the church.

Again the conversation died. Then Cass cleared his throat. "I wonder what's keeping her? Are you in the same classes?"

"Only assembly periods. It's just that I wanted to ask her something."

He was about to add that perhaps it could wait until Monday; he was leaning forward in his chair; but then Martha entered the room, glanced quizzically toward him, then intensely at Cass, finally sitting on the couch, waiting, and Matthew was convinced that there would be a triangle of silence now, one more person adding to the burden. He folded his hands tightly against their sudden trembling.

"You know Matthew?" Cass said to Martha, almost as if to shatter some preposterous tale that they were classmates.

"Sure."

"Hello," Matthew said.

And Cass, "Suppose I get us something to drink?" He rose quickly, nodded inappropriately, then left the room.

Matthew watched Martha cross her legs, curling her right instep around her left ankle. He raised his eyes to her face, saying, "I'll tell you why I came over." But he didn't, he waited for some time before he continued. "The bazaar's coming up over at St. Stan's next week. I thought maybe you'd like to go."

"I'd love to."

"That's swell."

110

"Are you going?"

"Of course I'm going." He stared at her, immediately angry, yet trying to smile the feeling away. "Look, maybe I didn't say this right. What I'm asking you is to go with me."

She smiled, crooked her forefinger above her upper lip, then said, "I thought you were selling chances—something like that."

"Well, hell," he began, cutting it off, wondering if he had cancelled himself out by swearing. "Sorry."

"Why?"

He strained against his anger now, thinking: *You know damn well why I'm sorry: because I said "hell"*; then exhaled audibly, realizing that she was communicating what she no doubt considered vital—that she was not a child. Perhaps she wasn't, but her flip denial seemed almost an accusation that *he* was the child.

He said, "I thought next Saturday would be the best night; there's a dance after the fireworks."

She nodded reflectively, but he did not detect agreement in it. So he inhaled now, swelling his chest, filling out his cheeks to appear older, less gaunt.

"Saturday's fine with me," she said.

"It is? It is"; thinking: *This goddamn girl is confusing me*. He tried to extemporize a line or two, but Cass returned, balancing three glasses of ginger ale, offering one to Martha, then handing one to Matthew. Matthew almost placed his glass on a small table, then caught the prohibitive gleam of the polished wood, finally circling the glass with both hands, resting it on his knees. Vaguely, he felt that they were both managing him, that he was a crapshooter denied the dice.

"That's better," Cass said. "Matthew? What have you been doing with yourself?"

"Working. Going to school."

Turning to Martha, Cass asked, "Will you be graduating together?"

She shrugged her shoulders and directed the question back at Matthew with her eyes.

"No. I don't go full time, so I have another year. A year from February. I have to work," he added.

Cass nodded and toyed with the rim of his glass. "Do you have any plans for college? Martha's filled out four or five applications."

"I guess not. I never really thought about it. Anyway, I guess I'll get drafted sooner or later."

"You should give it some thought. It doesn't seem you can get along without it these days."

"You never went," Martha said. "You look all right."

"That was long ago. It's different now."

"I think college is silly," she insisted. "I'll go, but I think it's silly."

Cass smiled, and a trace of righteousness played across his lips, reminding Matthew of the conversation they had had years ago—not the content, but the style.

"I'll bet you really don't mean that," Cass said lightly. "Not when you think of the clothing bills you're going to send me—or of a campus and sororities and proms. Don't tell me you're not looking forward to that?"

"And to all the bad habits I'll pick up, like smoking and coming in at three A.M."

Watching Cass, Matthew's feeling of being manipulated was reinforced; it all seemed an act staged for his benefit, but its purpose was not clear.

Martha said, "Or maybe I'll flunk out."

And Matthew, flatly and without conviction, because he could not extend his imagination so far in their direction, "It sounds like fun."

Turning to him, holding his eyes, Cass said, "It's a different world from Southfield, that's a certainty. One's entire life changes —new friends, new ideas. Don't you think so, Matthew?"

"I guess. I don't know much about it." He no longer knew what to do with his glass; it had sweated, darkening the knees of his trousers. Finally he placed it on the floor, and as he straightened up he almost knocked over a table lamp, quickly catching and steadying it, then flushing deeply.

As if immune to Matthew's misery, Cass said, "So you don't think there's much chance for you? College, I mean."

"I just don't know. I have to take care of my father. He's sick."
He wished that Cass would vanish; but he was not even ready to refill the glasses, sitting entrenched in a corner of the couch, appearing to sip his ginger ale although the glass was as full now as when he had first brought it into the room.

Matthew rose, saying, "I'd like to stay longer, but I can't. Thanks a lot for the ginger ale."

He shook Cass's outstretched hand, then walked with Martha to the porch.

"How about eight o'clock?"

"Eight's fine." She touched his arm. "You'll have to forgive Daddy. He's a fussbudget."

"That's okay. See you. You're sure eight's okay?"

"Fine."

He went down the steps, peculiarly ambivalent, thinking: *I don't have to forgive anybody; I don't have to do anything.* Halfway across Washington Street he realized how Cass had choked him on his own anger. He tore a thin branch from a tree and whipped it along a row of hedges. A feeling of hollow victory gnawed at him, and finally, angrily, he tried to vault the hedges; but he caught his foot and crashed through the sharp branches, his face lashed by nettles.

"Goddamn," he gasped, "goddamn it all."


Martha returned to the living room, sat next to Cass, and finished the dregs of her ginger ale.

"Did you get your business over with?" he asked.

"What business?"

"Matthew said he forgot to tell you something after school."

"Not tell. Ask. We're going to the bazaar next week."

"A date? I thought that's why he came."

"Isn't it all right?"

"Why shouldn't it be?"

"I don't know. I guess I think you don't like him."

"That's silly."

"I thought you were mean—really mean—the way you kept bringing up college."

"Mean?"

"Because you know he can't go, not that he doesn't want to. You made him defend himself; you just kept *talking* about it. Couldn't you see he was humiliated? All that about different worlds . . ."

"I don't think I humiliated him. And besides, if he wanted to go to college badly enough, nothing could stop him."

"He works six days a week to support his crazy father. Don't you understand? Doesn't he have enough to worry about?"

"You certainly know a lot about him."

"We go to school together."

"Yes, you do. But—I was *not* mean. You're not being fair."

"I am," she insisted petulantly; and he sensed that she was girding for a fight that he had no desire to engage in.

"You win," he said. "Let's forget about it. I'm going out for some air. I feel a headache coming on." He rose and bent to kiss her forehead, but she turned slightly away causing his lips to brush across her temple and into her hair.

She said, "Are you going to Simon's?"

"No, just outside."

He sat on the top step of the porch and propped his shoulder against a post, gazing into the darkness. She had been right of course; he had been mean; he had known, guessed, why Matthew had come as soon as he had opened the door. And his first thought, his immediate reaction had been to prevent it. He had been overwhelmed by a feeling, instantaneous, reflexive, powerful—he could not explain it reasonably—but it had impelled him to speak of college, grinding it out as if it were a hymn: *different worlds*. He understood that, and so must Matthew.

Martha had divined his intention, but had not seen into its true depth, where scraps and shreds of memory fused into huge prohibitions. Not to consider religion—*different worlds*—no, not to consider religion at all. It was superfluous; because they would go out together once, perhaps even twice, and he would eventually and inevitably bore or bother her, and it would all die of attrition, of mutual accord or discord. Nevertheless, he could not conjure away Matthew's presence: tall, muscular, sharp-featured like his father; a man, really, calling on his child. A child despite the evidence of his senses: the calves of her crossed legs, rounded and womanly; her breasts and hips no longer flat and quiescent. (He realized, although he would not concede, that she had discovered her body years before, knew it when she explained, not by words, but by the simple active desire to change the most inconsequential piece of clothing in the privacy of her room; when she began to lock the bathroom door; when he discovered her first brassière, an unneeded girdle in the laundry; the box of sanitary napkins in the linen closet; and who had instructed her? She had no mother.) And now she was what a man would look at and want; yet it was only a boy, really, who was forcing this recognition from him now. He had seen it and could no longer deny it, even though the temptation was enormous; a boy and girl, growing, and if anyone had said five years ago that this boy and this girl would sit together in this house, he would have covered all bets, held his sides and bleated at the absurdity. But there was no laughter now; somehow the joke was on him. Williams' son—why must it be Williams' son?

But they were young; he seized the image of them as children and clung to it tenaciously. Let the month or two run its course —no harm. The slightest protest now would deepen whatever attraction already existed. He felt that he had said too much already; she had trapped him, caught him being mean and unfair. Was he that obvious? Were the alterations of his moods, his attempts at subtlety so much simpler to detect than hers? Was she communicating her belief that he had always been mean, ingrained mean? Or had she meant now, this moment, this one time?

He shook his head, repudiating himself, understanding that this visit tonight troubled him far less than the knowledge that she would soon leave Southfield, enter that different world, different even from his—where she would learn literature and languages and history, but more important, would discover herself fully, superseding, antiquating a locked bathroom door or a piece of underwear. And then she would leave him, and they would be separated by more than physical distance; and he would be alone. It was normal and natural and proper and it frightened him; and he would suddenly become old. Because he would be alone.

The door opened behind him, the beacon of light intruding halfway across the street.

"Daddy? Aren't you cold?"

"No."

"Mind if I sit?"

He palmed the step. She sat next to him, then kissed his cheek, and a trembling strangeness passed through him, some reaction within him that he could not grasp.

"I'm sorry I said you were mean."

Collecting himself, he said, "But I am. Mean as a devil in church."

"You know what? You're getting to be a funny old man."

And she smiled, and he turned his face, knowing that whatever it expressed now must be hidden from her.


After his dive into the hedges, Matthew suddenly began to laugh at himself, and his ambivalence swung toward pure pleasure. He did not collect his two dollars; he did not want to see them or sit in the square or talk. He loped out to Route 12 and hitched a ride in a trailer truck.

Jogging along, lulled by the swishing of the diesel, he thought of the distant Sunday in church, how he had sat near Martha, watched her. And now he imposed interpretations and significances upon the memory, believed that he must have known that one day it would happen this way (not even vaguely disturbed by the fact that he had of course known nothing). Watching the arc of the headlights, he was about to think something foolish, then let himself think it: *my girl*—knowing it was doubly foolish; she thought he was selling chances. Nevertheless he said it half-aloud, just for the sound of it: "My girl."

And the driver said, "What?"

"Just singing."

"What song?"

"*My Girl*," smiling in self-complicity.

"Must be new."

"You ain't kidding," Matthew said, and a few minutes later hopped from the cab at the foot of the hill and circled the house to the kitchen door.

He opened it, took two steps ahead into the darkness, and almost fell over something lying on the floor. He groped for the light and threw the switch; John Roger lay doubled up, insensible, his hands clapped against his stomach as if someone had kicked him.

Matthew looked down at him for some time, then lifted him to his shoulders, no weight, like an empty sack, and hauled him up the stairs. John Roger began to moan and blubber, and Matthew dropped him on his bed; he bounced once, seemed to disintegrate in a tangle of arms and legs, then fell calm. Matthew doubled his fists, wanting desperately to beat the senseless body still more senseless, but he kicked the bedpost and whispered: "Dirty rotten stinking old bastard."

In the bathroom he stared at himself in the mirror, wondering how anyone could love, like, or just tolerate the face peering back at him. Then he said "My girl," and threw a piece of soap at the window; he wanted to hear the shatter of glass. But the window was drawn up, frustrating him.

# 3

It rained Saturday morning; but the afternoon cleared, became deceptively warm for several hours, drying the puddles in the school yard, and the booths of the bazaar were moved outdoors. After sunset a mild chill set in and, although everyone wore jackets and sweaters, there hovered in the air a fading patina of summer—perhaps a vague smell, a different kind of sweat under clothing—creating pockets of warmth into which people walked, sniffed at, then reluctantly relinquished as they moved on.

The booths—containing gambling wheels of all sizes, dice cages, dart games, baseballs and milk bottles—were arranged in two square blocks in one corner of the yard, dissected by a wide aisle. The open section of the yard was roped off for the fireworks and rockets due to be blasted into a wide fallow field beyond the fence, and for the dance at ten-thirty.

The sky was clear black; even the fuzzed fusion of the strings of colored lights failed to swallow the icy sharpness of the stars. Through the rusty music of an old brassy phonograph, which amplified songs past recognition, the wheels whirred, clicked, slowed with tantalizing tensions of rubber fingers easing, pausing, then sliding into numbered grooves—while bettors strained their bodies and clenched their fists and twisted with body english and contorted their features into grimaces which burst into sheepish embarrassment when they were wrenched back to the reality that they had lost (or won) only a dime. The wheels spun again; the grimaces twitched again.

Matthew avoided the wheels and the dice games. They were dull; the player had no part in it; once the dime was placed on the numbered oilcloth only luck took control; and he did not believe, did not want to believe, in luck. At the end of the aisle he stopped by the baseball booth, protectively whisked Martha behind him, and carefully chose one of the stitchless, spongy balls. He planted his feet, stared ahead, then cranked up and threw— not accurately, but so violently that the pyramided wooden bottles smashed like tinder and shot off in six different directions. Someone in back of him cheered; the Holy-Name-Society man in the booth handed him a large overstuffed rabbit, which he gave to Martha. He smiled down at her, watching proudly as she weighed the rabbit, hefting it; but she could not find a way to hold it comfortably.

"I love it, but I can't carry it."

Matthew returned it to the man in the booth. "Can we leave it here until later?"

"Sure, be more convenient."

"You won't forget?" Matthew said.

"No, you go ahead."

118

Happy with an early victory, he impulsively snatched Martha's hand and led her along the aisle, searching for new conquests, sure that after such a start he could accomplish anything.

Breathlessly, she was saying, "I've always wanted a big silly animal like that to sit on my bedspread—you know, to prop it up against the pillows . . ."

But he was not listening; he stopped at another booth and surveyed the game, the object of which was to puncture a suspended balloon with one of three impossibly blunt darts. He dropped a dime on the counter, picked up a bundle of darts, and gave them to Martha.

"Let's see how good you are."

"I'm awful at this."

"Try. Come on."

She aimed by shutting one eye and wedging the tip of her tongue between her teeth; she raised herself on the balls of her feet and threw the dart with the thoughtlessness of someone waving at a foolish remark. Her awkwardness, as the dart narrowly missed impaling the attendant's forehead, was so silly and ineffably girlish that Matthew urged her to try again, in love purely with the sight of her. She trebled her concentration with the second dart, managing to miss the balloon by only a foot. On the final try she hit the balloon, but the dart arced lazily and powerlessly and the tip merely bobbed the balloon on its string.

"Try again?"

"Not me."

"Anyway, you hit it. You need a little more steam."

He clasped her hand again and pushed through the growing crowd, feeling alive and quick, threading, flowing through hips and chests as if he were playing a game of elusiveness, a fluid grace that made him appear to float above the ground, motionless in his speed. Yet when he sat or stood quietly, some tension crying for a movement betrayed him into spilling or dropping things or almost destroying lamps—anything near him. Now, as he penetrated the crowd, he gripped Martha's hand with a reflexive strength, suddenly aware that she was with him, that he was crushing her fingers.

She said, "Slow down," heaving her chest, laughing, panting exaggeratedly.

"I'm sorry."

They walked on slowly; he did not take her hand again, but she slid it through the crook of his arm.

"Where were we going?" she said. "Must have been some place exciting—or at least some place that won't be there in two minutes."

He was considering an appropriate answer, but when he looked at her she was smiling; he was aware that she was developing a teasing pattern toward him—by speaking calmly and gravely while she smiled. Somehow it did not annoy him as much as he felt it should.

Smiling back, he said, "I don't know where I was headed—I guess that's dumb."

"Why is it dumb?"

He searched for another answer, but before he found it, Billy Chase almost bumped against him, staring at Martha for an instant, then turning.

"Hi," he said. "This place gets dopier every year." He grinned, then, "By the way, I guess you forgot that deuce you won."

And Matthew knew that if he had forgotten the bet, then so would Billy; but Billy wanted Martha to know that she had been a pawn in a gamble, like the stuffed rabbit.

He extended his hand toward Billy, saying, "Thanks for reminding me. I can use it tonight."

"Actually, Frank still has it."

"Why didn't he give it to me in school?"

"Who knows?"

Matthew doubled his fist, hiding it from Martha in front of his chest. "Why did you bring it up if you haven't got it?"

Billy smiled a silly wan grin, one eye cocked suspiciously at the fist. "Just to remind you."

"Thanks." He turned and, as if challenged again, took Martha's hand with great deliberation and walked off.

Feeling thwarted, set upon and unable to retaliate, his mood turned surly; he set his lips and stalked silently ahead, definitely directionless now, but at least not moving quickly, heading without plan toward the periphery of the two square blocks, wanting with all his power to break Billy's neck. He could barely control himself; his anger needed release, but he could not show it. He ground his teeth.

"Matthew?"

He stopped. She pointed to the last booth on the square in which a priest sat selling chances for the St. Stanislaus Kostka convent fund. He wanted to say, just to jar his constriction: *Is that the same convent they were selling last year and the year before?*

"That's Father Nowak," she said, her voice freighted with personal meaning.

"Do you want a chance?"

She nodded, and stilled his hand as he reached toward his pocket. She bought the chance with her own money, leaning into the booth, while Matthew catalogued a mental file of irreverent comments.

The priest said, "Hello, Mart'a," thickly accented and resonant.

And as Matthew watched her sign the receipt, he thought: *Goddamn it, you'll kill the night; you'll kill everything, always getting so goddamn mad.* He inhaled deeply, letting the air trickle out through his nose, calming himself, and as Martha left the booth she said, "He's my confessor. Do you know what I mean?"

"Of course I do. You tell him your sins."

"I didn't think you knew." Then, "Oh, why shouldn't you, for God's sake. I always feel it's something nobody else knows about —like a mystery or something."

He was suddenly intrigued by her sins. Having sins somehow made her less formidable, more approachable, and for the first time he thought about sex with her. Oddly he was no longer angry; his throat was free.

They bought Cokes at the refreshment stand, then sat in some camp chairs near the school building. They drank without speaking for several minutes; Matthew blew a small plume of steam from his mouth, watching it immediately vanish.

"I don't understand much about this sin thing," he said. "It sounds sort of funny to hear you say you go around sinning—like everybody does it all the time."

She perched her chin on the mouth of the bottle, saying, "Everyone does. Really."

"Isn't a sin supposed to be something terrible? I didn't think anybody went around saying they did something terrible." He scratched his head; the sitting, the immobility constrained him; he began shuffling his feet along the ground. "Look, ain't sins supposed to be secrets? It's funny the way you just said that: 'He's my confessor.' Like 'He's my plumber.' It's like saying you commit all kinds of sins."

"I suppose down deep I was saying that without thinking about it. Anyway, everyone does commit sins. It's no secret; why shouldn't I say it?"

"I don't believe in it, that's all," and he finished his Coke, clanking and scraping the bottle on the pavement in front of him, sanding it. "I'm sorry. I know you're Catholic and all."

"Do you know something? You say 'sorry' more than anyone I ever met in my life. If you don't believe in it, just say so, you don't have to apologize; I won't go to hell for listening to you. My father's best friend is an atheist. He doesn't believe in sin either. They've been talking about it for as long as I can remember and never had a fight." Her voice pitched higher. "Believe what you want. I won't suddenly lose my faith."

"Then promise you won't get mad if I say something."

"Promise."

"I don't like priests."

"Why?"

A variety of blasphemous answers occurred to him, but he smiled and said, "I haven't figured it out, for one. Number two, I'm probably no damn good. That's why."

She said nothing, just placed the unfinished Coke on the pavement beside her and leaned forward, her face expectant.

He said, "Anyway, you couldn't commit any sins," realizing that it was what he had wanted to say from the beginning, that she was perfect. He flushed, grateful for the dimness that masked his color. He had nothing more to say.

122

"I'll tell you something," she said, "if you promise not to tell anyone."

"Promise."

"I'm not very fond of priests either." She paused, then softly and complicitly, "This is silly, but do you know why I confess to Father Nowak? Because he smells good; he eats something that smells like violets. It *is* silly, isn't it? But Father Karel has bad breath and—well, it's all so stupid but I can't help it. I confess that—what I just told you—whenever I think of it."

"Is that a sin? If he has bad breath, he has it, that's all." He wondered about his own breath, and for a moment turned his face slightly away from her.

"Maybe it's not a real sin," she said, "but it's uncharitable. It's like saying a priest isn't a real priest unless he's good-looking or chews bubble gum."

"I wouldn't think anything about it."

"I do, an awful lot, because Father Nowak is a killer. He lectures all the time—even if I haven't much to confess. And he gives the longest penances in the world. Once I had three venial sins and he made me say twelve Our Fathers and twelve Hail Marys. I was so mad I wanted to scream. I even cried a little." She sighed, sitting up straight. "But I keep going back to him. . . . Maybe I don't particularly like priests because every time I go to confession I think of halitosis."

"Halitosis?"

"Bad breath."

"I know—but is that really what you think of? Boy, that's weird."

Laughing self-consciously, she crossed her heart with a forefinger. "I swear."

"Well—look, we've sat here long enough. Let's go back and win a million rabbits."

He helped her up and spirited her back among the booths and into the crowd, his hand clamped on hers, she trailing behind him by almost the full length of her arm.

As if they had blown past him like wind, Cass saw them, could have touched them as he stood near Simon, who was aiming a hoop at a square peg around which was wrapped a five-dollar bill. He saw them melt into the people, then turned back to the booth. Simon leaned the bulk of his stomach across the counter, aimed again, and corkscrewed the hoop through the air; it struck the front of the peg and bounded away. He tossed another. For an instant it balanced on top of the peg, then fell to the side.

"Now hell," he said, "I had that one dead."

"Come on, Simon," the attendant said. "It takes more than that."

"Yes? Well if this circus wasn't being run by the church I'd swear you sort of unfitted the hoop from the stick."

"Fork up another quarter, Simon. *Undertake* it again"—roaring at his pun, slapping his thigh.

"That did it," Simon said, screwing up his face in mock offense. "You'll never get my trade again." He squared his hat and eased away from the booth. To Cass, "You want to give that robber your business?"

"No, I'm no good at quoits. Never have been."

"What then? I'm all ears."

Cass looked at him, at the shining eyes, the flaccid jowls, the absurd protruding eyetooth—and yet it was a young face tonight, somehow vibrant; he wondered how Simon could seize so much childlike happiness from a simple revolving wheel, a thrown dart, the cloying fog of buttered popcorn.

"You were pretty good at that horse-racing thing last year," Simon said.

"What horse race?"

They walked along the aisle.

"Where you bounce the ball into the hole and the horse jumps ahead a notch."

"Yes. All right."

They found the booth and raced against a field of twelve, pounding their fists on a padded knob, watching the balls leaping into various tubes, the horses staggering up a slope of imitation turf. They lost. Simon played again, but Cass stepped back and gave up his place.

124

He wished that he had not seen them—pulling her behind him as if she had lost her will; pulling and yanking, violent like his father. Yet thinking: *God knows, she uses her will on me often enough, her woman's will. Why not now, with him?* And what was worse, galling, she was laughing, enjoying herself as much as Simon, loving it, wanting just that: to be pulled behind like some Oriental woman trudging hangdog after her man. Except that Matthew was no slow-paced Oriental; he would plunge, with her behind him if he could, like a pistol shot into hell.

Simon edged out to him, holding a Jew's harp in his hand. He clamped it between his teeth, gave it a rattling twang, then dropped it into a pocket. "Won by three lengths," he said.

Cass nodded and they walked on again. Simon jostled his shoulder and he angered, then shook his head and surveyed the people around him, the booths, the multicolored globes of light, looking at nothing yet knowing that he was searching for her; not wanting to admit it, transforming the search into a massive loathing of the noises and laughs and smells. Stupid and meaningless. Everything. And Simon was being stupid too, terribly stupid, suddenly hearing him say: "What's wrong with you?"

"Nothing."

"You're working awful hard against having a good time."

"I just don't like it here."

"Got to get that convent built."

"Please. If you don't mind, I'm not in the mood for wisecracks."

"Why didn't you say you didn't feel like coming?"

"I don't know. It just occurred to me a little while ago."

"Fine with me. I've about had my fill. Do you want to go now or wait for the fireworks?" He squinted at his wristwatch. "They're on in ten minutes."

"Yes—we'll wait for the fireworks," and he knew that he was patronizing, but did not regret it. He felt morbidly tired; the muscles of his legs throbbed. "Let's get our seats."

They walked out to the clearing in the yard, glancing at several men who were uncrating fireworks from the cartons, then climbed into the bleachers set against the fence, finally sitting in the third tier from the top. Cass folded his hands, gazed absently at the people filling the empty seats, then turned to Simon who was toying with the Jew's harp.

"You don't intend to play that, do you?"

"Well, I was sort of considering the earth-shaking repercussions it might have."

"Why make an ass of yourself?"

Simon dropped the harp into his breast pocket and looked away, saying, "You're ornery in your old age. Look out you don't forget how to smile."

The floodlights dimmed, accompanied by a patchwork of applause and girls' squeals; then the first explosion: a jarring salute preceded by a puff of white smoke. Next a rocket that soared in a thin flame and burst red-green-white far over the opposite fence. A pinwheel began its jig, and as the brightness flailed in a circle, the bleachers undulated with red shadows. Cass saw them again, about twenty feet to his right, sitting on the bottom tier. They were close together, his arm cradling her shoulders. Darkness.

"There's a place in Pennsylvania called Rocky Glen," Simon said. "I once saw a rocket there that exploded into the American flag."

The next rocket, despite the wish for better things in Simon's remark, was a partial dud, or wet, fizzing an impotent yellow, trailing several streams of thin vapor. The bleachers lowed with boos. Then Cass watched a procession of Roman candles, each one goading him more sharply until he bit his lip and painfully curled his toes against the walls of his shoes. Another rocket surged upward, Cass recoiling with an unaccountable terrifying suspense as it rose higher with increasing brightness, and he felt the stirring of a dead memory, one he could not articulate; and then the rocket flamed out like the sun, searing the memory away. He looked away from it, his temples beating; almost nauseated, he saw them bathed in a reddish haze, and he wanted to shout: *No no no*. But sat mute, sweating, knowing now with a cancerous agony that someday she, like her mother, would be taken wildly and would respond wildly and all existence would be the frenzy and sliding and groping of flesh. It was all right; it had to be; yes, it was all right. But not with him, he prayed: *God, not with that one.* And in the fading light Matthew spoke to her, his lips moving quickly, and Cass bent forward foolishly, uselessly trying to hear; but he could only see the incessant silent movement of the lips. Darkness—the lips still moving in his mind's eye.

"I'll bet Korea's like this," Matthew said.

"Do you think of it a lot?" she asked.

"More than ever lately."

"Why?"

"I don't know. I guess I've just been thinking of joining the Army. Look."

Another, more brilliant pinwheel cut loose, spun, then snapped from its mooring and spidered along the ground before dying.

"Say," he said, "do you think of anything when they go off?"

"Yes. I guess you can't help it."

"What?"

"Foreign countries mostly. Standing on the deck of a big ocean liner. Going some place where everything's different. Like Paris."

"Have you been there?"

"No, I just imagine it. The way you think about Korea."

He nodded and squeezed her arm, almost jumping as a long string of salutes popped like machine-gun fire, signaling the end of the show.


The growing coldness forced the dance into the church hall. Matthew danced simply and determinedly, knowing only basic steps, and mainly by watching others. Martha was more skillful, but she gave herself entirely to his lead. He held her tightly (she had thought briefly that he would crush her), securely, his right hand on the small of her back, his left hand cupping hers against the hollow of his shoulder. She felt an appropriate sense of fit between them; so good a fit that she could not feel him unless she wanted to be conscious of him.

They said only a few words, and soon her head rested on his shoulder—the first time she had ever permitted herself to do this because she truly wanted to, not because it was expected. And she was grateful that they were not in the school yard, in the open space, the expanse of exposure; she might not have done it at all. Because wanting to do it caused her to regard it in a different way; it gave her a sense of secrecy, of a private feeling that she did not want observed or detected.

For an instant she let herself be conscious of him, almost to see if he were still there, and suddenly she felt that she could never play some childish game with him. Because he didn't ask stupid Billy Chase questions, she did not have to subordinate her wiser femininity to that level, not have to be forced into the absurd bondage of conditioned responses, not have to conjure tricks and gambits to demolish awkward hands. It pleased her, yet the pleasure was permeated by anxiety; something was changing, a feeling almost like the day she first menstruated, the day she noticed pubic hair; but this time transformation raced a long distance ahead of her power to catch and absorb it.

Because dancing with him might have been her first dance, feeling his thigh on hers, not drawing back from it or inferring some careless sexual overtone (another conditioned reaction), feeling his hand placed naturally and possessively low on her back, realizing that the sense of possession was hers, not necessarily his. She could not say if she had suddenly come to want this touch because of her own desires or only because the hands were his. Whatever the feeling, it was undeniable, immutable, and she gave herself to the fantasy that he was a strange dark prince who had appeared, unheralded, from nowhere and who was carrying her off; then the reality, the recognition of the childish drives still within her, the archaic still-dreamed-of prince, whose image had persisted since the first page of her first fairy tale, the immediate and perpetual acceptance of the legend that it must always be this way: the strange prince a synonym for love, the unreal and impossible prince who alone possessed the power to command surrender—all that the apotheosis, the everlasting memory, the initiation into the meaning of love.

But it was not that way; the fairy tale was a lie; every girl knew it yet went right on believing it, having to believe it, until the lie lived with greater intensity than the believer. And if you waited for the prince who would never come, you would never have impure thoughts or strange aching desires, nor would you have a real boy touching your real body, or even the thought of him. Did dreams count? Oh, yes, she had dreamed of it, thinking, lying half-asleep (only half, and that was her secret, her sin), what it would be like to have someone she loved there beside her, holding her; and that was impure too, even though she could not imagine her lover's face (almost, but not quite, the prince again). Sometimes she pretended with a pillow, and he lay there and held her and God knows they never did anything; they never even moved—just lying, warm. It was a need of the night, always; a pained, trembling stare into the darkness, knowing that if anything in the world were meant to be shared, it was a bed; just wanting someone there. It was not impure, how could it be? Yet she had confessed it all the same: twelve Our Fathers and twelve Hail Marys, mustn't ever think of it again. But she did—wilfully.

Her stomach was weightless, a hollow of anticipation, as if she had forgotten something important, just now remembering the act of forgetting, thinking: Is it this boy? Then burning, trembling, her voice dead in her throat, because this was no dream in her bed but something that could be, now, if she let it; he was holding her now and it was real. But why him? Why anyone? It wasn't possible to be a woman so quickly. Who had forced this on her, made her a premature woman as some people became prematurely gray?

Her thoughts, feelings, flowed into the ending of the last scratchy record, the crisp snap of Matthew's fingers, his voice: "Hey, we forgot the rabbit."

When they found the booth it was partially dismantled, the canvas rolled back from the frame, the equipment crated. The attendant was finishing a cigarette, ready to flick it away, when Matthew asked him about the rabbit.

Slapping his thigh he said, "You know what I went and done? Clean forgot it."

"Can't you unpack it?"

"No, I just haven't got it—haven't got any of them. I gave them all out."

"Well, look—you said you'd remember, didn't you? Can you get another one?"

"They're all gone." He opened a cardboard box. "Why don't you take a clock, a nice cuckoo clock? How about a set of ash trays?"

"Look, I just want the rabbit."

"Come on, take the clock. Here." He moved the hands and the cuckoo popped out and piped. "Why don't you take this?"

"Because I want the rabbit, damn it, that's why."

"Let's not get sassy now."

"Sassy, hell. I want the rabbit and I better get one."

"Keep it up, sonny, and you'll get something else."

Matthew doubled his fists, but before he could retaliate, Martha said, "I'd like the clock, I think."

"More than the rabbit?" Matthew said.

"Well—no, not really, but I'll take it instead."

The clock was placed on the counter. Martha picked it up and pretended to examine it carefully, then handed it to Matthew; he glared at the attendant, took her hand, and led her through the school-yard gate.

She said, "You get angry easily, don't you?"

"No. No, I don't. He said he'd save it."

"He forgot, that's all."

They walked past the darkened stores toward Washington Street, then crossed to the square.

"Let's sit for a minute," he said. They sat on the long bench, and after a silence he said, "I suppose you're right. I do get mad. Quick."

"Why?"

"I don't know. I'm sick of all these people running you down. Every place you move, they run you down. I'll tell you. I wanted to break that guy's head. I just got the feeling."

He shook his head and she touched his hand, struck with the intensity of his anger, yet expressed to her with such gentleness. She traced her fingers along his wrist, then stopped; she almost leaned against him, then caught herself and straightened up, saying, "It's very cold. And late."

They left the square; and on her porch, holding her hand, he said, "Can I see you next Saturday?"

"I'm not sure."

"Can you tell me for sure Monday? In school?"

"I," and she rebelled against the petty game she had instinctively begun—the parry, waiting to be coaxed—and she said, "Yes. I mean next week is fine."

They stood facing each other for a moment, then he swallowed almost audibly, kissed her fingers, and left her standing alone. She watched the darkness into which he had walked, then turned and entered the house, locked the door behind her and went to her room, thankful that Cass had not waited up. She set the clock on her night table, triggered the cuckoo once, then undressed and lay in bed. She prompted her secret dream, urged it, demanded it; closing her eyes to see if tonight the boy, the prince would become Matthew.

# 4

He made the effort: he did not drink all day; like an old ghost his hands quivered and his stomach soured, but he did not drink. He shaved, painfully raked a comb through his hair, found a clean shirt; and at five o'clock he sat at the kitchen table, his clasped fingers throbbing, and waited for Matthew to come home. He was prepared to proclaim his parenthood; he waited, preparing.

And when he came through the back door, John Roger asked him to sit down, and, hiding his hands in his lap, said, "There's something you should know, something I got to tell you," looking at Matthew, intimidated for a moment, then completely cowed and paralyzed to overcome it, watching the face staring back at him, watching it stare impassive and unfamiliar and truculent, then saying again with his rusty voice, "A lot of things have happened to us." Beginning badly and foolishly, trying once more. "I want you to listen to what I got to say," then stopping, trapped, his fingers twisting the knee of his trousers.

"Go ahead and say it."

"Things. Things ain't been going right. There's things we got to clear up between us."

"What do you want, a bigger booze allowance?"

"Don't you talk like that, hear?"

"Well, is that what you want?"

"Listen here. There ain't no wonder why I drink, is there?"

"Who cares why you drink? Who the hell cares at all? Now I suppose you want me to buy it for you. Why not just stick to bleeding the old woman?"

"I ain't asking you to pay for it. Cousin Hope, she . . ."

"She's willing to go on buying your medicine, right? Whoever she is, I bet she tells everybody how she keeps you from dying, how you'd be dead by now if it wasn't for her. What do you write her? That you don't want to be a drag on me?" He laughed bitterly, quickly cutting the sound. "I know what your scheme is. The way you knock off those bottles, you'll get back every cent you paid her for this goddamn shack."

"The hell with her, let her die. Listen. You know I always said you wasn't my boy . . ."

"No. Please not that again."

"Wait."

"Why? Don't I know the story? You think I could forget it?"

"That's why I got to tell you. Because I said it all my life. I never left off saying it because I believed it."

"Don't say it again. Just don't. Sober or drunk, you been poisoning me with it all my life. How many times? How many times are you going to do this?"

"I don't," he began—thinking: *That's not what I want to say, but I got to start someplace; where else is there?* "I mean I ain't going to say that again."

"Well, thank God. Now let me ask you something. When I was a kid you said I owed you a debt, that you'd let me know when I paid it off. Now—am I all paid up?"

"Debt? What debt?"

"You shit all over me with that debt and the whiskey's washed it right out of your mind. You better think hard. Am I paid up?"

"I don't know about no debt."

"Stop lying for just one time. Stop forgetting whatever you want to. 'I put a lot of money into you and you're going to pay it all back to me.' Now do you remember? Then I'd be free to go or stay. Whatever I wanted."

"You don't owe me nothing"—thinking: *When did I say that?* But knowing that he could have, probably had.

"So you think it's settled now. You can't remember, so it's settled. I'm free?"

John Roger turned his head, sorting through an impossible tangle of thoughts, saying, "Can't you just let me say what I got to say?"

"Sure, what the hell."

He tried desperately, but he could find nowhere else to begin, not in the middle, certainly not at the end; because to say it all, to give it meaning, he had to repudiate everything he had ever thought, felt, said. Almost his whole life.

Uneasy, he said, "It's just that all these years I denied you."

And Matthew, slamming the flat of his hand against the table, scraped his chair back and shouted, "Shut up. Goddamn you, I'm sick of this. Take that story and choke on it."

"Don't curse me, Matt. You better not."

"What'll you do, beat me up?"

"You talk to me like a man, hear? I got to have some respect."

"No. No you don't. I'm not your son; you never wanted me to be. So respect is one thing I don't owe you for sure. Not even as a man. I'll talk to you the way I want to, like one stranger to another. All right. I just met you—and I don't like you and I don't want to bother with you any more. Now good-bye."

"Goddamn, Matt, listen. Will you please listen?"

"To what? How much do you think I can take? What do you want from me now? Should I get down on my knees and say how sorry I am I got in your way? No, because that's what you owe me, except I don't want it. I've looked at you day in and day out, laying here, drunk, dreaming about who you're going to get even with, never asking me how I was getting along. Never asking or caring where the money was coming from or who cleaned the house, never even wondering what I wanted to be or could

133

do or what it's like to go to school and not have any friends because you have to work and every kid you meet passes you up a grade. You just sit here and maybe fart sometimes to let me know you're not dead.

"Did you ever care that I used to come home all bloodied up? Did you ever think you was to blame, that I had to fight because everybody called you names? Shit! I fought because they called you names. How do you like *that* for something crazy? Anyway, it didn't matter after I got taller than everybody and could give better than I got—and after a while I knew that what they were calling you was true. And now I just want to get out of here. I'm sick of this house and you and everything. Look, you"—reaching across the table and clutching John Roger's arm—"I been working like an animal in those fields. Day after day until I want to kill everything I see. I don't want to do that any more. And I worked in school as hard as I could, and where's it going to get me? Can you hear me, old man? I can talk pretty well and I can even think a little bit, and what I think is: I'm going to get out; I'm going to get the hell out of here. I can't wait any more. I wished I'd get drafted; but they'll never take me, not with me in high school until almost twenty and you probably writing somebody that I have to support you. So I'm going to make it on my own." He released John Roger and gripped the back of his chair.

Shaking his head, John Roger said, "You don't want to go and do that."

"You don't think I'm going to stay here like Ma? No—you won't ever hit me or lock me up or curse me, but the longer I stay here the more I'll get like her, and then when I can't feel anything, don't hardly know where I am or what year or day it is, you'll kill me too."

John Roger stood, leaned forward, his hand raised and trembling and paralyzed by rage, and then he slapped Matthew's face, watching it stare back at him, implacable, unmoved. He snapped his hand back to his lap, amazed at his sudden fear, amazed at his audacity; because he was afraid of his son.

Yet he roared, "I never did. You take that back," feeling shriv-

134

eled, torn, destitute, realizing that whatever he had meant to accomplish was past redemption now. He watched Matthew sneer, then say, quietly and rhythmically, "Killed her. Killed her."

"No," dully.

"Killed her, and that was a point for you. But it's the only one you'll get. I remember, old man. I remember sitting in my room and hearing her cry and you screaming at her through the door. I don't know what I felt for her before that, maybe nothing, because I was afraid of what you would do to me. But if anybody ever made me care for her, it was you. I cried for her. I honest to God got to love her." He nodded, his eyes slit. "And then she was dying. . ."

The voice blurred, reverberated with personal meaning, accused more through its pure sound than it could through words.

And deftly, cutting through like a delicate stroke of a scalpel, a soft word: "Murderer."

"No. No. She killed herself; she wanted to be some kind of saint. And I let her. *I let her.*"

"A saint?"

"Yes. She let me do what I done; she never said anything. She looked at me with them cow's eyes and I knew she wouldn't never lift a hand to hit back, not even yell back. Nothing. And I couldn't take it, couldn't never take it, and she knew that too. She let me shit on her and I shitted on her, and all that time she was getting back at me by letting me do it. When she died, I seen that maybe I never hated her at all, but she made me hate her because when I stuck my fist up to her face she never yelled to stop me; she just moved her mouth like she was chewing— but she was praying and she knew I couldn't stand that so she done it more. And when I seen her doing that I hated that God of hers more than I ever did, because she was using him against me and I wanted to kill them both. Just standing there with those lips moving and chewing and letting me punch her if I had a mind to." He began to mumble, holding a dialogue with himself, gesturing with his hands, his eyes trained on the table.

And Matthew said, "You call her a saint now."

"Yes. She wanted to be a saint."

"And you let her die. You wanted her to."

He did not answer, not knowing the answer, impressed only by what he had felt since her death: despair, abandonment, absence as intricate in its heaviness as thick cobwebs shrouding some corner; not even knowing if it was truly because of her.

"Calling her a whore," Matthew said, "for as long as I can remember. You made me listen to you call her a whore."

Again he could not answer. He stilled his hands, staring at them, the crescents of iridescent black beneath the cracked nails, the quicks gauzed by webs of bitten, peeling flesh.

"You couldn't even just let her alone," Matthew said.

"No, I couldn't. I couldn't never do that."

There was an aching silence.

Then John Roger, "You're going to leave."

"Yes,"

"When?"

"I don't know. I wish I did."

"Because you hate me so bad."

"Yes. I hate you so much I couldn't even kill you. Once wouldn't be enough."

"But not because of her. Because I denied you, because of that."

"It doesn't matter any more. If you got down on your knees and said I was your son, I wouldn't listen to you. I don't want to be your son. I don't need you; I don't even want your name. Look at me. Old man, look at my face. I look so much like you it makes me sick. And you know it; you always knew it. But you had to be a real man. You had to tell me I wasn't your boy. Well, go ahead, I don't give a good goddamn. Tell me again."

John Roger shook his head.

Matthew said, "I wish Ma was a whore. I wish she was so I could laugh at you and tell it to you over and over. But she wasn't and you knew that too; you knew it every minute. Well, it's all too late. If I had to call you Daddy I'd go crazy or puke all over myself. And it's too late for you to start crying. Here." He went to the cupboard, seized a bottle of whiskey, and banged it

136

on the table. "This is what you want. Here," pushing it against John Roger's clawed hand. "Drink up. Goddamn you, drink up." And crying himself, he ran from the room.

"I'm sorry I hit you," John Roger mumbled, then raised his eyes and focused on the bottle. He dropped his head, worming it into the crook of his elbow, sobbing, wondering if there had ever been better times, if there had been one moment in his life touched by happiness or peace, even by accident. Too late: to retreat, advance, even die. Because no matter how he could have told Matthew, it would have meant nothing. No matter where he began.

He coughed the mucus from his throat and lifted the bottle to his mouth, wondering if soberness could ever change anything. But Matthew had not cared about that either; it was even too late for that; so he drank and went out to the porch and sat in the dark, his teeth shivering against the neck of the bottle. There had to be better times. At least one. He tried to remember.

# 5

Simon swabbed his mouth with a napkin, then crumpled, smoothed, folded, and finally placed it to the right of his cup; stifling a belch with the back of his hand, he sank back in his chair watching Cass emerge from the kitchen with a pot of coffee. His eyebrows knit peevishly, Cass poured, then sat opposite Simon and dribbled a bit of cream into his cup.

"I'm sorry," he said. "She could at least have waited to pour the coffee."

"Never mind. As long as her cooking stays the same. Lordy." He blocked a belch.

"She could have waited," Cass insisted, slowly pumping a spoon into his coffee.

"One of those fieldhands ever got a taste of her cooking he'd offer you a dowry—and maybe half his pay thrown in."

Still petulant, Cass gazed at him, the corner of his lips a crook of disgust, then glanced about the room, mildly oppressed by the built-in womanish touches: tin-sheeted ivory-painted walls molded like bas-reliefs of forests; a ledge running the length of the walls about two feet below the ceiling, spaced intermittently with flowered china and unmatched pewter; a crewelwork picture of the Last Supper, whose Christ, etched in French knots and chain stitches, looked sinister, while the Judas looked fair. He blew at the tassels dripping from the huge, low chandelier, then said, "Maybe that's exactly what's happening." Smiling weakly. "Except without the dowry, the pay, even the cooking. Without any of them."

"You don't mean Matthew?"

"Did you see her run out when the bell rang? Ran. Full gallop."

"Well, she *did* say good night. She was polite enough if that's what worries you."

"I wish that was all that worried me. Politeness."

Simon tested the coffee with his upper lip, drank some, and said, "What then?"

"What do you know about him?"

"The same as you do."

"No," shaking his head. "No, I left him alone—remember? And when I did, I did it completely. I nodded to him in the street and I served him in the store. But that was all. I left him alone."

"What more can *I* say? First off, I never heard anybody get nasty about him—not even gossip. Sometimes you hear his old man mentioned, but never him. He must be pretty quiet; he just grew," snapping his fingers. "Grew and nobody noticed or watched or I suppose gave a damn. One day he was just there. Like Topsy."

"Like a feral child. You know what feral children are?"

Refusing to be patronized, Simon said, "Maybe he *is* wild; he could be. But he's not an animal. And if nobody in this town can pin anything on him, he's probably so normal he's crazy." He sipped his coffee. "I think he's all right. I've never had anything to do with him, but that's what I think; it's a feeling. Once, when I was driving back from a funeral, I saw him working in the fields—a patch near the road. He was hoeing with his shirt

138

off, and he caught a rhythm with that hoe—not violent or jerky the way most people do it . . ."

"I'd say he was violent. When he was here last week I was afraid he'd break everything he touched."

Undeterred, Simon went on. "Anyway, the hoe. He worked perfectly even, with the same length of the stroke, the same pull; and his muscles were rolling up and down his back in the same rhythm as the hoe. I could see how any man could envy that, let alone a woman love it on first sight. I never felt so comically old."

"Comically?"

"Exactly. I looked down at my pouch rammed up against the wheel and I had to laugh. I suppose I laughed because I'm not old enough to see the end and not young enough to feel ashamed of myself. I felt like Mr. Micawber or one of those other fat coots in Dickens—round as the moon, my stomach weighing more than all of him hoeing there." He balanced the cup in his hand. "It just struck me funny. I laughed and Adam Kossecki, sitting next to me, threw me a look like poison. I tried to stop myself; I tried to explain; but I knew he wouldn't understand. I just grinned. He asked me what was so damned funny and didn't I have any respect for his brother. And I don't know why, but it set me off again. I told him next time to sit in the back, which was a sure thing since there were no more Kosseckis left but him —if I wanted to laugh in my own hearse, I'd damn well laugh. He said next time he'd take his trade elsewhere. That got me for good; I could hardly see the road." He smiled toothily, then took his pipe from his pocket and clamped the stem between his lips. "Thank God for the boy, pure and simple. Another year or so and I might have been looking at that belly and moaning that I lost something—my youth—like that. Whatever. Now I think I'll put on another hundred pounds."

"He doesn't make me laugh."

"You just don't like him, do you, Cass."

"Probably not." He refilled Simon's cup.

"Ever wonder why?"

"Now and then."

"Come up with any answers?"

Ignoring him, Cass said, "There are obvious things. For instance, why didn't she ask him in instead of meeting him on the porch? No doubt because he wants to avoid me. I didn't even know she was going out with him again until last night. And then I had to pry the simple fact out of her that they were going to the movies"; thinking unpleasantly: *Are they really?* "Why, Simon?"

"Because she knows you don't like him. Maybe she knows that and doesn't want to bring him inside the house because of it. Or maybe she feels really grown up now, wants her privacy." But to Simon it really meant a flight into exclusivity, secrecy, the beginning of a defensive young love which somehow always considered the world at large oppositional; and he wondered why Cass could not see that. Or perhaps he did. And found it intolerable.

"Maybe," Cass said. "Always maybe."

"Yes, maybe. And maybe she knows you're a hardhead too. Maybe you make her feel uncomfortable with a boy. What the hell, Cass, she's no baby. If she senses you won't be civil, well— she doesn't want to subject him to it. If you make it that clear, you old fart, you deserve a back seat. Maybe a rumble seat."

Cass frowned.

"One thing I'm sure of," Simon went on, "you know Martha would listen to anything you had to say if she felt you had any real objection to him."

"Now *I* can say maybe. No, I don't think she'd listen. I'd like to tell her how I feel, but I'm sure she'd buck. I suppose I expected her to choose someone better; maybe I didn't want her ever to choose anyone in this town. No more than that."

"Where was I when you turned snob?"

"I said 'better,' and I mean it. Better for her. I know nothing can come of this, but it doesn't alter the fact that there are droves of other kids she can go out with. She can take her pick."

"She picked him."

"That simple?"

"Unless you want to complicate it," Simon said; thinking that

140

without a word Martha had, perhaps through the subtlest change of expression or attitude, indicated to Cass that not only was Matthew not simply another boy but that he was, in and of himself, more than any other boy or man could ever be. The communication had frightened Cass or caught him up short or even stunned him, because what in theory was supposed to happen to her had indeed happened. And he had never believed it, considered it, but locked it out of acceptance. He rebelled; he did not like it. He *was* frightened—of even that small indication of feeling on her part, only a week old and probably still largely unconscious, unexplored, a first tremor of romantic seriousness in a girl of seventeen.

Simon said, "Maybe she grew up too fast. You might not have caught up with her, don't understand her reasons, what this new woman part of her wants."

"She's not a woman."

"Where I was born, she'd be a married woman with a shitty-assed kid or two. And if she didn't have a man, they'd give her a couple more years, then give up on her, make her wait on granpap and do the chores. What do you suppose runs through the mind of a woman like that—if she still has a mind left?"

"I think I know as much about women as any man."

"Which I guess isn't much." He sucked on his pipe, finally drawing smoke, then secured it with his eyetooth. "You've been married; I haven't. So that makes us even; we know about the same. It's hard enough to recognize the man part of the boy when it pops out. And we're men. So what can we know about women? Especially when they still look like girls? And God almighty—what do they think when they're in love? I don't know; but it's more of everything than we can name or understand."

"It's true—about the love."

"Suppose you might not understand Martha, you can't keep up with her—just suppose it. Well, remember her fourteenth birthday and I bought her that doll? God knows I turned red as a beet. I took one look at her in her party dress and my mouth hung off its hinges. She grew up, on the spot. Her dress, her hair,

**141**

everything. She got to the point where she could hide the little girl in her any time she wanted to—a trick a man can't do with the little boy in him. I almost died with that silly doll in my hand."

"Holding it by one arm with that look on your face." Cass shook his head, then laughed.

Simon said, "And what did you get her, wise guy?"

"A set of classics. Abridged for children. But I never did show them to her."

"Because you saw what happened to that doll."

"Yes. I sneaked out the back and caught Harry Chase open. I bought her perfume and a vanity set."

"After—after me."

Cass nodded.

Simon said, "Maybe I don't have the experience, but I can feel a little bit what it must be like to think you see kids growing, think you're right there with them. But no, you're way behind. And you feel old and stupid as hell. You get old, and I suppose missing it all is part of being a father. You know you're old when you're not the center of your world any more, when you lose complete control, when the patriarch trips on his throne. You feel out of place, unneeded, an ornament in the middle of young people all of a sudden grown up, with their own minds. Then I guess you can go two ways—accept it and scratch your head and try to learn all over again or get obnoxious and hated by everybody because you start to panic and push and try to sell them on the idea that you matter more than them, that they owe you everything. Then you're really old-miserable, lousy old."

"I guess I've thought of that," Cass said defensively.

"When you think of Martha and the boy?"

"Yes."

"Then maybe you'd better find out which way you want to go."

"Meaning?"

"Meaning just that. Do you have any real reasons for not liking the boy?"

"Some."

"His father."

"I can't deny that."

"Overruled," Simon said.

"Overruled?"

"He's the spitting image of his old man, at least the way the old man was. You see? That's the way it is. A man looks one way, then changes, and you can't see that change, gauge it; then there he is again, the way he was to start with, reincarnated almost."

"Maybe it is the image. I'm not sure of that either."

"Is it the religion?"

"I haven't thought too much about that. Why should I? As I've said, nothing serious is happening between them—or probably will. I don't want to think about the religion part of it now when it may never turn up."

"Good—fair enough. But I'll tell you what I think. Give him a chance; give yourself a chance. Find out what he's really like. What the hell can you lose? Martha's a good, sensible girl. If she sees something good in him, maybe he's got it. Why not trust her judgment? She doesn't run around with everybody in town. He might be special for a reason."

"Then again, she doesn't run around even a little. I doubt if she's got enough dates behind her to recognize what's important in a man and what's not. Or worse, what's destructive."

"She knows what she wants now. Anyway," blowing smoke through his nose, "you sound like you've been reading one of those teenage guides for parents they sell for fifty cents in the drug store."

"There was a time when I did."

"Help you?"

"Sure. For proms it's permissible for the father to lend his daughter's date the family car. A sneaky way to get her home on time. Strange car equals responsibility."

Before speaking, Simon knocked his pipe ashes into a saucer. "Trust her. She knows what she's doing."

"Why does she need him? That's what crucifies me. Has whatever he's got visible to everyone or is it visible only to her?"

"So? Does it matter? A person goes after the things he needs. Always. It doesn't matter who else can see anything."

And Cass peered down at his cold coffee, the streaks of congealed cream striating the surface; thinking: *All this is so fair and objective and high-minded; but it solves nothing, just because it is objective.* And thinking, too, that no reasons were compelling enough for him to like Matthew; that even if he came to hate Matthew while she continued to need whatever unknown, imperceptible quality hid within him, then who would be wrong? Thinking: *Me? Or would it mean that whatever he possessed fit perfectly into some gaping wound of her own lack? What does she lack? Where is the emptiness?*

"How about some more coffee?" Simon asked.

Cass stood and went out into the kitchen.

And Simon: "What kind of movie did they go to?"

"I don't know. Simon? I think you might be wrong."

"About what?"

"That there might be something special about him."

Gazing toward the kitchen, Simon said softly, "You try so hard. So very hard."

"What?"

"I say, could be. Anyway, who knows? Listen. Make it strong like Martha does."

# 6

They saw *An American in Paris* at the Regency in Bluefield, then silently drank ice-cream sodas and, tacitly, mutually agreed to return to Southfield. They caught the last bus, an old wreck that rattled and bucked, whose door opened manually. Sitting in the rear, they listened to the snores of the one other passenger, a farmer slouched in his seat, a sweaty hat clamped over his eyes like a lid, his short explosions of air dissecting the sick retching of the ancient motor.

Then Martha said, "Paris." Just that, staring through the window at nothing, occasionally refocusing on the dark glass itself, examining her reflection which, through an optical trick, seemed to possess a crescent of mustache across the upper lip. "Paris," she said again, unaware of her dramatic breathlessness, then turned to Matthew. "Daddy took my mother to Paris on their honeymoon," suddenly struck by the sound of the word, drawing in her upper lip contemplatively and pronouncing it silently several times, as she always did when for no apparent reason a familiar word became strangely, eerily silly and vaguely embarrassing. Honeymoon. Honey. Moon. Honeymoon? She said, "He was there during the First War too. I wonder if it's really like the picture?" She relaxed her face dreamily and looked at Matthew, as if expecting an answer.

"Tell him to see it. Then ask him."

"He never goes to the movies," pausing; then, "He took my mother to the movies on their first date," wondering, as soon as she said it, if some slight unclear parallel existed between her father and mother, herself and Matthew. Had she been thinking of that? Was that why she had ruminated about honeymoon? She twitched her brows and peeked at Matthew in the dark window.

"Did they have movies then?" he asked.

"Charlie Chaplin, I guess. Things like that. I often wonder why he never told me what they saw."

"Why do you wonder?"

"Oh, sometimes I feel as if my mother died last week. Sometimes I feel sure I knew her. You know—daydreams. And then sometimes I feel I never had a mother at all. I guess Daddy thinks she was a saint and he wants me to believe it."

"Do you?"

"No."

"But why do you wonder?"

"Oh, that. I suppose because Daddy told me everything about them, every little detail, everything they did." Then she flushed, saying quickly and confusedly, "Well, not everything"; flushing more deeply, angry for the unpalatable impulse that had prompted her qualification when he had not, could not have, drawn an inference. He understood what she had meant; his nodding, serious head had told her that; yet perhaps she secretly sneered at the ethereal relationship, the purity that had seemed to conceive her, a phenomenon she could no longer believe in. She was grateful that he had let her remark pass.

But as soon as he became silent she wanted to hear his voice. He had said little during the evening, his face at times brooding and intractable; in the theater she was frightened that he would slip away, that she would turn her head and find him gone. He had touched her hand once, and although she had drawn it away, simply letting it rest on her lap dangerously close to the insides of her thighs, he removed his hand almost immediately. She had thought of her thighs when she was calm enough after the contact to half absorb herself in the film; needing calmness, because unlike the night at the bazaar, when he had gripped her hand as he might the handle of a package, his touch in the darkness had prickled her skin. Even sitting in the bleachers with the expiring rockets coating them with darkness, his arm around her shoulders, she had felt nothing like this, his hand unexpectedly, unerringly, quietly finding hers. Had he taken his hand away because she had not responded, had not held it? And then: why think of her thighs?

Her hands were nervous now; pressing her knees tight together, she started as he said, "Do you remember that time in church?"

"Yes."

He nodded seriously, adding nothing. The bus stopped and admitted a passenger, the door tinning shut behind him. As the driver mulched gears the man seemed engaged in a scientific survey of the seats. Finally he sat behind the driver and began to talk.

Martha looked at Matthew as he watched the man, saw his set, apprehensive face relax. She smiled, also glad that the man had decided not to sit near them.

"I thought a lot about that day," Matthew said.

"Yes?"

"I don't know. I never went back, that's what I was thinking."

"Didn't you like it?"

"I don't know that either." He folded his arms across his chest, saying, "I suppose my mother wanted me to go back, but I was afraid my old man would hit her." He nodded. "I guess that was it. Then again, maybe I didn't go back because I just didn't want to. What I mean is, I've done a lot of things I wanted to and the hell with everybody. I kept thinking about Ma—all the time. Maybe I was just too young."

"You can try again."

"No. I don't think I want to now. I guess I just don't believe it. Anyway, at least I met you there."

He turned from her quickly and rubbed the side of his nose with a forefinger. As she watched him, the dregs of her nervousness vanished. She was less insecure. He had said, in so many words, that he liked her; and she realized that it was what she had wanted to hear. Now it was easier for her to think that in the theater he had been nervous too.

"Why did your father want me to go to church so bad?"

"He never told me, really. You're not angry at him now, are you?"

"No. It's just that back then he asked me if I ever felt I needed to go to church. I swear, I thought about that for nearly a year, used to ask myself every time I went upstreet and passed by the church. I never had the need, not one time. So I just gave up on it. Once I damn near told him. I went to the store for something and I almost came out with it. 'Mr. Nowell, I don't ever feel like going to church, so I can't be a Catholic, can I?' Just like that. But I never did. After that first time I wondered why he never asked me to go again."

"Did you want him to?"

"Hell, I don't know. Maybe. I kind of liked him."

"Still do?"

"Since that first time I never said more than ten words to him until last week."

"Maybe you'll feel like going back someday."

"But will I ever have to?"

"No one says you have to do anything."

"You're a funny kind of Catholic." He smiled. "You even want the priest to smell good."

She returned his smile and tossed her head. "You still might go back—that's the missionary in me, the good Catholic. Anyway, even atheists go back to church, most of them," suddenly thinking of Simon, thinking further, knowing that whatever church he had belonged to would never see him again. Yet there was a forthrightness and solidity in his ungodliness that baffled her, but convinced her that his belief in—what—not truly ungodliness but some tangible force that he shared with no one— was as unfailing and honest and direct as her father's, even Father Nowak's belief in the God of the church. And she had often thought of, contemplated, a private God like Simon's; not because he or it fascinated her (how could it? she could not even identify it) but only because Cass was often annoyed by it. He tried to shut out Simon's God (again, she knew the God was nonexistent, but she knew no better way to describe Simon's involvement), even tried to prevent him from discussing their God. But when they did talk of it, Simon eagerly and Cass with a profound vertical furrow dissecting his forehead, Cass did not allow her to hear it, not with gruffness or prohibitions but with excuses, reminding her of homework and bedtime. Yet, she admitted, she was fascinated; perhaps just because she could not hear, was not allowed to.

Unconvinced, she said, "Some of them go back."

"Well, I wish I was an atheist or a Communist or something I could put my finger on. At least I'd know what it is I'm supposed to go back to. The big trouble all my life is that I had to tell everybody I wasn't anything. Nothing at all."

She wanted to say: Don't worry. But it was gratuitous; it was obvious that he did worry, often, she could see it in the pinch of his eyes. She sighed, then stifled a mock yawn with the back of her hand, hoping to change the subject.

"Tired?" he said.

"Just from sitting."

"It won't be long now."

"No. Matthew? Do you really want to go to Korea? You said you did at the bazaar."

"I said I might join the Army. I guess it was just talk." He shrugged his shoulders. "Sometimes I do want to go."

"Why should anyone want to go to war?"

"Because there are times when I feel like shooting at somebody."

"Do you really mean that?"

"Yes. Sometimes. Mostly I'd just like to get away from here."

"Southfield?"

"The whole thing. I don't know why I stay around. I just don't. Anyway, you want to get out of here too. You said so."

"Not to war. Not to shoot people."

"I said *sometimes*," he snapped. Then, calmly, "I really don't want to kill people. I only think of that because the Army seems the one way out—and there's a war on. So, one and one equals two."

"It's because of the fields, isn't it?"

"My father too. I can't lie about that. But I do hate the fields. God, I do. Not the work itself—sometimes it feels good, just when you're doing it, when you're daydreaming. But it won't get me anywhere. It just doesn't mean anything, not if I do it every day for the rest of my life." He rooted his eyes on the sleeping farmer. "It's like going around in a circle—really, it's like that. I mean, in fact. You plant one field in the spring, then plant all the rest, then you're back to that first field to get rid of the weeds and the small leaves, and you go right ahead to the next one. Then back to the first field again for first picking, then second picking, then whatever the hell else is left." He dug a fist into his thigh. "That damn first field. It's always there, never burns up, never goes away. Sometimes you get so dizzy with the heat under those nets you wish you never started that first field, wish you started the second one. And then you think how stupid that was—you're really dizzy then—because no matter where you start, that place is first and you'll always go back to it. It's like living and dying in the same place, like never getting out of bed."

He glanced up the aisle and saw the passenger behind the driver looking back at him; he turned to Martha and lowered his voice.

"School is getting like that too. Always a term behind. You know, I used to be good at almost everything except music. English was always my favorite. Not the grammar, but honest to God, I even liked *Silas Marner*. Now I don't care any more, it all seems so stupid." And half to himself, "Stupider when I see *him* every night."

"Your father?"

"Who? Yes." He played his eyes over her face, then said, "I'm jealous of you."

"Me?"

And suddenly he smiled and pressed her hand, saying, "Is that a sin?"

"Not jealousy, really. Envy is—a deadly one."

"Maybe I still do like your old man in a way."

They left the bus at the Southfield square and walked slowly up Washington Street, finally sitting on her porch swing, sitting in the chill night, listening to a hardy renegade cricket, she trailing a foot on the floor to still the grating of the rusty chains.

He took her hand and said, "I wanted to hold it in the movies, but I thought you'd get mad," tracing his thumb along her wrist, saying nothing more. And she wondered if she could ever understand why he hadn't held it, really why. He circled her wrist and her skin prickled again, knowing that the feeling was everything *but* the cold air, feeling the prickles mantle her legs and arms, feeling weightless and giddy enough to giggle and ruin it all. But she didn't, because she knew that it would happen exactly as it did, almost felt the distance between them torn away, his lips touching a corner of her mouth. As before, with his hand, she did not resist when his lips pained hers, just released the tension within her and rocked in the swing until he clutched her body, one hand hard and moist on the back of her neck, the fingers penetrating her hair. And with a lurch of strength she circled his waist with both arms and locked her hands behind him, pressing and torturing her fingers, tightening her forearms against his ribs until the pain she forced on herself unhinged her lips, crushed them through his, boring her mouth into his until she felt the heat of his tongue against the inside of her cheek—drawing him toward her so that now he could not resist or stop or draw back—accepting the strangeness and fear and comfort of the nervous weight inside her. And she would have cried out, but the pain in her fingers, the crushing, numbed her; her fingers lost their grip; her mouth was empty.

He drew his head back and she thought: My God, what have I done, hearing the hideous, telltale creak of the chains which might wake her father, which would. But as if he felt her fear and possessed the remedy, Matthew leaned forward and kissed her eyes; no one had ever done that before, tasted her tears. She rested her head against his chest, peaceful in the belief that the kissing of her eyes, the stillness of his body and his hands on hers was evidence that whatever he was thinking, it was not that she was a tramp; because for an instant she had thought it, as soon as her mouth closed, in that eternity of half-regret between his movement away from her and the touch of his lips on her eyes. She had thought and felt it, realizing in a rush of confusion and bitterness and undirected anger that somehow, tacitly, by a process she had never been aware of, she had been taught to expect such a reaction from a boy, a man. She had been conditioned to it, somewhere learning her automatic self-recriminating response. But it was not true, not for them.

And then she was embarrassed, thankful for the darkness. Embarrassment, that too—false.

Finally she thought of sin. What she had done was a sin, her own, not his; and if she wanted sin so badly then she must be beyond penance or salvation. Yet sin was part of a composite vision of her experience: of first confession and communion, and children disobeying parents and swearing; what she had done was an act apart, the conditional clause in the catechism, divorced from the pure sensation of feeling, the smell of his body, the willing destruction of the fine-print chastity she had read but discarded, the destruction of her little girl's fairy prince and all the stuffed-toy guardians against life, the bloodless image which she felt she must cling to even in womanhood. He had made her cry, and only he could stop the tears.

"I never want to be alone," he said.

"No."

"All week I looked at myself in the mirror, wondering how you could like me."

She lifted his hand to her cheek, feeling it curl under her chin, hold her, draw her face to his. Gently—she held his head with her hands so he would kiss her gently.

# Five

## 1

Stirring sugar into his coffee and biting luxuriously into a piece of thickly-buttered toast, Simon watched Harry Chase tack black-and-orange Halloween streamers along the frame of the mirror behind the soda fountain, covering each knot of the crepe paper with a witch's mask or a cardboard pumpkin. Harry Chase eased himself from the footstool and stepped back several paces, contemplating his work. Dabbing his lips with a paper napkin, Simon glanced toward the display window, his eyes attracted by a sudden alteration of light; peering in, but not at him, was a small wizened face with slitted eyes and a white-wall haircut, which illusorily suspended the ears from the rim of a black hat. Then, as if floating, the face turned and drifted on, bobbing into a globe of red water, vanishing behind a placard, plunging into a globe of blue water, disappearing again beyond the window frame.

"Did you see that?" Simon said.

"What?" Harry Chase answered, flicking his eyes along the streamers. "Is something crooked?"

"Never mind." Simon left the store.

The man stood two doors away, leaning forward on tiptoe, craning his neck toward a shop window. Simon watched silently for a minute, then clucked his tongue, wiped his forehead with a handkerchief, and called out, "Willy? Is that you, Willy?"

He turned from the window and stared, his body smaller and more crooked than Simon remembered; he wore a cheap black suit, at least two sizes too large, which hung from his shoulders like a cloak; his tie, black too, was awkwardly knotted and half-buried under the collar. A prune, Simon thought; no, a dried gray cocoon.

"Hello, Simon. I guess it is me."

"Hell now."

"I came back, Simon."

"It looks that way."

"You took on weight. I guess people are still getting them fifty-dollar funerals."

"Yes. Fifty dollars."

Willy came forward and jerked out his hand; Simon paused, looked at it, then shrugged and took it, feeling a rub of sandpaper on his palm.

"Time flies, don't it?" Willy sat on the edge of his suitcase, a pasteboard monstrosity which would have disintegrated under a normal weight.

"The years pass," Simon said.

"Town looks different. Modernistic."

Simon grunted and lighted his pipe; he said, "Never thought we'd see you again."

"Would of come back before. Spent two years extra."

"How's that?"

"Got nervous. Antsy. Couldn't stay out of trouble is what they said." He squinted, flagged his hand over his eyes, and peered up the street; he held his gaze on the soldier's monument standing green and pigeon-dropped, then nodded. "Lots of cars around. Lots of stores. Women all dressed nice."

"People have a little more now."

"Is that for sure? No lie?"

"You got eyes."

"That's just fine. Awful good news. I wondered about that all these years."

"You wondered?"

"Couldn't hardly sleep for worrying."

Simon puffed slushily on his pipe.

Willy said, "Now tell me true, Simon. Nobody's poor?"

"Maybe a few." He tapped out his pipe. "Well, nice to see you, Willy. I have to go to work."

"Want to dodge me, Simon?"

"Do you really want to know?"

"The way I figure, you should be proud to be seen with me."

"It's the high spot of my life."

"Maybe you don't like my suit, Simon? I know it ain't the best, but what do you want for nothing? Anyway, I don't see no cutaway on you. Not unless that stomach of yours is part of your pants and not just fat. They didn't give me no five-course meals where I was." He cackled, but there was no smile. "The menu was kind of short."

Simon shook his head.

Willy said, "I come off the bus and the first thing I see is a bank. And then a saloon. And then all them cars—red ones and two-colored ones—and stores and women, and I says to myself: well, shit, this town really made it. It went places. One thing I didn't see was no Welcome Home Willy sign, no brass bands with girls in them little shorts that show their pussies. Why, Christ, I saved the town. Didn't I save it?" He laughed expressionlessly, pounding his knee with the side of his fist; then abruptly ceased, setting his lips. "You remember? I saved it." He spat at his feet. "Shit."

"Good-bye, Willy."

"I got to get a room," rising, lifting his suitcase as if it were empty, then shaking himself like a wet dog, his body wheeling half around before his coat followed the movement. "You be in your place later?"

"Maybe."

"Well, you better. I got a lot of things for you to hear. We're going to be good friends, Simon." He nodded, then turned and walked down the street, his head plunging forward and back like a pigeon's.

Simon returned to the drug store, followed by Harry Chase who had been standing in the doorway, listening.

Harry Chase said, "He talked crazy."

"Was he ever sane?"

"Why did he bring up the bank? You don't suppose he's planning to rob it, do you?"

"I couldn't say."

Simon paid for his toast and coffee, bought a can of tobacco, and walked slowly to the funeral chapel. Inside, he sat at his desk with his elbows propped up and spread the blotter with the month's bills, staring at them absently, convinced that in a vague way Willy's return was pitiable, yet wondering if his appearance served as symbolic knowledge that everyone was driven to return, physically or mentally, to what was familiar and comprehensible no matter how painful. Call it obsession: the criminal back to the scene, or the elephant finding his graveyard.

He looked off toward a blank wall, wondering if he could feel what he had just thought; he didn't, not honestly. He could not truly decipher the element of need in Willy's return.

Perhaps there was something else: Willy back, searching for revenge, not realizing in the illusive immediacy of his bitter memory that years were accumulating, dying, that everyone connected with that night so long ago was dead or dying too or just gone. Which they were. Except Simon. And Willy back from where? From prison obviously, or a work farm, or some place that sickened of him and drove him out of sight.

He bent over the desk and neatly stacked his checks, placing them one by one into envelopes, wondering if he were turning miserly because the postage-paid envelopes pleased him. Then he went to his room and dozed in the armchair.

He could not have known how long Willy had stood looking down at him; the room was almost completely dark except for the diffuse glow of the small table lamp. For a moment the face seemed some meaningless remnant of a dream, a vague half-awake impression; then he blinked and pushed his body erect, saying, "How did you get in here?"

"Through the door," Willy said. "Better lock it if you take a snore. Liable to get robbed."

"You could knock."

"That's just it. When doors is open I kind of just walk through." He sat opposite Simon, worming himself into a corner of the chair; sitting in the dimness, still in his black suit, he seemed a darker, animated shadow, like a blanket draped across a frame. He crossed his legs, an incongruous white sock dazzling out into the light.

"Comfortable?" Simon asked.

"Just fine."

"What do you want here?"

"I got a nice room over by Mrs. Sych—Shz . . ."

"Szczepanowska."

"Good at them Polack names, ain't you Simon?"

"I live here."

"Real nice room she gave me. Shit, but nice."

"I said, what do you want?"

"I was wondering. All that time talking to you in the street, I says to myself, why don't he ask me where I been all these years?"

"Maybe I don't care."

"That's just what I says to myself: Maybe he don't care. And then I says: Maybe I better tell him anyway. I been in jail."

"No shit, Willy."

"Can't get around them prison suits, can you? Knocked out knees and a paper ass."

"Willy, I don't want to talk to you. Just tell me what you want.

Quick. Or I'll kick you the hell out of here. You must have sneaked around the chapel as soon as you saw me sleeping, so you probably saw that big bronze coffin. Well, I'll tell you. If you don't speak up in one minute I'm going to take you and shove you inside that thing and throw you in some hole."

"Whee," whistling through his teeth. "Sure got it in for me, ain't you?"

"Yes. Exactly. Now—*what?*"

"I don't guess you'll be throwing me in no hole, Simon. Gee whiz, that chaplain up to the jail told me forgiveness is next to God. But I guess you still got it in for me from way back."

"What do you want me to do? Rehabilitate you? I wouldn't give you a nickel. Not when I know damn well that if there was a body out there when I was asleep, you'd take it and try to hock it. Not when you sit there like a crazy monkey with some idea the size of a beebee shot busting your brains apart."

"Aw, Simon—don't you believe a man can change?" He cocked his head and threw out his hands, looking genuinely offended.

"Not you. You're not big enough to change. You just get smaller. Someday there won't be anything left to see."

"Now that's where you're dead wrong. Fact I'll show you how much I learned traveling around. Like I bet you don't know much about Fallsville, do you, Simon?"

"Fallsville."

"Beautiful spot. Pop., five thousand, ninety-two."

"What about Fallsville?"

Willy plucked a black notebook from a coat pocket, darted his tongue at a forefinger, and rippled the pages. Pausing, he said, "Nineteen twenty-two or twenty-three, the exact year ain't too clear. Hear you stopped there. Just passing through, sort of." Simon said nothing, and Willy, "Maybe you heard of this fella named Lucky while you was there. Maybe you even run into him."

"Well?"

"See, this Lucky was some kind of preacher. Got in lots of trouble, then run off. Nobody ever did know where he went to. Had your last name, Simon."

158

"It's a common name."

"Seems this fella had a sign with your first name too." He sniffed. "Oh now shit, Simon. Why don't you admit it. They said they never could forget your face, not with that tooth and all. Said they checked up on you." He flipped two pages. "Let's see. Said you was run out of a couple more towns. Then there was a little fella, guess he was eight was all, up in Indiana. Something about," arching over the notebook, squinting into the light, "about mo-les-ta-tion."

Reflexively, Simon lunged forward and knocked the notebook from Willy's hand; Willy bent, retrieved it, and tucked it back into his pocket.

"Some of that's true," Simon said. "So what?"

"The little boy?"

"Not that. Now you get out of here."

"Whyn't you tell me the rest?"

"Tell you?"

"Hold on. They found out about you, checked back, like I said. Because of the other boy. The one in Fallsville."

"What boy in Fallsville?" About to wash him away into the street like a bad memory, Simon listened now. Nothing had happened in Fallsville—humiliation, derision, but no accusations.

"The one you tried to cure or heal or something."

"I never did that."

"Name of Bridges. Twelve-year-old. His old man done all that checking on you. Even took after you with a gun. Never could figure out how he messed up with Fallsville thirty or forty miles from here only. I could of told him right where you was, but what the hell."

"You're lying."

"No, Simon, not me. No. Got the proof, all right. Met the kid's old man in a saloon, half drunk to death. Told me the whole story. Real sad. Kid drowned."

"Drowned?"

"Seems he got shook up at what you was preaching. Went and got himself drowned in some river trying to baptize himself. Did it right in front of his pal. Said he was going into the river to get

159

God to fix his leg. Crippled or something. Walked right in after the rain. Boom."

"You lying bastard, they never listened to me in Fallsville. They almost killed me. There was no boy there." Simon heaved out of his chair, hunched, almost leaning against Willy, who clucked his tongue, saying quickly, "Didn't think you'd of believed me. Wait." He produced a cracked billfold and removed a fragile yellow newspaper clipping. "Kid's old man said I could have it. Said it didn't matter no more, not after all these years."

Simon took the clipping with the anticipation of imminent sickness, and held it close to the light; and unless Willy had somehow contrived to bribe a typesetter, what he had said was true. The story was there, a ridiculous graphic attempt at small town luridness, and his name, printed twice. He sat again and covered his eyes with a hand, feeling Willy slip the clipping from his fingers.

"You must of gave him one hell of an idea," Willy said. "Unless you came right out and told him to jump in that river. He had a bum leg. Couldn't swim a inch."

"Oh, Jesus," Simon said.

"Well, as soon as I found out I was coming right back to tell you, but that's when I had my trouble. No sense talking about that. No sense at all. You could say 1933 wasn't my best year."

"He looked for me? The father?"

"Hell, yes. Couple of years, he said. So I says: Why don't you call the cops, and he says he did, but they didn't do nothing about it. Something about no crime being done. Legal crime, anyways."

Simon uncovered his eyes and dropped his head on his chest, saying, "Now you told me, you better go."

"Yeah. Well. Like I said this afternoon, we're going to be good friends from now on."

"Friends?"

"Because I don't guess you want everybody to know all about that. I don't guess you do—right, Simon? And then I figure I'd like to live a little better; you know how it is. I mean, what the hell. Share and share alike. Time you had a silent partner anyway."

"Get out, Willy."

"Now, Simon."

"Get out or I'll kill you."

"Simon, you ain't thinking straight."

Simon lunged forward, tore Willy from the chair, and bent him backward until he gasped, his breath rattling.

"You'll get out now," Simon shouted. "Now, you son-of-a-bitch."

"I'll tell everybody, the whole town. They'll lynch you."

"I don't care who you tell. Tell anybody you want. But when you tell, you better run like hell—some place on God's earth where I'll never find you. Because if I ever see you again, I'll kill you. I'll break you apart like a piece of dried horseshit."

"My back!" Willy screamed. "My *back!*"

"I want to break it. My God, I want to." He dragged Willy through the chapel, jerked open the door, and threw him halfway across the sidewalk, hearing him bellow as he scraped along the concrete.

Crying, Willy said, "I'll get you, you fat fuck," shaking his fist, twitching. "I'll get you when I'm ready."

Simon stepped outside; Willy leaped to his feet and, wailing, ran off in the direction of the square. Then Simon looked up the street, and seeing only a boy walking through the light of a distant street lamp, closed the door and returned to his living room.

Sitting again, he stared, numb and sick, into the darkest corner of the room, biting his lips and scouring his face with a handkerchief, thinking that the memory he had tried so desperately to destroy would never be stilled now, not with this, the dead boy. How many others maimed or mad or dead, he could never know, whose families had searched for him with guns and clubs and whips, searching under rocks, in brothels, in saloons and railroad dumps, but never in the honest, the clean places. Never in the open. And how close had he come to being trapped? He clenched his fists and shuddered.

The boy in Fallsville (if alive, how old now—forty-two?) did not need to die, at least in one sense; there would be no solace even if he had been pulled from the river and rescued. No solace because on his crippled leg he had been driven there; not by honest faith, no matter how fanatical, but by deception and corruption. Had he, Simon, such power after all? Power to push even one so far?

And so he was a murderer; he felt that, and there was nothing to palliate the fact, nothing in the coincidental accident of that death to soften remembrance and shame and guilt. The old life was there, always, rooted in him like his eyetooth, its prominence accommodated by a hole in a pipestem. It was not meaningful that he was no longer what he had been; nothing could be obliterated or justified or even rationalized by the relinquishing of his Bible or his collection-plate hat or his lies.

Willy. The agent. Somehow there was justice in that.

Now he knew: the belief that only he himself had suffered had been stupidly illusory. And there was nothing to do; again, as it had been thirty years before, a feeling of immobility, encapsulation, stagnation. He could only live with what he knew, waking to it each day, and it was immutable, unalterable, whether or not Willy lived or died, telling or not telling. Even if he were drummed out of Southfield there would be no atonement in it; at least he could not think of it as such. Because he did not seek atonement; he did not believe in it; it could neither repair nor negate what had been done—unless you needed it because you feared punishment or damnation and believed that God could forgive anything, even murder, without restoring the life of the murdered. A trifle. Forgiveness must come only from the boy, who would be a man now, who was dead. Otherwise nothing. A man could not forgive himself; what he had done only added to what he was, did not subtract from it.

And so it had caught him, the old life, and now he was powerless, would always be unable to recall even the isolated pleasant moments. He could do only what he was doing now: crying, sobbing into his hands, for the first time in almost thirty years wishing he were someone else. Anyone.

John Roger lay on his bed, sleepless eyes staring, the blanket huddled up under his chin, his hands clasped on his chest; he had stumbled into bed at dusk, driven by the incandescent pain living in the small of his back. The pain eased but, afraid it would return, he had not moved except to shift the position of his legs quietly and slowly as if there were someone in the room who must not see, as if motion were fatal. He lay there for hours, and when the sudden November wind battered south from upstreet he caught the faint quarter-hour tolling of the churchbells. At first he fought against the sound, then surrendered and listened, counting between the peals—nine hundred seconds— and it was at the seven-hundredth and fifty-fifth second past eleven-thirty that he heard the almost inaudible creak of the downstairs door, then the soft tread of Matthew climbing the steps and moving along the hall to his room.

It was a ghost's sound; a ghost, when he lay there needing flesh and blood. Again he wanted to leave the bed and tell Matthew what had become so hopelessly distorted two weeks before; but he hadn't the strength, nor the strength to risk another rebuke of hate. He wondered why he had the need at all; he could not understand its power; somehow the need simply to say "I'm your father" meant salvation. Yet when he thought of the word (obsessing him, not a moment without it), he could not define what it meant for him; it drifted like a wisp of vapor between dreams and living. Perplexed, frightened, he controlled nothing within him; he was driven, as the pain had driven him to bed; he would not even show surprise if his mouth suddenly began to speak against his will.

Finally, defying his ritual, he turned his body and wedged his head under the pillow, trying to divine why he must always think of it (realizing that his denial of it for twenty years was merely the reverse side of a coin, that he thought of it even then), trying to divert his mind, laboring the thought that a man always had memories to fall back on, cling to, when life became too heavy, when he wanted not to exist. There must have been better times; like a gambling wheel he spun his memories, holding his breath, waiting suspensefully for the pointer to stop, waiting because he did not know himself where to stop. Better times. When he was ten?

Ten: Sitting in the parlor of the Episcopalian orphanage, insignificant among the floral-papered walls and the floral carpet; the brown fading antimacassared chairs and the polished yellow piano, which was locked and never used; listening at the crack between the sliding doors to his Aunt Schooner (he never called her Aunt Willa, she was too large and mannish) talking to Mrs. Demmers, the rector's wife; just waiting for Aunt Schooner's visit, and so he listened.

She saying, "Yes, I suppose he'll have to be a—a . . ."

"Ward of the state. It's a pity; he's a good boy."

And hearing Mrs. Demmers say it, he felt proud, yet a cheat as well, because he had always caused her trouble: hiding in impossible places or breaking windows, and once he had even vomited in the dining hall. She was a good woman to say it, he thought.

She tsk-tsked and said, "Would you like me to tell him?"

Tell him what?

"I don't think it matters. He never knew his father; no one did, not really. The Lord knows I grew up with him and I never did."

"As you wish. Only I do think there's an instinctual feeling about these things—between a child and father. Even if the relationship is in name only."

"Well, I couldn't say about that, Mrs. Demmers. But now he's gone, we just can't afford to keep the boy here."

"Isn't there Mrs. Williams? Have you contacted her?"

"No, we don't have anything to do with her."

He heard the scraping of a chair, a pause, and finally Mrs. Demmers' voice, farther away, said, "Johnny was a love-child, wasn't he?"

"I suppose that's the way they put it these days."

164

"Perhaps you should contact her. She must feel something."

"Must she? Well, no, I'm sorry. He never saw fit to marry her—it killed Mother, you know, it surely did—and she never saw fit to remind him to. I couldn't—you understand, of course—couldn't have anything to do with a woman like that."

"I'm thinking only of Johnny. There are times when pride . . ."

"The Lord knows, we are too. I suppose you know my brother's support money never came to enough?"

"No, I had no idea."

"I suppose they needed the money for themselves." She grunted peculiarly, almost a nasal whine.

"Shall *I* contact her?"

"No, my husband and I made up our mind. If she doesn't care without being forced, well, we just can't manage it."

"Then you realize that unless she steps forward, Johnny goes to a state home—not of your choice."

"I've heard there are lots of nice places."

"Well. I imagine you'll want to see him now."

"That will be fine."

John Roger ran from the door and sat stiffly on the sofa, his posture so rigid, his eyes so diverted that Mrs. Demmers might have known that he had heard; she glanced suspiciously at the door as she let Aunt Schooner precede her into the parlor. Aunt Schooner strode directly to the sofa and, as he half rose, battered him back into the cushions with a coarse, attacking kiss; she seized his shoulders and held them tightly while she scanned his face.

Then, "Well, Johnny-Cake, have you been a good boy?"

"I think so." He looked toward Mrs. Demmers for confirmation, but she was staring out the window.

Aunt Schooner sat and dragged him beside her; she took his hand and pumped it, not shaking it, greeting him, just swinging it because she could not keep still. She set her thick eyebrows, which struggled to meet in the tweezer-scarred center, looked down her large broad nose, and billowed out her upper lip with her tongue. Then her jaw drooped, exposing huge squarish teeth, and he saw fresh webbed wrinkles at the corners of her eyes.

She said, "Your Uncle Paul and I both know you like it here," waving vaguely toward Mrs. Demmers, "but you'll have to leave soon."

"To where?"

"Oh, another nice place." She puckered her lips sourly, then whispered close to his ear. "Maybe even nicer than here."

When she drew back he looked directly into her eyes and said, "Is my father gone?"

Mrs. Demmers turned from the window.

"Why—yes," Aunt Schooner said.

"To where?"

Her face vacillated between a smile and a grimace. "Well, he's passed away."

He began to cry. It was not what Mrs. Demmers had spoken of behind the door, not that at all; his feeling was more than instinctual; it was nourishment, solace, wonder, and weapon. Because no one at the orphanage had a father, and John Roger invoked him, called him down, conjured him—as if he were God—on the heads of his tormentors; comforted and buoyed himself with the illusion that someday his father would come to reclaim him. It was his strength, which he refused to surrender even though he was despised for it, because no boy could deny the existence of that mysterious father; they tried, but Mr. Demmers told them otherwise. So he was not an orphan, just a short-term transient in an orphanage; and it gave him a peace and security that he would never again experience.

That he had never seen his father signified nothing; it left him free to idealize him, mold the man in the image of his choice. thing he knew concretely: his father was happy. One Christmas at Aunt Schooner's house he heard her say to Uncle Paul, "He has no right to be happy. How can he write that to us—how?"

And Uncle Paul, "Well."

"Why does he write at all?"

"He's not my brother."

And ignoring him, Aunt Schooner said what John Roger had heard her say so often that it was the first word he had ever searched for in the dictionary.

166

"It's that whore did it to him." She pronounced it *hoor*, and so the dictionary never defined it for him.

Uncle Paul, rustling his newspaper: "I guess she makes him happy. I guess she does, if he says she does."

"A whore?" And the solid, yet hollow thump of her fist against the hardness above her breasts.

He thought of it while Aunt Schooner seemed confused by his contorted, crying face; and Mrs. Demmers standing silently, profiled against the window, the wind buffeting the lace curtains against her hips. And no matter how his tears supported her insight, it was more than instinctual; it was practical. He clung to the practicality at the state home and said his father was alive; but he could not lie well and no one believed him, and he finally admitted that his father had abandoned him; and when he admitted it, he seemed to die.

One day, years later, a social worker asked him if his father were alive and he said, "No. The son-of-a-bitch is dead." But that was later, when he was seventeen.

When he left Mrs. Demmers and entered the state home he did not attend chapel the first Sunday, and the dormitory head was penalized; he dragged John Roger into the toilet and jammed his head into a urinal and flushed it five times, then broke a rib and two fingers. In the infirmary an attendant held him stomach down while another mounted him and stole the last remnant of virginity that was possible to steal. When he was fourteen he ran away and, after four days and nights of hunger, tried to rob a newsstand. He was sent to a reformatory where they didn't hit him for not attending chapel. They just hit him.

He would never turn the wheel again, because he could never win; more, he could never not lose.

Then he left the bed and went to Matthew's room, first quietly, then shuffling his bare feet and coughing so Matthew would hear him, not think he was being sneaked up on. He knocked at the frame of the open door.

Matthew sat on the edge of his bed, his arms folded and resting on his knees; he looked up, then away.

John Roger said, "You been gettting in kind of late."

"I suppose I have."

"It ain't good for you."

"Don't worry. I'll get to work in the morning."

"That ain't what I mean. That ain't it at all."

Matthew shrugged his shoulders.

"You got a girl or something?" John Roger said.

Matthew stared and suddenly smiled, a mirthless grimace that chilled John Roger, made him cringe. "Not me," and turned off the light.

"You ought to get more sleep." He retreated into the hall, shivering uncontrollably, walking on the balls of his feet.

# Six

The strangeness of an unpremeditated, coincidental plan, which became a plan only because the event accompanied a wish, then the convergence of the elements, the event and wish dovetailing, locked.

She watched Cass leave for Simon's bundled against the dregs of the day's snow, his great boots tight on his calves; he was gone, hidden by the thin wet mist. And when she made no preparations to dress against the weather, neither laying out her coat nor searching through the closet for her boots, she knew—as if she had submitted to the weight of objective evidence—that she would not leave the house with Matthew, had never intended to. And realizing this, she felt that she had disposed of Cass by design, sent him away to be replaced by Matthew.

She waited quietly in the empty house, aware suddenly that she was sitting rigid as death on the edge of the couch, stretched on a rack of something akin to terror, her knees torturing each other, her hands twisting and kneading the frilly cushions, finally startled into full consciousness by the jarring pain of a broken fingernail. She examined it, filed the torn edge with her upper teeth, then leaned back, short of breath as if she had run a great distance.

It was a strange way to wait for him.

They wouldn't leave the house, she knew that; yet the decision was not harmless, merely not leaving. Nothing so simple, so passive. She was not leaving because she was going to make something happen, which was also a component of the plan, the foundation of the wish that magically united with Cass's night out.

She steadied her breathing, shook herself, and bit her lip, almost cutting through the skin when the doorbell jingled; the surprise, the snow-stifled porch preventing a single warning footfall robbing her of the last vestige of her tenuous composure. Reflexively, panicked, she bolted from the couch, then stood noiselessly until the jingling came again, and when she opened the door she immediately (as if denying another human presence) attended to the stillness of the air and the death of the snow. Matthew stood on the step, zipped into a miserably thin Army-surplus field jacket, his hands jammed into the side pockets.

Closing, then locking the door after him, she said, "You'd better warm up for a while," and when his eyes questioned her, she realized that she had made an ordinary statement in a tone of funeral gravity, almost as if he were an object.

"It stopped," he said. "It's not so cold now."

Standing awkwardly in the foyer, she could not look at him; and then, mercifully, he zipped open the jacket, flapped away the beads of water, and hung it on the clothestree.

"We're in trouble," he said. "The busses can't make it to Bluefield in less than two hours. We could flag down the Greyhound, but getting back—I don't know."

She could smile now, because whatever lay at the roots of her obscure, terrifying plan, she was at least partially vindicated. They simply could not go; the busses wouldn't let them.

He smiled back and she said, "Go over to the fire," pushing him playfully. She brought a kitchen towel for his hair, watching him scrub violently, then fold the towel over the nub of an andiron. He carefully examined his boots, also Army-surplus, to see if he had spotted the rug. Satisfied, he sat and stretched his feet to the fire.

"I don't think we should try to go," she said. "Not if we can't get back."

"Maybe that's a good reason to go." He grinned, flushing slightly.

"Because you hate Southfield so much?"

"Well, I wasn't thinking of that." He seemed even more embarrassed.

Painfully, she realized that she had not responded to his teasing because somehow she had not recognized it. She tried to rescue him. "A good idea. We can eat supper at a fancy restaurant with two waiters and another one for the champagne— except there isn't any such place in Bluefield—and everyone will look at us and say: 'What a good-looking couple.' " And then, impulsively, "And we'll stay in the Bridal Suite at the King Philip House." She blushed and hoped he would understand her fantasy, the lightness and play she hoped she had injected into it, not its almost satirical seriousness. She averted her eyes, fighting against a reaction of prudishness, hoping he would say something reassuring, even funny, because lately her gravity was a strain to bear; she was enervated by the moral weight she imposed on every thought.

He kissed her instead; not seeing him rise, she simply found him above and behind her, leaning over and nuzzling his lips in the hollow behind her ear.

"That sounds nice," he said. "But we have to get married or it won't come true."

She laughed, clean and silvery, giddy at the blessed relief of tension. But she broke no spell. He did not go away. She gazed up at him, peculiarily sensitized by his upside-down face; then he was next to her, cradling her shoulders. Looking at his face again, she could not fathom his expression; and she knew that if he felt as she did, he could not decipher hers. They could only look back into themselves for even a vapor of meaning; and there, within, they would find fright. But they would not talk of it, admit it; and the silence, the blasted reservoir of words became by the necessity to somehow tell, completely kinetic, bodily. She knew that a word now, any word, could restore reason and balance and sobriety, could fragment the opulent dream they had launched together. A hot drink, cocoa—one word—the cocoa in the kitchen, heat to melt the fright, the taste of cocoa, safe and childish and chocolaty, a taste to tell her age by.

But words were skeletons and his body loomed against hers, and her mouth opened to receive his tongue. The way it happened, his tongue lightly atop hers, she thought of communion; and the intrusion of the image, its sacrilegious analogy, presented two choices: flee or bury the thought. She buried it, buried it by burrying her tongue, extending it until it wrenched, feeling him twist away slightly under the spell of what could only be his own need to flee. And then she realized that he was attempting to conceal the effect of her tongue. But she did not pity his panic or embarrassment, still desperate to annihilate that analogy, forcing him closer until he surrendered his shame and she felt the supple resilient hardness prod at her thigh; and accepting it, meeting it, not with shock or withdrawal, but with even more painful thrusts of her tongue, blockading his, passing, glancing, as she found the hilly hidden corners of his mouth. It was her response, and she gave up; she could not blame him nor project responsibility on him; because the permission she had given him had supported his courage.

She felt his hand under her sweater pause for an instant as if the touch of her back were enough for him; but it moved on and found the clasp between the wings of her shoulders, and her body stretched forward and she felt, although it could not be, that her breasts had swollen, become engorged, filling and straining as if they were bursting from her chest. His fingers mangled the clasp. She winced under the stinging rake of a fingernail, but she would not help him. It must happen *to* her; she must not aid it. He must do it *to* her; she could escape into that—*beyond her will*. To her, not with her. Her only comfort.

Then the clasp came loose (she could not resist—*beyond her will*) and her imprisoned, growing breasts were free, suddenly weightless. And when his hand touched them, exploring tenuously, almost afraid of its callouses and roughness and power to hurt, yet hurting nevertheless, she clove to him and stood, holding him so that he could not think she wanted to escape. They stood together, she walking, leading him to the couch in the far corner of the room where she could extinguish the lights, because she could not do this in the light, and even the undulating glow of the embered fire disturbed her. But she could no longer think of it; her sweater was already free of her shoulders; a moment of darkness and fear, and then it passed over her head, her brassière falling forward, the thin straps gliding down her arms. Still happening to her—*beyond her will*. She closed her eyes, imagining him in a posture of appraisal, feeling the air chill her flesh, even more chilling with the space between them.

Now she could stop. Without contact, free of his touch, she could stop.

But she sat on the couch, feeling him lift her ankles, feeling her shoes leave her feet—and then her left foot held by his hands, his fingers playing down the instep. A pause, no contact again, and again the chill, more frightening than the closeness. He opened her skirt and she felt his hands on her hips tugging at the bands on her skirt and underwear, his fingers working into the soft pliant hollows above her hipbones, tickling her.

She pressed down into the couch; he must do it *to* her—*beyond her will*. And suddenly she despised herself because she was feigning death, making herself a corpse, offering him ashes and dust purely to murder her own feeling. So she bit her tongue until it pained, almost to confirm her living, then raised herself and covered his hands with hers, helping him to pull everything away from her nakedness; feeling, as the bundle of cloth slid over her feet, the slithering friction of her stockings against her calves, the slight obstinate tug as they came free over her heels.

Cold. She needed a blanket.

With her eyes closed she could sense his pause, knowing somehow that he was not appraising her now, only himself; then heard his buckle grate, and reflexively tensed her thighs, doomed to his decision.

She needed a cover—a blanket. Cass always brought her a blanket when she was cold. She loved the open window, the occasional drift of snow on the sill; and she needed him to bring her a blanket, tuck her, cocoon her in its folds. A kiss on the forehead.

"I'm worried," he said to Simon.

"There's no reason to."

"There's every reason to."

"You want to go home? The minute you got here, you wanted to go. Your eyes haven't left the door."

"Only because they're alone together."

"No movie?"

"There's no bus service."

"You mean you checked on it?"

"Yes. I checked."

"Cass, for God's sake."

"She's my daughter. I have the right to check."

"So? They're probably playing Monopoly or Parcheesi."

"Please."

"Well, somebody buys those goddamn games. They make enough of them."

"Can't you see you're only making it worse?"

"Then what are they doing?"

"Never mind. I shouldn't have mentioned it."

"You talk like you didn't know her. At all."

"It's not her I'm worried about. I know *her*, Simon. It's him. Just him."

He thought: *I'm ruining it, killing it; it will never go further than this night, not now. She'll pretend it never happened and*

174

*I'll walk out, and there won't be anybody again. Again, like al-*
*ways—nobody.*

Thinking it only because he could not stop, not when he saw
her lying in not enough darkness in the burnt orange light from
the fire, the shadows curving and pulsing across her body, and the
hair between her legs even darker, the one dark part of her; and
suddenly he did not care, because this was the thousandth time
in his life that he hungered powerfully for something, and for
the thousandth time vacillated because he had never felt the right
to take anything. He wanted, pure and simple, to take something—not leavings nor charity nor two-dollar Army surplus nor
the horror of a dead life in a dead house. And she was helping
him; and she was whole and new.

There had been a moment—he had paused with his hand on
his belt—he had almost run from the house. And now he stared
at her, her body strangely rigid, stiff at the knees, her head
thrown back as if her neck were broken—and for an instant he
hated her for believing that he would hurt her before he even
touched her, as if he possessed such destructive power, a dirty
and despicable power. He did not care if she was a virgin, did
not even care about the certainty that she was about to give herself to him before she was truly a woman; he did not care for
any of her pain, in the body or the heart; he did not care about
her fear.

He hardly saw her now, blinded by the thought that he got
the leavings, the Polack farm girls, the whores who stank and
mocked him by washing his crotch; Jane Nartiewicz, the drooler
he had gone to on a dare (proof of what the world thought he was
fit for, what was his proper due). And the fear each time, and
the questions: Why? Why? When he wanted none of it.

And finally he looked at her again and somehow loved her because she was not leavings, and her smell was flowers, even a bit
too strong; thinking that if anything could clean him, could root
the Williams out of his soul and body, it was her; thinking again:
*She's waiting for me.* And for a moment the dirt swirled up and
wrenched out his tears. Then he set his teeth until he felt the
pain rattling his head, tore down his pants, and because he knew
nothing of gentleness or tenderness (only the vague words, the

**175**

wishful words of love moaned out so plaintively by girls in movies and books) he covered her, opened her thighs, and entered her.


"One day you'll have to understand what you really feel. Comprehend it and deal with it. Because now you don't, and that's what tortures you."

"I know what I feel. I feel I'm not acting like a father. It's in my power to, and I don't. I feel weak, sitting and letting this foolish, impossible thing die of attrition. Why not just end it now?"

"Cass, please look at yourself. Look at what you're making of this. Two kids having dates, like ten million others. You've got your thoughts on a proposal of marriage. You're fighting against that day."

"I am, damn you. Yes."

"I can't even tell how you're saying that. Whether you're surprised, whether you agree—I don't know."

"Neither do I. For the love of Christ, Simon, what's wrong with me?"

"All your life you've had her to yourself. You can't admit you'd be alone without her. Alone—maybe like me."

"I don't know."

"You sold yourself short; you could have had much more. Another marriage, another child—and her too."

" 'This is my castle and you are my king.' She used to say that."

"When she was a child."

"She's my flesh and blood, Simon. I love her. God knows how much I love her."


He was hurting her; the prince was hurting her and she could not stop him, lying dead, almost recoiling from the pressure of his body and the slippery, liquid sounds of their rubbing stomachs. And of course the pain, tightening her body against it and pretending the body was not hers; yet it was convulsing under his jagged, arhythmic driving. Her left foot was crumpled and lame on the floor, and she did not know how it got there, not her body—*beyond her will*. And worse, feeling nothing but an intrusion, a cutting, knowing that she did not dare anesthetize her body completely because she needed the pain: sin-free pain (O my God, I am heartily sorry . . .). *Bless me father. For I have sinned. I committed. A sin. Of impurity. Alone. By myself. No one else. Abused myself alone. No one else.* That was all right—alone, no one else—but not this. And princes never hurt, so this must be real flesh; thinking of words scribbled on walls of the gym, in the toilet of the Regency: prick. But it didn't prick. It tore and bludgeoned. Thinking how she fought him, how she let him, wanted him, and now forbade him. Thinking: *I'm insane;* gasping as he sucked her breast into his mouth, biting; feeling his hands crawl beneath her so that all his weight was on her now and her breath came short and asthmatic, her chest caving. Then why take this pain. *Why?*

She began to cry, not at the pain but because she must be insane, because she could not tear away from him, just lay there neither taking nor giving, doing nothing and thinking: *Not insane. Dead.*

He was frantic now, terrifying her with motion; then lunged and stiffened as if a knife had been plunged into him, jerking to a stop as if he had died rigid in midair; and her feeling, she could not be sure, of something warm deep inside her. Then he collapsed and she could feel his touch on every point of her body, not just his whole diffuse weight, hands where hands had never been before, his mouth where no mouth had been. And suddenly she felt him leave and he was doing something with his hands that she dare not see, because now she did feel (odd that she felt only when he left her), and the throbbing increased and her leg sprang from the floor and tried desperately to circle him, but it did not arrive in time. Her knees sickled and her stomach rose; and by the time he lay next to her with his head on her breasts, begging her forgiveness, crying, kissing her hair, the prince had died in the pain and her mother had left the kingdom of heaven and become a woman who had lain with a man in bed —and felt. A woman.

She said, "I'll never let anyone else do that again."

Again, he said he was sorry.

And she let him cry on her breasts, saying finally, sensing his agony, "I won't leave you," and kissing him she was neither insane nor dead, just different, and frightened of her power to make him cry.


Kicking through the snow, Cass paused at the door, noticing the broad footprints that had preceeded him, hardened into molds by granules of frost; prints that had come and never gone away. He breathed deeply, steadied himself, then entered the house, startled by the clarity of her greeting as he pried loose his boots.

They were sitting before the fireplace playing Monopoly; and he could not believe it, nor could he believe that his shame was propelling him to run away, hide; his ears burned deep beneath the remnants of iciness, and he remained near the door, away from the lamplight. He dredged up a smile, his eyes staring at the little green houses and big red hotels and the shiny bone dice; and he felt that he should leave and re-enter—to check his reality. "Monopoly," Simon had said.

Finally he shook Matthew's hand, declined to join them for cocoa, and went to his room. And later, sitting propped in bed, his eyes blurred on the pages of a book, he heard Martha knock, enter, and say, "Daddy? Can Matthew come for Christmas dinner?"

"Yes," he said. "Yes, why not?" Not hearing the command in her voice. He turned to the window and, confused, said, "Turn out the light when you leave."


## 2

At the first shirring of bells she crumpled forward and brushed Cass's elbow, her heart aching dully, her knees like pulp on the foam-rubbered kneeler. She drooped her head, yet stared ob-

178

liquely, furtively, at the priest who was all but lost in the tiny forest of angel-haired pine trees cluttering the altar; his arms, poking from bell sleeves, plunged through pots of poinsettia into the tabernacle, his hands searching for the chalice. Shuddering, she begged for control, before she was seen trembling, before anyone interpreted what she was about to do. She needed to cry, crying would calm her. She almost decided to, just for the relief; she could somehow pretend that the Mass and Christmas and plaster saints were so unspeakably beautiful and stirring that she simply cried from the joy of it. But checking her, the small unresonant organ initiated its pageant of once-a-year hymns: "Christ the King Is Born." Father Nowak dazzled his fingers through the golden receptacles, thumb and index finger suddenly conjuring out the white opaque host. And as he turned to the pews and the bells sounded and everyone struck their breasts with lightly doubled fists, she stared at his eyes which, in the confessional the day before, were to her supreme gratitude invisible behind the darkness of the screen.

It was not his potential sermon on purity that she had knelt in terror of, because when she had told him, he had not been outraged or overwhelmingly hurt, nor did he groan or admonish. The fear and misery she had felt, thinking of the ways in which she could make a *sin of impurity—with someone* sound casual, was nothing compared with his question afterward: *Why?* Because she could not answer him. Mentally, she tried: *Love? Beyond my will?* But what she said was: *I don't know;* her mind circling backward, remembering how she knew that she would do it, how she had calculated it. More, how she had examined the couch and her thighs and found no blood; her body had already been prepared; somehow her virginity had been taken long before. *Why?* he asked again, and again she answered: *I don't know;* then sobbed and begged him not to confuse her, reassured by the scent of his violet breath in the blackness. And where he was cruel about a simple lie, an uncharitable thought, he was gentle about this; he spoke of universal sin and how all people in their mortality were expected by God to fall, but were also expected to rise again, and how God's truly chosen were always those who were instructed by their sins and were hence cleansed of them forever. And she must promise never to do again what God had ordained only for the sacrament of marriage. She promised, happy to escape the amorphous yet incredible punishment she had feared, the uncanny terror replaced by a flood of grace. And for the first time she understood what grace was—not the mysterious convoluted magic that cleansed or made one like Christ but simpler, more essential; it was the banishment of anxiety and fear. And it was also power; if God forgave, so must everyone. So must Cass.

And so she promised; she promised, recited her Act of Contrition, performed her exquisitely prolonged and punishing penance, and that night, before decorating the tree, walked with Matthew to Cass's closed store where they got a set of unsold lights and a box of shiny blue ornaments, and where she let him kiss her and touch her breasts, and she satisfied him with her hands while he groped with his. All in less than a minute. Returning to the house, the grace gone and the fear twisting within her, she hid her face and hands from Cass and fumbled with the box of bulbs and the prickly boughs of the tree.

And now, once more, in less than twenty-four hours after her penance, a mortal sinner. And when she received the host into her mouth she would commit not simply another mortal sin but deliberate desecration and sacrilege. She thought of grace again and of how idiotically wrong she had been, because she could not make excuses to Cass, could not pretend illness or that she had foolishly eaten something, a simple inadvertent act which would not allow her to take communion. She had to do this, perform the desecration, because she and Cass had received together every Christmas, and she could violate that ritual less than the commandments of the church. It was Cass to whom she owed her guilt and redemption; the grace of God was illusory; it was Cass she expiated for, Cass she did her penance for. It was clear now: if he forgave her, then everyone must. Even God.

He touched her elbow; she started, blinked, and looked into his face; he knew that she had not been following the Mass, had not heard the bells summoning the communicants. She rose with him and left the pew, dead, fighting against feeling, because no matter the feeling it would grow like a cancer into abject panic, the wild oceanic convulsions powerful enough to make her run, scream, soil her clothing, or drive her mad. She preceded him along the aisle, imagining his eyes searing through her, because of course he must know; and she felt that he was permitting her to damn herself in his presence.

She knelt at the altar, her steepled hands pressing up under the rail, watching through half-shut eyes Father Nowak gliding toward her in his gold and blood-red vestments, doling out wafers to extended tongues. She clamped her eyes tight and waited, and she suddenly thought: *He isn't coming to me.* The time grew and swelled and she began to panic, convinced that he, too, knew what she had done—and he was standing above her, examining the devils in her soul, accusing and condemning; and she, her face like a hideous caricature of a lecher, her tongue hanging crooked between bloated lips. But then the heavy scent of violet and the airy touch of the host on her tongue. She took it in and, unlike the stories she had heard as a child of the inmates of hell who had done what she had just done, it neither burned nor turned her to stone nor struck her dead, just softened and clung to her palate and briefly gagged her as it always had before crumbling down her throat. And the organ moaned, whined, and finally roared: "Joy to the World."


Hours after dinner, the living room was still heavy and full, the uncurled, dying ribbons from packages scattered about the floor. Cass prodded the fire; a log dropped, showering sparks up the flue in a fine iridescent dust. He gazed for a moment at the ceiling, beyond which Martha must lie in bed, the creak of her footsteps long gone—he was at least sure of that. Then he looked at the tree, finally pouring himself a large glass of the port Simon had brought.

Simon sat opposite him, his jacket open across a mound of white shirt dissected by Martha's Christmas tie. Their eyes met briefly and Cass said, "A funny Christmas." He drank some wine.

Simon watched his eyes drift off again as they had for well over an hour, as if he were taking inventory of every piece of furniture, every figure in the carpet. And finally, as Simon knew they would, the eyes found the sprig of mistletoe suspended by a hollied ribbon from the dining-room arch. Knew it, because under the pale sprig Matthew and Martha had kissed; knew that Cass would return to it because their kiss had been tense, self-conscious, prolonged only a split-second longer than the usual Christmas kiss, but long enough to attract attention, to somehow freeze the room, to turn them all into a cast of characters in a tableau. "How about me?" Simon had said, and the tension creaked loose. But perhaps his remark had been less effective than Cass's sudden, unseen disappearance.

Under the mistletoe, kissing, Simon admitted that there was something between them after all; something that compelled the holding of the kiss despite their knowledge of Cass's hostility, something they could not help or control. So Cass had been right; they could not help revealing the seriousness of themselves; revealing what Cass had insisted was there all along. And Cass? The only one who could not admit its appeal.

"Funny," Cass said again, turning from the mistletoe.

"Nothing funny about that turkey," Simon said.

"Whenever you're stuck, whenever you want to duck out, you praise the world of the flesh."

Simon grinned, yet he knew how accurately the remark had struck, because now he found himself responding guardedly to Cass, forcing himself to counter that depressing gloominess with increasing superficiality. So very often now. "Yes," he said. "I suppose I do. Why worry when you can eat?"

"But you *know* what I mean by funny, don't you?"

"I guess I really don't."

Cass grunted, slightly sarcastic and disbelieving, then said, "Well, they're involved. Surely are, aren't they?"

"Hm?"

"Involved and you can't deny it. But I'm not sure how I feel about it. That was some kiss, wasn't it, Simon?" He was smiling peculiarly, his upper lip drawn back, showing his teeth. Was he going to cry?

"They're good-looking kids," Simon said. "When I was their age I was an ugly little fart." Thinking: *But like that boy. Somehow I was like that boy.* The thought puzzled him; he knitted his brows.

"You're avoiding me, Simon," still smiling.

And suddenly Simon was overwhelmed with impatience and vague, diffuse anger; he did not want to hear about this boy any longer; he did not want to play the sounding board, to sponge up this irrationality concerning two ordinary adolescents who were beginning to assume the significance of Adam and Eve on the brink of causing the fall of man. It was not real, this problem, not real at all, because almost every boy found his girl; but in this house it was seen in the context of darkness, a darkness that glowed with the intensity of hellfire. And he was weary of it, weary of grown men who must discuss it, weary of the father who stared hang-jawed at his child with utter incomprehension and a naïveté that Simon was beginning to feel masked sheer malice, if not some tortured sickness. Simon did not want to talk of it and, feeling his temples hammer, almost shouted: *For Christ's sake, stop!* But he thought of Willy Kling and Fallsville and the boy being sucked to his death by the mud of a river bottom, and he shouted nothing. Just hoped there would be no more of this, no more because he would be driven away by complete disgust and helpless rage; and he wanted simply and quietly to say: *I have my troubles too—and they may be bigger.*

"Things are always confusing," he said shortly, filled his pipe, and impaled the stem on his eyetooth. He believed what he had said, because out of his own confusion he had offered Matthew a job, even more confused because not only didn't he really understand why he had done it but because he had no job available. *Somehow like that boy,* he thought again.

Cass grinned the strange doglike grin again and said mockingly, "Maybe we'll have a marriage soon."

"Cass. He sat at the table and only used one wrong fork, which

I wouldn't have noticed if your eyes didn't glare his way. He didn't slurp his soup or his coffee. He made nice small talk. He called you 'Sir.' Maybe I'm no judge. Maybe I gave him a job just so he'd rob me. Look, he was a respectful guest and he kissed his girl under your mistletoe, in plain sight. If they get married, I'll rent a cutaway and you'll rent a cutaway and we'll do what a thousand people do every day: kiss the bride and congratulate the groom. And amen. Amen, amen."

Cass stared at him for a time, not diverting his eyes even while he sipped his wine; and Simon could not fathom if the gaze communicated repudiation or mockery or the unbearable defensive superciliousness to which Cass had always been prone and which was becoming increasingly accentuated, ubiquitous, insufferable. Then the enigmatic features sagged; the jowls collapsed; the mouth hung partly open in dumb confusion. And Simon thought: *Maybe it isn't as simple as that; maybe to him it is the fall of man.* Thinking again of the drowned boy, questioning his right to judge, even advise a man who was at least not a murderer.

"I can't move," Cass said finally. "I want to scream and wail —louder and louder, until the pain goes. Somehow goes away." His wrist crumpled and some wine sloshed on his thighs. Listlessly, he set the glass on a table and brushed his fingers at the stains. "I just don't know, Simon. I wanted it to be better."

"Just let them live. Alone, together, any way they want to." Then he leaned forward and almost shouted, jarred by the roar of his own voice, blinking in wonderment, "Just so we can die in peace, for Jesus' sake. Just let's die in peace, if we can't live in peace, if that's all that's left to us. I can't watch you bleeding to death any more. If you don't let them alone, you'll kill us."

His eyes wide, Cass said, "Us?"

But Simon could not explain: that somehow he and Cass were identical, that Matthew and Martha and the boy in the river—they were all the same, even old man Williams in the rotting house. Everything meshed and fused in a piper's dance to the slaughter, and the possibilities for willful destruction were infinite, with not a single moment of just living or merely peace.

And he said again, "Just let them alone."

184

And Cass, as if Simon were some charismatic oracle, said, "Yes," his eyes clouding, his face immobile, the tears suddenly leaking down his cheeks. Yet he denied the tears; his face was carved from stone, and he stared past Simon as if he were neither crying nor even alive.

And Simon thought: *My God. Sweet Jesus, we don't even know how to cry.*

*Just let them alone.*

Simon's words plucked at his memory like an implement of torture; they whirled and danced through his brain until they threatened to fracture his eyes with hallucinations. *Alone*, synonymous with *apart*; he wanted it that way; but no matter how he construed it, *alone* meant Martha away from the house, away from him, free to destroy herself, and he helpless. More: aiding and abetting the beginning of the end of her life.

He sat for what seemed centuries amid the memorials of Christmas: the boxes, ribbons, tree, and the mistletoe which mesmerized him like a cheap hypnotic device, hanging like a noose from the arch. And it seemed to him, as he rose from his chair and tore the mistletoe from its tack, crushing it between his fingers, that he had come to his decision intuitively, discovered it in a deep well of unconsidered emotion, without thought or plan.

He would end it, not, as he truly wished, with the ferocity of his destructive fingers annihilating the pale green leaves, the gray-white berries, but with realism and civility. With no.— Directly to Matthew—No.

No. He said it softly several times, feeling the pleasurable contact of the tip of his tongue as it tapped the palate—a short, striking, definite blow. No.

He pried the tack from the wood, trying with a heavy rub of his thumb to obliterate the tiny hole, the desecration of his house.

Uneasily, fumbling to hide his hands, Matthew sat watching Cass. And Cass gazed back steadily, a tight half-smile twitching at his lips. Matthew wondering if it was a real smile or just some odd tic, feeling himself the almost dead object of an examination, an appraisal. He regretted having come; yet he could not have refused Cass, not with the distance already so thick between them. But it was really Simon who had told him to lay down the broom and go.

Looking at Cass, he wondered why this man was destined to act out some role in his life, why he had materialized after so many years, somehow prodding him, crossing, recrossing his path. Yet this time he hadn't crossed it at all; this time it was Matthew who had sought him out. Because of Martha, because of her, he was prodding Cass.

He sat still.

And then Cass said, "I'd like to put my cards on the table. I imagine you know that my wife died when Martha was born. Well, at first I didn't know what to do about her—a man doesn't know about babies. But finally I decided to give her everything I could, raise her the best way possible, make up for the lack of a mother.

"Well, God knows how impossible that is, so perhaps I went overboard. I don't know, and it's really not important. What happened was, despite all my fumbling and ignorance, she grew up fine. And now I want the best for her—more than ever. Because she's worth it. She's used to it and expects it. I want her to go to college, and she can go to the best. She deserves to get out of this town, to go somewhere and develop and see life, and not become stuck like my generation. And some day she should have the opportunity to choose a man fit for her, someone who, God knows, should have a broader outlook and understanding of life than any of us have here." He paused, as if gauging some intended effect, then asked, "Will you agree with me on that? Does that sound logical?"

"Yes. Who doesn't want to get out of here?"

"And that's why—I'm being as honest as I know how—that's why I'm worried about the relationship you two have."

"We just go out together, Mr. Nowell."

"I know, and that's all right. I've welcomed you into my house. I like you. It's just that Martha's going through an age now when young girls are impressionable. Do you understand?"

"The meaning of the word? I've heard it," drily.

"And I know how cooped up she feels in Southfield. As you say, who doesn't want to get out of here? I *want* her to get out, but girls are romantic. They have dreams about running away and getting married—all that. She may think you're some kind of romantic hero, something like that." Digressing, "Sometimes I think even the poorest movies get something of the truth about these things. Anyway, you're her first real boy friend and that means a lot to a girl, her first romance. She gives it all the loyalty she can muster up. Do you understand?"

He understood perfectly: that he was not wanted here, that he was being told, with graceful cruelty, to leave. Perhaps he could nose around the back door like a dog pining for a scrap, but no more. And what really angered him was Cass's style: devious, smooth, unmanly, sneaky, as if he couldn't be honest, as if he could not even try. Cass hated him, but couldn't or wouldn't tell him, and Matthew wondered if his reaction were anger or purely contempt.

He said, "You don't want me to see her."

"I wouldn't go that far. You both have the right to see each other if you want. But I don't think we ought to let it get out of hand. Not since her college plans are almost a reality. Not since you're both just kids."

"Kids?"

"Well, you're much older in many ways; you've had a lot to bear—a lot of responsibility. And she's apt to be swayed by that too. Frankly, you're not the usual Southfield boy." He laughed, but it seemed insincere. "Crewcuts, silliness. You see . . ."

He went on, Matthew listening for a time, becoming sick with apathy, withdrawing because Cass was not speaking of him or Martha or of anyone he knew or ever heard of. He was holding a soliloquy, a tortured and complicated one, and therefore meaningless to anyone but himself. And after a time Matthew thought of Martha, but she gave him no relief from the droning impossible words because she was precisely the object in the center of their weird oblique involvement, dangling between them like a prize over which they must clash and fight.

Suddenly he felt only anger, the storm of words had finally clinched their purpose. As usual, the anger seemed trapped within him; and as usual, the feeling was brutally painful, insufferable. But now he refused to punish himself.

He broke in, "You haven't put any cards on any table."

"Excuse me?"

"I said, you haven't been honest. What you want to say is 'Get the hell out of my daughter's way.' That's what you want to say."

"I didn't mean to make it sound that way."

"When a man says he wants to lay his cards on the table, he doesn't hang on to the deck so hard."

"Are you calling me a liar, Matthew?"

"No. Because I don't think you can help the way you say things. I just don't think you can help it. So let's just forget about it. You don't want me around? I'll go." He stood.

"I'd like to get clear what you mean."

"You don't know how to talk to people. Why don't you just say Martha's too good for me, that I'll ruin her or something? That you don't want me around? Why did you have to get me to say it for you?"

"That's pretty fancy, getting all that out of what I said. You seem to like to misinterpret me."

Doubling his fists, Matthew said, "Look, mister, don't shit on me. Just tell me straight. Don't shit all over me with words."

Matthew's rage tensed through his body, his eyes glowering at Cass, who merely sat, the peculiar almost-smile back on his lips, then vanishing as he said, "You really want to know, don't you? You don't want to spare yourself any pain at all. You want it thrown right in your face."

"Yes."

"Nobody here wants you. Should Martha take up with someone who's lived like an animal for twenty years? Ignorant, poor, ambitionless? I'd be a madman to permit that. I haven't worked year after year at the most idiotic job in the world to see her a slave in this town, a slave to a field hand for the rest of her life. God knows you probably can't help what you are. But be it by yourself. Do you think you can live like an animal in that filthy house, with that degenerate so-called father of yours, and have the right even to *look* at my daughter? Just go your own way, back into your world. Leave us alone now."

Their eyes met, and some strange, unpredictable knowledge passed between them. Cass's face was sprung loose with surprise, almost fright; and Matthew realized what Cass had just come to know: that his voice had raged out a plea, not an insult.

"I don't understand you," Matthew said.

"Get out."

"Nobody understands you."

And Cass bellowed, "I don't want a bastard near her!"

"I wish," Matthew said, "I wish it was in me to kill you"; then turned quickly to hide his tears and slammed through the front door.

The shaking of glass in the frame jolted through the house, slicing into Cass like some exquisite physical pain. He shut his eyes, pressing his fingers against the lids so tightly that patches of deep color welled out of the darkness; and when he removed his fingers and blinked, Martha was standing in the foyer, in the chill of the open door. It was suddenly important for him to understand why she had left the door open; how many steps she had taken to return home from wherever she had been (where?); why she had chosen to wear her white coat and not her blue. His head dangled crookedly, a ball of spongy pain on a weak ligament.

"I heard what you called him," she said. "The whole world heard what you called him."

"You spied once before," he mumbled.

She squinted and arched her neck, as if peering into a dark room, attempting to make out some indistinguishable shape.

"I called him what he is," he said; then, "Close the door."

189

She obeyed and, without removing her coat or hat, sat in the chair Matthew had occupied. "I don't understand why," she said, "why you did that."

"Because I won't let you make a tramp of yourself. I tried to be civil with him. It was a mistake. He doesn't understand civility. He acted exactly the way you might expect: swearing and cursing like an animal."

"You provoked it. He's not like that."

"He's nothing but hate and violence."

Martha moved to the edge of the chair, the snow from her boots melting into the carpet. Finally she said, "You've lied to me—always."

"Lied?"

"That you could call him that after all your talk about love and tolerance—all that. You never believed a word of it. You lied."

"I won't be called a liar, Martha. Not by anyone. Besides, what I said to him was nothing. That was just my anger. It's the other reasons that are real."

"Reasons for what?" The simplicity of her question stunned him.

Was it possible that she had no idea what he was driving at? He refused to believe it. She was being perverse. He said, "Reasons why you shouldn't see him again."

"You don't know him," she answered, as if there had just been no communication at all between them.

"Better than you ever could," he said.

"You can't give me a reason. Not one."

"I don't choose to catalogue his defects. You've had your little misguided fling with him, now forget it. Look at you. You're sitting there calmly enough, that's proof you can't be feeling so much indignation."

"I'm sitting here this way because it's what you've taught me. Be reasonable, calm. Emotion clouds logic and destroys the soul."

"I never said that."

"That's how it was heard."

He rose and went to the fireplace, then kicked softly at the bot-

190

tom log. He turned to her and propped his elbow high on the mantlepiece.

"What the devil is this all about, Martha? What is all this rebellion against me?"

"There's no rebellion. It's just that you invited him into the house, you never gave me reason to think you disliked him. And now *this*."

"I tried to talk reasonably with him."

"But why did you have to talk with him at all? It's my business."

"Because you showed you couldn't handle it."

"You don't know that. And that's another lie."

"Lie?"

"Always boasting how you brought me up to think, to make choices. You never believed that for a minute. Or if you did, it was about things that didn't matter to you. Like I could choose one course over another at school, or a new skirt, or the pattern of my wallpaper. But no other choices. Nothing that intruded on what you had in mind."

He shook his head.

"You never asked me how I felt about Matthew," she said. "Never. Not whether I really liked him or, if I did, why? You just knew I felt some way, and that way was how you had to see it. For some horrible reason you needed to see what you saw, and you needed to crucify him today."

"Don't analyze me, Martha."

"You taught me. When you want to understand something that's unclear, something that bothers you, analyze it. Take it apart."

"I wasn't talking about people."

"If not, then what? Analyze which college to go to, what flavor ice cream to eat? That kind of really important unclear thing?"

"You've got a lot to get out of your system, haven't you?"

"I guess I do. More than I ever thought."

"Go ahead."

"Stop being so rational all the time."

"I won't be an animal."

191

"Oh, God," she said, and turned away from him. Then, "I don't intend to listen to you. I'm going to see him again. As much as I want."

"No, you're not going to do that."

"I choose to," she said haughtily.

"Just keep quiet and listen to me, and that's the end of it. When you don't know what's best for you, what's even permissible for you, then it's my business to straighten things out. You and he just walking in the street together is ridiculous."

"Why? Why am I so special? I'm not a princess. I'm not even pretty."

"If you can't see what I mean, then I'm sorry for you."

"Then you won't tell me the truth—about why you really want to keep him away."

"Look, Martha, enough is enough. I've let you talk, but obviously you're not reasonable enough or old enough to understand the real issues in this. You're angry at me for some reason that has nothing to do with this. For the last time, the boy is doomed; he's going nowhere in this world; he'll be a millstone around your neck."

"We're not getting married."

"Praise God, and I don't want to think that you could ever dream of it. Just some foolish way to break your heart."

"Dear God, Daddy, you're doing this to him and me because of your dream, not ours. What is it you're afraid of?"

"Maybe it is my dream. I have a right to dream. Every father has a right to dream about his children. Your mother and I had such a dream, and thank God I knew her part in it, what she wanted for her child. That kept me from making too many mistakes, that little bit of knowledge I got from her: what a girl is, what she needs."

"Stop it, please. Stop invoking her like a saint. She wasn't a saint; she couldn't have known everything you say she did. No one could. No one could be so pure and holy and wise."

"I've stood this long enough I think."

"My God, that's really it, isn't it? You won't be satisfied unless you can reincarnate her. Your feelings about me are the same as your feelings about her. You really can't make the distinction."

"Feelings? What feelings?"

"That's it. I'm her. Her, not a real daughter. Her—all over again. Completely. You won't rest until somehow I become her. You just don't know the difference. Even the same name. All these years I just thought . . ."

"Feelings?" Cass roared. "What do you mean by feelings?"

"I thought it was a tribute—my name after hers, the saintly, wonderful, wise woman. But it wasn't that at all. I'm not your daughter. I'm her in every way. You want her all over again."

He strode to her chair and flailed the back of his hand across her face. Her head jerked back, her white knit snowcap springing away from her hair.

"You accuse me of that?" he said. "Of that?"

She stared at him, the cheek he had struck burning crimson. And then she said, "God. What else did you think I meant besides some absurd memory of her?"

Through the paralyzing fear of what he had done, implied, believed she had meant, he cringed before her unbelieving, gaping eyes. "I thought," he stammered, "it was—you said 'feelings' —I thought because you were angry, you meant . . ."

But she ran through the foyer, through the door, and soon he felt the chill bellowing in again from the porch. He went to the door and closed it, and with his hand on the knob and his dead eyes trained quizzically on the floor, said again, "I thought you were saying—you see, 'feelings' meant to me that . . ." And then he plunged his head forward against the door jamb, and the impact, stunning him far more than was possible, left him sagging against the wall; and he remembered that he had not mentioned the great reason to her, the reason that was most important, must be most important: that the boy did not believe in God. Appalled and frightened that he had somehow forgotten it, he almost opened the door and shouted it out into the snow. But suddenly he saw that he had unknowingly picked up her snowcap and carried it to the foyer. He felt the rough wool between his fingers; then, as if it burned him, he recoiled from it, hanging it quickly on a branch of the clothestree.

After he finished sweeping Simon's floor (Simon looking pained, muttering) Matthew went home and paused briefly at the kitchen door, seeing John Roger and the dried-up little man, Willy something, who had for some reason come to the house, who had amazingly become John Roger's friend. They were talking, John Roger's posture awkward, thumbs twiddling, unused to the company, like a rusty clock jarred into action and surprised it could still move. The little man's hands fluttered like a bird's wings.

Shrugging, Matthew went to his room, his wish to kill Cass long gone, because it had all turned out exactly as he could have predicted, and more. More, because he had not even stopped when he had passed Martha on the porch, had not even told her what had happened. Had not even said hello. So of course now she would listen to Cass, and that would be the end of all of it.

Of course, too, it was as Cass had said: he was stupid, an animal, not even entitled to a piece of a scrap at the back door. Finally he lay back on his bed; anyway, he would speak to her. Cass was right: it could go nowhere; but he would stick with it, if she permitted, until it was inevitably ruined, until he had nothing at all but the dirt under his nails. And even that would belong to the fields or to Simon's floor.

# Seven

At seventy-five cents an hour, three boys from the high-school service-and-citizenship squad began to spring clean the soldiers monument. They hacked away with stiff wire brushes and paint scrapers and yellow soap, but the crusts hardly budged. They could only inch down through a few layers of pigeon droppings, transform the dull white to a moldy gray, then survey the result. Essentially nothing. The warrior maintained his unflinching optimism, the eyes staring almost heavenward beneath the rim of the obsolete tin pot, the arm still cocked, a quarterback about to spot pass with a grenade instead of a football, the leggings on his calves like steel bandages. But he was still crusty, and now gray, and always a flaky green. Disgusted, one of the boys thrust the middle finger of his right hand into the air, and another boy calculated the age of the soldier as fifty-three at the least. And then they turned away; it wasn't their war; he wasn't their kind; and they left him to the pigeons.

Through the bay window of the drug store, between the globes of tinted water, she could see Matthew sweeping in front of the funeral chapel. The three collusive, complicit, giggling voices echoed past her like a shallow current of nonsense; she was lost in him, in the violent, mesmerizing scuffing of the broom. "In spring," Harry Chase's voice twitted, "a young girl's fancy lightly turns to thoughts of—ice-cream sodas." The explosion of giggling jarred her from the window, and she knew that they had been watching her. They went on giggling, sucking straws. She wondered when the same sounds had ceased trickling out of her own well of silliness, when she had ceased laughing altogether. Quickly she joined them in leafing through a pulp magazine whose floridly colored cover blared forth a pair of heavy-lidded grappling lovers. A voice softly read: "Never had she responded so completely to any man's lips. His kisses set her heart ablaze." They giggled, knees thumping against the underside of the table, and she turned back to the window. And finally the giggling crescendoed into hysteria and drove her out of the store.

Driving the hearse back from the cemetery, Simon sniffed at the breeze cutting across the fields, swung over the county bridge, and turned his head almost reflexively toward the weather-honed old house stuck on its hill. As he passed, he saw something scuttling away from the porch, something small and black, but larger than a crow, and then the house was behind him. He blinked. Willy Kling? No, he was getting old and woefully astigmatic; he hadn't seen a thing. Just an association with something. He wrinkled his nose at the air again and felt the warmth of the sun wash obliquely through the windshield. But finally he shook his head, knowing that it had been Willy. He felt slightly haunted and drove faster upstreet.

196

Cass left the church and headed toward the store, seeing, as he turned the school-yard corner, Father Nowak pursuing a spotted orange butterfly with a wide-mouthed gauze net. His cassock flapping around his legs, he bolted through a row of hedges and vanished in a sound of crackling twigs. The butterfly reappeared, Father Nowak close behind, and with a flick of the net the chase was done. Father Nowak peered closely through the gauze, regarded the frantic orange blur, then with infinite gentleness set it free, watching it dodge away in tight circles. Unable to interpret what he had seen, Cass walked on, his hands bulging his pockets; and suddenly he found himself at the door of his house. He stood confused, deracinated, directionless, then turned and went to the store.

# Eight

Halfway to the door she almost stumbled, then wheeled suddenly and lay on her bed, her eyes trained on the open window, gazing at the dusky treetops bleaching, quietly, almost imperceptibly, from green to gray; they too trapped in the ambivalence that hemmed her inside the room. Gray-green, in-out—it seemed the same; it didn't matter.

April: in the year of Our Lord 1951: but she could not understand this spring, had not met it head on; it had simply come, dragged and limped in, as bleak and dingy as winter slush. Yet it should have become the springtime of her life (she had read it somewhere), if she were loved. It limped in, bloodless, a dying robot; and she accused it of every pain she could remember.

Oddly, crossing her mind was a parade of *Vogues* and *Glamours* and *Seventeens*, their frosted covers flung open, their pages slowly turning, manikins in spring raiment (impossible to wear) smiling untroubled smiles, their faces insanely distorted with joy. She blinked; her right leg twitched spastically as if kicking the fantasy away. Only to be replaced by another: hiding the magazines in school as if they were pornography, pictures to build a future on, hidden messages implying secrets shared by married women. And the immortally young girls disguising their gaunt cheeks and saber-pointed elbows and distended rib cages with coats of tinted varnish and baggy tweeds pinned to tightness with secret clamps (perhaps *that* was the secret). Ideal bodies—for a morgue. She blinked again, but the leg did not twitch.

She lay quietly, a mortal sinner, a perpetrator of sacrileges, and she did not care. She was too weary to care. She closed her eyes and counted aloud on her fingers the number of times they had made love, so weary that her mumbling seemed to creep from under the leadness of her eyelids; as if, when she reached the end of the count, she might fall asleep or die. And again the girls with the clamped clothing scuttered past—the pinned-up tweeds.

She had forgotten how many times. But except for the setting, each was no different from the last—or would be from the next. There was no pain, but there was also nothing to take its place. And he would not be gentle because he could not be, his face bristled, his arms like rippled rage, and she thinking that they did not even have the comfort of a house, a bed. It was a fitting symbol, exactly appropriate, that it had been happening lately in King Philip's cave: the barbarian Indian, the rape of the white maiden. She had almost tasted the symbolism last time, letting him plunge into her and screaming inside that this was not what loving meant, not being used on the floor of a dirty cave, on the greasy smell of an old Army blanket. She had pulled away from him, jerked to her feet, and stood immobile, staring toward the faraway gray patch at the mouth of the cave. She wanted the warmth of the early spring outside, feeling only the perpetual cellar-damp crawl and ooze along her thighs. Dully, her hands knotting into the bunched skirt at her waist, she looked down at the underpants strangling her right ankle; hemmed, she remembered, with tiny yellow roses.

She began to cry, and then tremble, because this was not what she had ever dreamed of, because she could not even feel degraded, not if she rolled naked in the dirt of the floor. Dimly, she saw him sit back with his hands outstretched, palms braced against the ground, and she sensed the pain and bewilderment darkening his face, judged his feelings by her own—if he had withdrawn from her. But her empathy fell dead; she could think only of herself and the hatefulness of what they were doing, and thought suddenly that it might all be different if she could feel something. Knowing too that she would not permit herself to feel, remembering the first time they had lain against the wall in the deepest corner of the cave like two squirrels or field mice, and the brush of her hand on the sick slime of the rocks. They had heard a flurried scrambling and heavy breathing from another part of the cave; they stopped, listening, she frightened and amazed by the voice of a girl trilling from a high echoing squeal to a low strangled quaver: ooooooooooo . . . What had she felt in the weirdness of that sound? Wondering about it even when Matthew returned to her, entered her, and she lay there half dead or at least insensate, imaging the four of them lying together in an amorphous undifferentiated mass, struggling and grunting. For a moment she could not recall her name; and then Matthew was finished. Finished, and they lay there in the darkness waiting for the others to leave. But they didn't; they moved, minute after minute of perpetual movement, moaned and gasped, and a startling hiss of torn clothing. She tightened her thighs against the sound, against the ripping . . .

The memory welled up in her like a sickness and she prodded at the underpants with her left foot, then purged herself of all memory, breathed deeply, and began to draw the yellow roses up past her knees, covering herself, thinking: *Killing myself, mutilating myself*; thinking how she had taken communion again with Cass, this time striding willfully to the altar, kneeling, taking the host on her tongue with a morbid delight in the knowledge that no stark death awaited her, that she was leaving no possibility unexplored in her search for damnation.

Straightening her skirt over her hips, letting it fall into place, she looked down at Matthew and whispered, "I can't do this any more. I'll meet you; I'll do anything you want, but not this. Not this, not any more."

He said nothing. She perceived the demand in his silence; whether or not it existed, she perceived it. She prayed that he would speak because she knew what he must be thinking: unloved, worthless, dirty, needing her like a child. She could not tolerate that, neither his self-torture nor her denial of his feelings. Caught and mangled in a trap they had constructed together; she believing in her omnipotence, in her mythical desirability, and because of it, forced to give him his prize. All to let him feel clean while she dirtied herself. It was past her understanding, and her ignorance enraged her.

Still he did not speak, and the dampness of the cave began to thicken like a malodorous blanket gathering at her throat.

"I don't want it this way," she said, conscious of the whimper in her voice. "I want to be home where it's warm and clean. This isn't me here in all this dirt. Matthew, this isn't me."

He leaned forward on his knees and pushed his face into her thighs, but still did not speak.

"Say something," she whispered.

He rubbed his cheek against the stubby tweed of her skirt. She drew back and screamed, "Goddamn you, say something," her voice bounding about the cave, returning to her like a blow in the face. Then rage beating at her head, she pulled down her skirt and tore her underpants away, a hissing rip in the darkness. She grasped his hair and brought his face toward her, moving her body against him with the anger mounting and bellowing in her temples, and with a short, stifled scream, she felt. Felt, trapping him with her hands, degrading him like a forlorn dog. And then she drew back her hand and, crying for both of them, smashed it across his mouth. . . .

And again the frilly girls from *Glamour* and *Vogue* and *Seventeen*, their perpetual parade across a movie screen of dreams, the

**201**

sugarplums and Cinderellas of growing and grown women, the agents in the continuity of fairy tales. She opened her eyes and turned toward the window again; the trees were almost invisible in the darkness, only their topmost branches spiderwebbed by the moon. She rose, the weariness oppressive now, bound her hair with a light scarf, and left the room. Down the stairs, walking trancelike across the foyer, barely aware of the voice from the living room.

"Where are you going?"

She turned blankly and with a conscious effort focused on Cass sitting in the armchair, looming somehow like a broken-down bear, a caricature.

"Out."

"I'm surprised. Surprised you're not lying."

She merely stared, a pain working into her eyes.

"I know where you're going," he said again.

She nodded; his words seemed disjointed, unconnected; she could not follow him.

"Go back upstairs."

She moved toward the door, so slowly that he was able to leave his chair and block her. She looked up at him, unable to judge if he were frightened or frightening.

"You can't meet him," he said.

"I'm not meeting anybody," she answered, almost as a final protest, knowing that it was useless to lie, past the necessity of lying.

"The other times," he said, "the other times you thought I didn't know."

"You spied on me?"

"Spied, skulked—anything you want to call it."

"You're insane," she said without expression. "Like me, like your daughter. Insane." Oddly, she wanted him to strike her, yet felt that no matter what she said, the flatness of her voice would subvert him.

He said, "Go upstairs."

"No."

He crooked his fingers under her chin and lifted her face; and his voice, as calm and soothing as the hand on her skin, "Tramp."

Their eyes met and she said, "You don't really know. You don't really know at all."

"Happy birthday," he whispered, withdrawing his hand.

She was eighteen. She hadn't remembered. Strangely, she hadn't remembered. She thought of gifts.

"You have no father," he said. "Only a keeper." Then, "Do what you want. From now on, do anything you want."

Nodding, pausing, then nodding again, she said with complete detachment, "I said you really don't know. We've had intercourse."

And when he did not retaliate, simply leaned against the door with his eyes shut and his head slowly shaking, she went back to her room. She locked the door, stood aimlessly for a moment, then bit her fingers until she silently screamed, wishing that he would have beaten her: hands, breasts, all the offending parts and places. But he hadn't. Wouldn't.

She lay on the bed again, alone and terrified, images of Cass at the door, of Matthew waiting in the cave, all swirling through blazes of color. And finally, like a child, she closed her eyes tightly so that she could not be seen.

Two thoughts occurred to Cass: he had fainted or had suffered some sudden attack of somnambulism. He found himself on the porch swing and could not remember how he had gotten there. His analytic hold on the world, his symbol and machine of control, was crushed, useless, a jumble of broken, crazily spinning cogs and wheels, telling him that it had broken under the strain of his use, that whatever he had considered life, it had not been real—not ever. His existence was not even a shambles, a mistake, a philosophical failure; it was nothing.

So the thought of Martha meant nothing now, because she, too, was a shadow cast from his emptiness. Only the first Martha had been palpable, and the memory of her suddenly seized his lips, pulled them awry, and tormented them into a sneer. The overwhelming cynicism and rage he had had to check, or at least appraise and vitiate whenever it appeared, filled the hollow of his stomach, and he spat. Because of her, his wife, he had never existed, because he had sunk himself somewhere in the heart of her desire, never to emerge again. A stud, he thought, no more; and there was no sense inventing more palatable embellishments on her sexuality. And what could he expect from his wife's daughter; why should she have grown differently? The same itching, the sucking of the male into them. Except that with him, in marriage, morality lived in a drugged satisfaction; God knew how many she would have lain with if he had not responded always, incessantly, until he ached.

He hated her now, and he was not shocked, not remorseful; he hated even her indelible animal capacity to conceive and bear a child so late in life. And how appropriate, how predictable that year after year she could have squirmed and lunged in orgastic explosions, yet died the one time she had permitted a sperm to outrace her, catch her off guard, pre-empt pure pleasure. Died, but left a legitimate heiress.

He savored his bitterness and hate, even smiling his new smile: sinister and doglike, a corner of his lips curled, his teeth protruding maliciously.

He remembered clearly his intense joy when he had demolished John Roger. How incredibly, frighteningly good it had felt to slash and kick and bury his rage in someone's body, to feel the slushing of once hard bone, the spongy retreat of flesh, the heady, winey blood erupting through the skin of his knuckles.

He should have sired sons. They would have grown violent.

And then he laughed. Because a violent one had come for his daughter, the violent one who long ago he had in some oblique way tried to forge into a son. The pure and violent son who would permit no woman to rape him, to dredge the manhood from him.

The laugh ebbed to the doglike smile, settled, and he rose from the swing and walked hurriedly along the street, his hands clenched, his arms stiff and locked at the elbows. He began to count his steps, finally barging through Simon's door, standing erect and tense and, as if he could not arrest his momentum, swaying slightly forward.

And Simon, looking up from his desk, the lamplight foggy with oceans of pipe smoke, grunted.

"Someday," Cass said, "I'll kill you. Wipe you away."

"Cass?"

"They fucked." Staring into the billows of smoke, inhaling its heavy, soporific odor, the room seemed a kind of weird church. And he said, hollowly, with an almost caricatured biblical righteousness, "In their own dirt, their own dirt."

"What are you telling me?"

"You know. You knew that one day I'd come and tell you this. That this would happen."

Simon rose, his face eclipsing into the darkness, the swirling light glaring against his shirtfront. He said, "Because I didn't want you to stand against them? You want to kill me for that?"

"No. Because you deprived me of my manhood. You prevented my violence. You preached softness and weakness at me when violence was rightfully mine."

"I preached nothing."

"What was in my power to stop, you allowed, and I listened to you. I let you take the last measure of dignity from me."

"You better go."

"You don't know how the animals act, do you? The bitch in heat and the panting, drooling dog who smells her? You don't know because you're a eunuch. You copulate with corpses."

"The battle's out in the open now, isn't it? It's always been there, hanging over our heads. Well, you might as well stop using your daughter to beat at me. There's no need of it any more." He paused, then, "You are a sorry son-of-a-bitch. As sorry as I ever saw."

Cass wheeled and left, almost halfway across the street before he heard Simon thunder, "Come ahead. Come back and kill me!"

And then the booming of the door, the crackling of the glass pane. Nothing but the wash of moon with its odd brownish pie-cut spot, mantling the helmet and shoulders of the monument, and the grenade-bearing arm hooked and clenched like the fulfillment of a curse.

# 2

The little crumpled black man, the twisted Adam's apple, the fluttering hands first intimating at the crotch then ending somehow in tiny nipping tugs at an earlobe.

John Roger grunted. *Shit.* In the good days—no, just the old days—he wouldn't have spit in his direction, wouldn't have looked at him unless he felt the need to disgust himself. But now? He shifted in the kitchen chair, sitting erect, a parody of stiffness, so that his kidneys and perhaps his liver pressed against a rung of the backrest. It was better for the pain; somehow it was better if he pressed it.

He wouldn't have spit at him. Now he fed him whiskey. He lined up two glasses, each differently shaped, then pushed the almost filled bottle between them, producing a kind of warped symmetry. Alone, squinting at the black crow on the label, he tried to recall when Willy Kling had first come to the house; leaning forward, he strained for a thought, then quickly moved back against the rung. Who knew when he had come? One drunken night he was there at the door like a black potato sack delivering itself. And then they were drinking together and he was hearing stories about Southfield, drinking more wildly than ever before to blot out any mention of the place, yet unable to silence the clucking black mouth, somehow unwilling to. And with the tilting of one more glass, it had no longer mattered; and he capitulated and listened, even swapping a story, hearing his voice rasp through the rusty hinges of his jaw. And then one night he talked and the other listened. Talked.

Once he would not have looked at him. But now he talked to him, and the act was miraculous. Somewhere wedged into the crusty black turtle shell lived a man seven sizes too small who sat and listened.

Seizing a glass, rolling it between his palms, he ruined the symmetry of his construction. Thinking that no one had ever listened to him, respected his word. And that was almost too terrifying to dwell upon, because in reality it was impossible to live hour after hour, talking millions of words, without even one mattering to anyone. He strained again, trying to conjure a single memory in which he had spoken and someone had listened; then winced again as his back came loose from the chair, jerking rapidly, wondering why any effort to remember provoked physical agony. Or perhaps why any effort caused him to bend forward, leaning not until he tumbled into a memory but until the pain hammered at him like a warning against pitching into some dark howling hole in his mind.

*Shit*, he grunted, angling his back into the chair, suddenly and inexplicably awed by the feeling that he might begin to talk to himself. Suppose someone sat opposite him now, someone compelled to listen. Who would he choose? A swell of dazzling hate, a turning of his memory, and he realized that what he wanted to say would smash forth in torrents of rage and loathing. Try something else. A stranger, some woman he had once leered at on a moving-picture screen. Who? Light hair and cupid-bow lips and long eyelashes that batted like a wind-up toy. Oddly, he imaged Aunt Schooner sitting across from him.

"Bastard," he mumbled, and she vanished.

How was she like a woman in a moving picture? Phoney, was all.

And then there was Esther, sitting gray and plaintive and martyred, her eyelids flickering, dusting the tabletop with almost imperceptible swirls of her feverish iridescent pupils.

"What?" he said, turning slightly away from her. "What the hell do you want to come back for?"

She was forcing him to conjecture. He set his face imperiously and beat the side of his thumb rapidly against the seat of the chair.

"Look—what the hell? I'm just sitting here. You ain't there, so don't start up with me." The word *sorry* crossed his mind. He squinted again. She was still there.

"All right, you don't need to show me anything. Anything at all. Don't I know? Whatever it is, don't I know it? Now look you, Esther."

207

And he leaped forward, knocking a glass on its side, his mouth
jutting open, watching the chair filling up with black, hearing
it say, "What are you talking about? Or to?"

"Nothing. You came in on me too quick."

"I opens the door and says to myself, 'Who's he talking at?' "

"No, nothing. It ain't nothing."

"I figured maybe you was praying out loud. Like that."

"No. Pray? Ain't no praying here. Never was."

Willy snatched up the toppled glass, swirled the rim on the
point of his elbow, and poured it half full. "You?" he said.

"What? Yes. Sure."

Willy poured for him; John Roger tossed it off and refilled the
glass almost before the first razor's edge cut his stomach. Then
a burst of comforting, alive warmth. Drinking more slowly, he
gauged Willy, vacillating, wondering if he could ask something,
if he should. Then fortifying himself with a quick swallow, he
said, refilling his glass, "You ever hear of anybody that seen
things?"

"Seen what things?"

"That maybe wasn't there."

Willy clucked, paused, then said, "Yeah. Oh, yeah. Up to the
hospital once—I was minor infected in my leg. I seen a fellow
—what do you call them—with d.t.'s."

"I heard of them."

"He seen bugs. Shit! Like this," spreading his palms as if he
were judging the size of a huge mythical fish. " 'Least he said
like that. Spiders, he said, and once a cockaroach."

"No."

"Listen what I'm telling you. That big," again spreading his
hands.

*Not so bad, then. Only her. Better than a bug that big.
D.t.'s?*

"Used to holler out at night: 'Get 'em fuggin' off me, get 'em
fuggin' off me.' Yaaa."

*Only her. Not so bad at all.*

"What did you do?" John Roger asked, drinking again.

"Weren't nothing you *could* do. Just lay there and listen. No, wait. Yeah. Once somebody gave him a bedpan in the face."

"Spilled it on him?"

"No, it was empty. Hit him with it." He pounded lightly against his forehead. "Right there. Made a noise, like a clong, you know? Donnng." He grinned, and his Adam's apple mulched, as the corners of his lips screwed upward.

*Hit me, I'll kill you.* Strange thought.

"Fellow was only like about twenty too."

*Matthew's age.*

He drank again; as he looked over the rim of his glass the face before him undulated, features fusing, dilating, constricting.

"Young," he remarked.

"For that, yeah."

"What happened to him?"

"I ain't got no idea. My leg healed up and I left. Told them it weren't right for a man like me—minor infected is what I was —to be laying there in the same room with a crazy man."

*Crazy man. Only crazy men see things? Ain't crazy.*

"You don't have to be crazy to see things."

"I'm telling you. He was crazy."

*No.*

"You don't. I'm telling you."

Willy relented. "Guess it's how you look at it," he said lightly.

"I guess so."

They drank. There was little sense in looking at Willy now; the face radiated like an erratic light globe: dimming, glowing, dimming. He blinked, the needles of numbness probing along his body, then into the joints and bones.

From the quavering light, Willy's voice: "I ever tell you about the undertaker?"

"No."

"You like him?"

*The undertaker. What undertaker?*

He tried to think. He remembered nothing about an under- taker but would not admit it. "Don't know him that good—to like him nor not to like him."

"Your boy works at his place. You got to think something about him."

*My boy and the undertaker. It snapped into place.*

"Yes." he almost growled, his teeth grating. "Yes, the son-of-a-bitch."

"I thought you said . . ."

"Yes. I know that bastard."

Willy grunted, clucked, clucked again. "You know what he done once? He preached the Bible to a kid in Fallsville. Kid drowned himself."

"What?"

"Yes. Went to the river and killed himself getting baptized. Ain't that some shit?"

*Same thing with Matthew. He beat me up. My nose. Broken.*

"Goddamn son-of-a-bitch."

Willy's voice edged sharply. "Did you know he was a preacher? In the old days?"

*More whiskey. Keep in mind. The rain barrel. Almost drowned me. Broken nose.*

"What?"

"A preacher."

"Yes. Preacher."

*Preached. Matthew. Catholic. Knee-bending son-of-a-bitch. Nose. Broken. Esther—she saw. Blood in the sink.*

"I ain't sure why you don't like him."

"Son-of-a-bitch." Thickly now, his tongue butting into his teeth and gums, jamming into his cheeks. He poured a glass of whiskey down his throat without swallowing.

"Hey! Easy, why don't you? It ain't water."

*Pain in the back. Gone. Him and Esther. Knee-benders. Matthew. Seen my blood in the sink. Seen the nose.*

"Why don't you like him?"

"Was after my boy. You know he was after my boy?"

"Yeah? Hey, what do you know? Small world, ain't it?" He clucked, incredibly, like the faraway hoofbeats of diminutive horses. "Like the kid at Fallsville?"

"What kid? Fallsville? Fuck Fallsville. He tried to make my kid the way he was. I fought against him."

"You don't say. Well, well. You sure about your kid?"

"Goddamn. Ain't no man calls me a liar."

*Oh, yes. After my boy. That's why. Why he went against me. Why he won't look at me.*

"Well, let me tell you something, J.R. He's—you know—still after your boy."

"What?"

"Yeah. Honest to God."

"Preaching? At him? Matthew?"

"Well, it ain't the kind of preaching you come by in no church. Like the kid at Fallsville. Only now he's after older ones it looks like. Sure looks like he's after older ones now."

"What do you mean?"

"I guess it ain't so easy to believe."

"Believe?" He pounded the table with his hands, hard and flat. "Believe what? What? I don't even know what it is—what the hell you're talking about."

"He's after your kid, for Crissakes."

"What the hell are you telling me about?"

"He's a queer, J.R. He's a queer and he's after your kid."

*Queer. Him!*

"I seen your kid just a bit ago. Going up to the mountain, to the cave. Ain't the first time I seen him go up there."

*Cave?*

He blinked, rolling his head like a dog shedding water, seeing the black shape fuzzing in the light, faceless. He tried to focus, to catch and fix the blur; if he could fix it, pin it, he could talk to it. But he couldn't.

"Nah, nah. No, what the hell. What . . ."

"I'm telling you. They go up to the cave. You see, the way I got it figured, he took your kid in to work for him so's they could stay right there. See, that way nobody would think a thing about it. But they're still using the cave to do it. Anyway," tapping his temple with a forefinger, "I got that figured out too. See, they . . ."

*Them. In the cave? Together? Do? Do what together?*

"What in the cave? What?"

"Jesus, I told you. He's trying to make your kid a queer."

Queer. Cave. Oh my God, so that's why. What he always wanted from Matthew. Queer. A queer beat me. Broke my nose. Even a queer beat me. Even a queer. He began to cry.

"Hey. Hey, hey—what the hell are you doing?" He quickly snuffled, sucking back the mucus. "Ain't doing nothing."

That low. That low, even a queer could. Broke my nose. A fruit. Dead. I should be dead. Can't never die. Nor even live.

"If I was you, goddamn sure I'd do something. Fellow, a queer, trying to make my kid. Made is really what it is. Jesus, I'd sure do something."

Matthew. No girls. Told me. One night, told me. Looked funny. God, God. No. Yes.

"He ain't. My boy ain't queer."

"I'm just telling you, J.R. Just telling you, is all."

Wagging his head in denial, he felt his neck wrenching, cranking out of control. Trying to stop his head, he threw up his hands and clutched his hair in clumps, long matted hair he hadn't taken scissors to in months. His head bobbed now, trembled, then steadied on the flabby shaft of the neck.

No girls. He told me, looking all funny.

Throwing back his head, he bellowed—no words, no sense, a raw hideous wail. The blurred black shadow sprang back, the chair squealed against the linoleum.

Kill him. Best thing. For me and Matthew.

Eyes rolled, pieces snapping into place, the sound of metal in his brain. Hearing: Kill him, the heat plunging, coursing through him, better, wilder, more fantastic than whiskey, anything. Bellowing again, he tore from the table, loping, almost running to the closet. Jarring open the door, he scattered rags and boxes, unrecognizable objects and pulpy forms that clattered and spun and blasted against the walls, spears of dust biting his eyes. Then, pulling as if against a powerful counterweight, he drew out the old shotgun and two shells taped to the stock, all wadded with rags. Snapping away the rags, he ran his hand along the twin barrels, feeling the grit of the grease which had hardened to gum, its rancid stink faint in the air. Then suddenly he ceased fondling the metal and whirled on Willy, expected to see the wisp of black filling the chair; but it was empty. His eyes jerked to the door where Willy stood or squatted, he was not sure. Only that it was black and small.

"You said cave? On the mountain?"

"Yeah, yeah. What are you going to do with that thing?"

Untaping the shells, he jammed them home, then snapped the joint of the gun and waved the barrels toward the door.

"My boy ain't no queer. Son-of-a-bitch other is. The priest." He touched a memory. "Priest and his nun."

"Priest? Nun? What the hell are you saying?"

John Roger laughed mirthlessly, pumping the gun unsteadily; Willy dodging away from the line of sight.

"Him and that daughter. The king and the queen, and him a queer."

"You're making me crazy," Willy wailed, almost stamping his feet. "Who are you talking about?"

"The daughter. His pimp is what she is."

"He ain't got no daughter, for Crissakes. He ain't got nobody." Suddenly his eyes bugged, his throat spastic with erratic, wild clucking. "The undertaker. The fuckin' undertaker! Didn't you hear what I said?"

"Son-of-a-bitch beat up on me. Wanted my boy all along. Broke my nose."

"You ain't even talking to me; you don't even know I'm here." Then, screaming, "The undertaker. Not who you think."

John Roger levelled the gun at Willy's chest, saying clearly, oddly sober, "The cave."

"Simon, Simon, Simon," Willy stuttered hysterically. "Simon Forbes, the undertaker, is who I mean, mean, m-mm," gagging on the word. And recouping for a moment, "Put that thing down; get it away from me for Crissakes. Forget it, forget what I told you. I ain't even sure. I was just telling you what I heard. Just because I seen him go up to the mountain, just because—look, for—, for—, for—, forget it."

"Get the fuck out of here. I wouldn't shit on the best part of you."

"Look, J.R. . . ."

"You called my boy a queer, didn't you?"

He cocked a hammer. Willy bolted at the sound, screaming, running, vanishing through the door as the burst gouged and splintered the wall. John Roger shot backward, his body slamming against the pantry door, the pain sluicing through his whiskied numbness, his hands flailing at the gun, which squirmed as if alive. He slid halfway down the door, his knees crumpling outward, the gun butt bludgeoning his right knee. The acid odor of the smoke cut at his nostrils and eyes, freeing mucus and tears. Dazed a moment, he finally groped up along the door, his free hand on the knob, then stood and rattled out a cough. He spat, scrubbing his face with a sleeve. He stepped forward tentatively, then staggered across the floor, gripping, hefting the gun, lurching out into the yard, pitching forward into the night for some distance before planting his feet wide and steady on the ground. *The cave.* He turned, skirting the rear of the house, climbing a sloping path umbrella'd by black trees, stumbling on stones and snaky roots, finally emerging on the two-lane highway which curved for more than a mile to the base of the mountain.

He began to walk, his feet sickling inward, his body moaning along in the right lane, an explosion of uncontrollable momentum plunging him like a damaged brakeless vehicle across the double white lines. *Thermometer factory: spinning.* Once or twice the gun butt scraped against the blacktop, grating; he jerked the barrels up, clearing the gun of the rasping sound. Again the rasp and, snapping his arm, this time he rammed the barrel ends into the soft flesh under his chin; his knees buckled, he wobbled, stopped, then cringed at the ghostly play of his shadow in the pale wash of the moon. Cradling the gun in his arms, he walked on.

*That day. Went to protect my boy. From kneebenders like Esther. Didn't know what it really was that he had to be protected from. If I knew. Only knew. No. Would have gone with what's in my hands. No broken nose. No blood. Only his. My son. Yes. My son. Mine mine mine my son son mine mine mine . . .*

He shouted at the moon, at the darkened wedge that seemed to regard him suspiciously.

"Because, goddamn it, he's all I got."

*He'll see now. See he's my son. Won't listen to words. Show him. A gunshot and he's my son. Believe it then. Got a father. Me. What's twenty years? Made a mistake. Who don't? Got to see it now. Matthew. Got to know it. Turned queer. Why? Me? My fault? Should have killed long ago. Everybody. Esther? Never killed her. Never. No. Forget it, can't set nothing straight thinking on it. Goddamn son-of-a-bitch. My nose. Broke. Queer broke my nose. Blood. In the sink where they saw.*

Headlight beams destroyed the flood of moon, coming from behind him, even more blurred by the sweat in his eyes. For a moment he wanted to leap into the ditch at the side of the road, but he could not get his breath—the grip of a great powerful fist wringing his chest. Panting, he turned to the nearing lights, jouncing like wild, hungry, silver-yellow eyes blazing excruciating light. He stood rooted, easing the gun out of sight against the back of his leg. He waved with his free hand, then heard the shift of the motor, from purr to jangling rasp, gears sputtering crazily, meshing in agony. The lights, closer, seemed about to burn him to death, then mercifully cut low at his waist. A tattoo from the horn. But he stood firm until the car stopped, then lumbered around to the back door and yanked it open.

"What's wrong?" the driver said. "What the hell do you want?"

But John Roger cocked the second hammer, thrusting the barrels forward. He slumped into the seat.

"Oh my God," the driver mumbled. "Look, I ain't got any money. Maybe two bucks is all."

"I want to go to the cave. Up to the mountain," saying it almost as if he had just hailed a taxi.

"Look, mister, turn that thing away and I'll take you to Boston if you want. Please. Please take it away."

"Ain't going to hurt you. Just you take me up to the cave."

"There ain't no road up there."

"There is a road. Drove it once." He pumped the gun.

"I mean it don't go all the way up."

"You take me as far as it goes," again the almost placid, businesslike tone.

The driver glanced at the barrels pointed at his nose, then up at John Roger's face, and finally turned toward the road. He clutched, ground the machinery into a protesting whine, then set off.

And John Roger thought: *Blood. This time his. Not mine. Not this time.*

Settling, he began to regulate his breathing, pressing his back into the seat against the pain.

# 3

Sitting on the old Army blanket, his shoulders propped against the wall of the cave, Matthew gazed out at the moon; the amber wedge he had been watching for hours had lost its definition, spreading along the rim like a stain on a blotter. He had stayed, although after ten minutes he knew, as surely as if someone had told him, that she would not come. Listless, weary, nowhere to go. Shutting his eyes, he laid his head back against the rock wall.

He had understood its inevitability: if not tonight, next week. Because it was ruined. He knew it was ruined when, walking that afternoon to Simon's, he was magnetized by the window of the Army recruiting office on the first floor of the town hall. He stood, halted, his hands dangling like lead weights, like a man who had lost not only the contents of his pockets but the pockets as well. He almost went in, almost signed the papers and let them take him away. But he couldn't; somehow they would stare at him, refuse him as if he were insane, pronounce him a Williams, unfit. No one wanted a Williams, not even to die. His thoughts seemed idiotic, but he felt them as if their reality were unquestionable.

He didn't go in. They would get him anyway, when he finished school—in June, still two years behind everyone, still not finished.

Maybe they would never take him; maybe he would finish high school when he was a hundred. He could have told them he was quitting. But he didn't; he couldn't go, wondering why his whole world was dead and he could still not bring himself to leave it.

Because of her. Even though he knew it was ruined; he could not believe it. Could not believe it no matter how irreparably he had damaged it, pressing his intolerable hunger on her, afraid to touch her now because she would cry or push him away with her silence. He almost welcomed the times she had beat at him with her fists; at least she was not abandoning him in a wordless, motionless hell. At least she cared enough to hit him.

And suddenly he was angry, bitterly resentful that she considered herself so pure and special and delicate that she had to guard her body like some secret treasure, watching it as if it were something she had been loaned and entrusted with, not hers at all. Even angrier: why had she let him do what he did only to punish him for it? Punish him even while she let him, giving him a weird new feeling that he was being used as a tool in a battle of which he had no understanding. He winced as his head bumped back against the wall.

No, the blame was mainly his. He had sworn to himself that he would touch her gently, just hold her if that was all she wanted. But his vow was impossible. He touched her, and it was not good enough; he had to take her, pry into her. And it was not that he became lost in her, that his wildness obliterated reason, that in some sudden way he plunged into unconsciousness. Because he was keenly aware, his senses honed to the quick, that he was grasping her, wrenching her body, gripping her flesh with the intention of giving her pain, at times revelling in the hurt he knew he was inflicting, feeling the rigid battling of her body, the tightness and constriction fighting off his invasion. So he gripped more tightly, heaved his weight against her, pressed. He wanted her to scream, to cry.

His eyes bulged as if he had just discovered some new unfathomable mystery in the darkness. Why? Why did he want to hurt her? Because she was so high, so exalted that he needed to destroy her? To soil her with his body? Whatever it was, he recognized the doom in himself: to break whatever he loved, to lose whatever he was driven to keep. Yet she could have helped him to understand; if she cared for him, she could have helped. But she didn't; for some reason she wouldn't. Perhaps she wanted to be hurt.

Whatever it was, had been, it was over. She was not coming; she would never come again. And suddenly his thoughts no longer mattered; he was surrounded by her smell, and his fingertips remembered the warmth and softness and the places they were always so afraid to touch. Thinking that no matter what happened to him—live, die, become great through some freakish magic—he would never have her again, never have it exactly that way, the way he needed it.

He began to cry, letting his body rock, losing himself in a frightening feeling of oceanic giddiness. Because she was everything to him. He lay on the blanket and scrubbed his face against it, hoping to feel some vestige of her. But it was over, and now he was nothing. He would walk the streets and fields, thinking always of what was. Almost twenty years old and only a past. He would sneak to the railroad station in September and hide behind the luggage trucks and watch her leave for college, watch her kissing people good-bye, and strain toward her face and body as she vanished. Then slink away. And then nothing.

He cried into his hands, then abruptly stopped, hearing the scuffling drag of footsteps. Hers? He rose to his knees, peering toward the entrance of the cave framed in the moonlight, hearing the click of metal, seeing someone there, bobbing. And then the harsh, hollow voice, icing his body, "Come out. Come out of there."

Why was he wavering? His words, the sounds had not come out with the force he had intended. And he was trembling because of it. Perplexed, he stared into the cave, awed by the blackness.

*Black. Undertaker?*

His tongue shot through his lips, scouring them, then his teeth grating them.

*Undertaker?*

Something was wrong, but he could not plumb the core of it. His head ached and burned with spears of soberness, the immunization of the whiskey peeling away.

*What undertaker?*

He squeezed the stock of the gun, fighting an overwhelming sense of panic, as if he did not understand why he was here. The pieces which had snapped into a configuration as he sat at his table came all undone, scattered like buckshot.

*Fat man at the grave. Esther's grave. Driving her in the hearse.*

And then he wanted to run; his hands shook, the gun impossibly, frighteningly heavy; his breathing tearing out of him in small explosions.

*Broke my nose. A car full of Polacks. From the cemetery. Him!*

His eyes bugged, seeing the figure of a man appear at the mouth of the cave. Almost defensively he stepped backward and thrust the gun ahead of him, trying to lock his knees against falling. Terrified, he watched the figure come toward him, then stop, hearing, "Oh my God. You!"

And then he was sitting down, sprawled, the shock of smoke eating at his eyes, then gone. The figure had snapped, twisted, shot back into the cave; there was nothing in front of him now. He blinked, blinked again, then said in a small questioning voice, "Matthew?"

# 4

Since the gunshot came from the summit and the cave faced the town, they all heard it: a roar tinning away like sheet lightning, spiraling down in lesions of ringing sound.

They could not help but hear it, a night without sound, a night made visibly quiet by a moon floating huge, cloudless, and ivory white, spotted with a single dark stain, an eye within an eye staring the voices of motion into hiding, escape; crickets, field mice, rabbits—all gone; and even the hurrying of the river slid into liquid silence, as if it had suddenly reversed against itself, locked struggling and swirling and moonswept.

Sitting in the dark of the funeral chapel, tucked and hidden away in his armchair, Simon heard it; heard it and leaned wearily forward, listening again as if it might only have been the beating of his brain, the pumping of his heart. Minutes passed, the silence almost returned; he rose, hearing the age creak and tool at his joints, and snapped on the light, looking immediately at the large wood-cased clock above his desk: 11:16. And then a pair of clear shouts, the sound of feet whirling past the door, the crescendoed gunning of a car engine.

He switched off the light and went outside. People in knots of twos and threes emerged from the backs of stores, trotting up from their houses on Washington Street—all seen, revealed as never before: older children in various sleep clothes, men in half-buckled trousers and long-john shirts, women in bedroom slippers still securing their bodies in robes, the moon silvering their hairpins and curlers. The sheriff's car shot by, squealing first around the square, then left into Washington Street toward the highway, the mountain road.

He worked the stiffness from the small of his back and crossed to the square, the soldiers monument before him stove black, then hardening from silhouette to pale and pronounced, featured. He stood there a moment, listening, then sat on the bench and looked up at the mountain; but he could see nothing and turned slightly toward the people who were walking to the town hall where the sheriff kept his office, all knowing that whatever had happened would be reported there. Their talking sounded flat, dull, cluttered, all monotone. He watched them move in a kind of bleached unison, united only by direction, some walking on the sidewalks past the row of stores, others in the middle of the street.

Gazing off toward the mountain again he caught a glimmer, not a light, more like a small mirror weakly reflecting; probably a firefly, he thought, scuttering across the backdrop of blackness. Then he saw the twinkling headlights of a car; they disappeared; appeared again; and some distance behind them another car repeating the same interplay of light. Then almost a siren: a scooping moan cut suddenly, quacking weakly and foolishly into nothing. Now the crickets took up a bleat of dryness—meek, parched throats.

After a time that let the stiffness return to his body, he could see the pinpricks of bobbing flashlights peeping in and out of the darkness, and he knew that they were in the cave. Vague guesses tugged at his acceptance, found no response; he simply stared as if he had suspended thought and feeling, as if for a brief moment he did not permit himself to exist.

One of the cars began its descent. He watched it dip from the crest, its lights bubbling through the trees as it wound down the road, vanishing for its final sweep around the circumference before it emerged on the highway.

And then he rose, creaked again, left the square, and walked to the town hall, pushing through several people to the top step, waiting under the combined glare of the portico globes and their fluorescent boosters, which warped lips purple and skin an angry yellow. Crowds were all alike, he thought, remembering a murder in a Southern town, a child strangled by a tramp, and when the tramp was tracked and caught the people paraded through the streets with placards and misspelled signs: BURN HIM—HANGINGS TOO GOOD—WE WANT JUSTESS—and setting scarecrows ablaze on lampposts. They almost lynched the tramp, almost tore down the jail; until the city newspapers sent photographers, until they all began to enjoy posing, held the signs higher, but vengeance gone from their faces, only jubilation, peering into camera lenses, waving, smiling, performing absurdities for the reporters. And all the next day buying newspapers by the dozen to scissor, paste, and send clippings to relatives and friends, their own faces circled in crayon with arrows saying: ME or HERE WE ARE. Righteousness the path to perpetuation . . .

"Here they come," someone shouted, a car veering into the square and pulling up at the curb.

It was a Massachusetts State Police car, new and shiny and weaponlike; a trooper left the driver's seat and opened the rear door. The sheriff's deputy backed out, drawing a man after him from the seat, forcing him to straighten up as he half fell against a fender.

A shout: "Well, God, look who it is."

Another: "What's he done, hey?"

Laughing: "I guess he's out of retirement now."

John Roger stood without help then, his eyes not even blinking in the light, the light itself severe on his face, neutralizing the color of his scraggly cheeks, molding the hollows and rents of his face, fiercely purpling old scars and a furrow at the bridge of the nose, casting broad black arrows straight into his eyes. Suddenly there was a flurry, and Simon watched the jarring tangle as the chain of the handcuffs somehow pinched and gripped the pocket of the deputy's shirt. Then they brought him up the steps, John Roger in the middle, staring ahead, his feet limp and twisted inward, dragging. The trooper carried a shotgun in his left hand, the twin barrels protruding from a wrap of newspapers; pausing, he turned to the crowd. "Why don't you all go back to bed. There's nothing to see."

"Don't you be so sassy," someone said. "You people have been here a year and mine have been here sixty. Keep sassy and we might not let you stay."

Again laughter. A hoot.

The trooper shook his head, the deputy saying, "Straight down the hall and up the stairs"; the trooper continuing on into the building, pushing John Roger ahead of him.

"What's he done?" a woman asked, her question buttressed by a small echoing chorus.

"Nothing," the deputy said, his face contracted at the mouth and eyes. "Now go home like the man asked you."

Simon plucked his sleeve and said, "Can I come in, Adam?"

"If you want, Simon. It's your privilege."

And as he entered, Simon heard a voice behind him, "It's a killing all right. They need the undertaker already."

"They always got to know everything," Adam said, locking the door, then leading Simon along the hall, past the small auditorium, and up a short flight of stairs to the sheriff's office.

The trooper, removing the handcuffs now, said, "I think he's off his head. Hey, old man, what day is it? What year?" Pointing to a stain in John Roger's groin, "Don't you know how to ask for the boy's room?"

But he merely stood, still staring into a vacuum with the dead expression of someone looking not at nothing but at the unseen, unknown reflections of his own mind.

"Simon," Adam said, "do you know Cass Nowell's number offhand?"

"Three-one-eight."

Adam sat at a rolltop desk and pushed the shotgun away with his forearm, then unscrambled the telephone from a heap of ledger books and papers. He dialed, waited, then, "Cass? Adam Bratny. Could you please come over to the office now? . . . Yes, well I know it's late, but Taylor told me to call you . . . Well, didn't you hear the shot? The whole damn upstreet's outside . . . Well, it does concern you . . . Taylor says it does, now don't say no . . . Cass . . . Cass, I don't want to have to have Taylor tell you . . . Yes, now. All right, as soon as you can. Please."

Simon listened, but watched John Roger—shoulders knotted up almost under the straggle of long hair; his hands clenched wrist to wrist in front of him, as if the handcuffs still secured them. Now, in normal light, his face was matted with stubble; glistening stripes of drying tears hung like mucus from his eyes, curving with the hollows of his cheeks, vanishing into the wings of his nostrils; a bead of liquid trembled on the tip of his nose.

"Let's go," the trooper said.

"Here." Adam left the desk and opened a door which gave into a small room containing a single barred cell. He snapped on a green-shaded light hanging limply from the ceiling by a frayed insulated wire, then creaked open the door of the cell.

The trooper prodded John Roger through the room and into the cell, then returned to the office while Adam locked first the cell, then the outer door; locked it and leaned back against it, nervously bringing his arm up and scrubbing his forehead with a sleeve.

"Where is there a doctor?" the trooper asked.

"Third house on Washington Street. Take a right—if he's not out there with the rest of them."

"We'll be back now," the trooper said; and left the office, the clack of his cleated heels reverberating down the stairs and through the empty halls until the front door slammed.

"What happened up there, Adam?"

"Enough to make you sick, that's all." He went to the desk, and as suddenly as he had brought his arm up to his forehead, jerked open a drawer and removed a pint of whiskey; he raised it high to his lips, the light diffusing through it like a two-tinted prism: amber, yellow bubbles. Replacing it in the drawer, he began to speak, but was interrupted by a head thrust through the door, a man saying, "A few of us folks . . ."

"Get the hell out of here," Adam shouted, going to the door and seizing the man's arm, escorting him bumpily down the stairs; Simon hearing his protests, Adam's curses.

And when Adam returned he said, "I'm shook up and I ain't afraid to admit it either."

"Adam, did he kill somebody?"

"He did, all right."

"Who?"

"Simon, you got every right in the world to be here, but please don't ask me who it was. Taylor said I mustn't tell anybody. They'll be bringing the body down in a few minutes, and then you can ask . . ."

"Why did you call Cass?"

"Please just wait for Taylor."

Simon went to the window and parted the venetian blinds, looking down at the people still clustered by the portico, some of them sitting on the steps.

"They still out there, Simon?"

"Yes."

They were silent for a time, then both were jarred by a noise from the cell, a short raw-wood screech of moving furniture.

"What the hell's he up to?" Adam said. He rose and opened the door, going up to the cell.

John Roger sat on a cot with his back to them, his hands invisible, his head bent almost between his legs. His body moved softly back and forth, rocking, hunched; he was mumbling to himself, only the sound audible, more a wordless drone.

224

Adam tried to peer over the humped shoulders, saying, "Hey." But there was no response, the droning ceaseless, the rocking more jagged.

And coming away from the bars, Adam's head struck the hanging lamp, and before his slipping fingers could still it, it wobbled elliptically and violently, flashing insane arcs of shattered light against the walls of the room, the bars, his face, the old man's back; then he caught the rim of the shade and steadied it peacefully on its cord.


When Sheriff Taylor and the state troopers brought the body down from the mountain there was no place to keep it—neither hospital, infirmary, nor morgue—so they carried it past the people and into the town hall. It was shrouded in an old Army blanket already mottled by glistening damp stains stanched and drying, growing darker before their eyes, until soon the blanket would merely appear dirty, caked or spattered with pitch. They laid it on the floor outside the sheriff's office and covered it with still another blanket.

Taylor and two troopers entered the office, the one who had brought in John Roger now blinking wearily, the other standing tall, straining in his shirt, businesslike and blank. Taylor nodded to Simon, then waved Adam out of the chair by the desk and sat down, creaking; he tilted his hat back on his vein-hatched globular head, fingering the accents of wet, flattened hair which sprouted in sparse twists. He grunted, said, "He's got to go to Bluefield, sergeant. We're never too ready for things like this. All we got is one cell for drunks and such." He jerked his head toward the locked door. "I suppose you have got him in there, Adam?"

"Right. Locked tight."

Addressing the troopers again, Taylor said, "It'll hold him as good as the drunks, but I won't take any responsibility, not when I've been asking for a real jail for years. I'll put a call through to the police in Bluefield. Let them stick him right up that county seat of theirs."

"Look," the sergeant said, "I'll radio the barracks. They'll pick him up."

"For all I care you can take the old bastard right now. Makes no difference to me."

"We would if it was absolutely necessary, but I think he'll be all right here for the time being. We still have patrols to finish and then there's the body. It would be hard to handle it now." He trailed off, then, "No, you might as well keep the whole thing in a package. Unless you think you'll have trouble with the people."

"Them? Not a chance. The whole place is nothing but a schoolhouse for gossipers. The ones outside are the worst of the bunch—the town people, if you know what I mean—the real smart ones." He fished clumsily in his shirt pocket, his searching fingers beating through the cloth like an erratic heart, then drew out a cigarette and lighted it with a kitchen match struck on the sole of his shoe. "No trouble at all."

"One last thing," the sergeant said. "I'll have to make out my own report and send it on to the barracks. They'll give it over to Bluefield. I think we can say we apprehended him in severe mental strain."

"Yes, fine." The sheriff rose and shook the sergeant's hand. "Listen, I want to thank you boys."

"So long as you haven't got any more crazy ones in this town."

"Now that'll be hard to tell, won't it?"

The troopers left, cleating down the stairs, Adam following them to lock the door.

"Well, Simon," Taylor said, "it's been a night."

"Who was it?"

Taylor ground his cigarette into the floor, then stretched, finally scratching his dark, ringed armpits. He said, "Let's take a look. You'll probably get him before long." They went out into the hall, Taylor saying, "I sent the doctor home. I knew there was no chance, but I had to make sure." He squatted over the body and furled the blankets back to the chin, tucking them in under the shoulders. "Simon?"

"Oh, goddamn," Simon said. "Goddamn, what a misery. I

think I knew it. I think I knew it from the minute I heard that shot." He took his eyes from the body, then doubled his fist and lightly punched the wall in a reflex of frustration. "I knew it and I didn't want to believe it."

"You knew?"

"That's why I stayed to see, because I was hoping against it. Sometimes you trick yourself, you think you can change what you know has been done."

"Look, Simon, I'm the last man in the world to ask anybody to fink out, but did Adam tell you anything? I mean, I wouldn't mind you knowing; it's just that I told him to keep his mouth shut."

"No, I knew, that's all."

"Then would you mind telling me how?"

"I can't, because I don't know. Because it was a feeling I can't explain to you." Looking again at the body, "What a waste. Lordy, what a stinking waste."

"All right, we'll talk later." Pointing to the chin extending over the edge of the blankets, "He got a little of it in the face. Must have had his head bent." He drew the blankets up and rose heavily. "The rest of him isn't exactly appetizing."

"Piss-poor word. What's the difference now?"

"All right, it's the ugliest, dirtiest thing I've ever seen. He took a twelve-gauge straight in the chest. When we got up there the old man was standing in the cave holding the gun on us. For a minute we just stopped dead—figured the other barrel was primed. He could have got one of us without an aim, we were that close. And then that goddamn sergeant walked right up to him and took the thing away, just took it out of his hands like the old bastard was asleep on his feet. He wasn't holding that gun on us at all—and it was clean anyway. Goddamn glory-boy sergeant couldn't have known it was empty. Then when I saw what happened I was embarrassed; I could hardly look."

"Embarrassed?"

"No, maybe ashamed. I can't put my finger on it; it's just a feeling. I kept thinking, what kind of man would do it? I couldn't

**227**

help myself; I had to ask him. Made a damn fool of myself asking it. I couldn't get a word out of him; he was stoned."

"I wonder if anybody ever knew what kind of man he was. Or is. I wonder if he knows himself."

Rounding the edges of the blankets with his foot, nodding toward the body, Taylor said, "How long was he working for you?"

"Not long."

"He went out with Cass's daughter, didn't he?"

"Yes. When he could."

"I've got to see Cass, to get it clear in my mind. They'll probably want him for a statement. His girl, too."

After Taylor dragged the body into another room, they went back to the office where Adam was spooning coffee into a pot already hissing on a hot plate.

"Say," Taylor said, "did you call Cass Nowell?"

"You told me, didn't you? Said he'd come over as soon as he could."

"All right." Then to Simon, "Now would you please tell me how you knew about this?"

"I said it was a feeling." Thinking, wondering with a curiosity no less insistent than Taylor's how he had come to have the feeling. Something about doom, he decided. Some people were doomed and you only needed to wait before it happened. He began to speak again, but his voice was suddenly muffled by knocking at the front door, the flat of a fist pounding, shaking the knob in a rattle of metal.

"Oh, goddamn them," Taylor said, barging out into the hall, double-stepping down the stairs, then unlocking and throwing open the door. Cass Nowell, his fist still raised, lurched inside.

"What's going on?" someone shouted.

"Just a minute," Taylor said to Cass, and walked out to the lip of the portico, facing the people who had remained, waiting, milling about the bottom step. "Go home, the whole lot of you. You ought to be ashamed of yourselves."

"What are we paying you for? For secrets? We got a right to know what happened."

228

"All right, damn it. But then go home. Old man Williams killed his boy."

He turned and went back inside, kicking the door shut with a long swing of his leg, saying, "Try to do a job and they throw your pay up to you," wanting to say more, but stopping, staring at Cass clutching a window ledge for support, his eyes covered by one hand; asking finally, "What's the matter, Cass?"

"Matter? No, nothing's the matter." He walked directly down the hall, Taylor behind him.

# 5

Cass came through the door of the sheriff's office, almost backlashing it into Taylor who reflexively warded it off with his forearm. Oblivious to Taylor's offended protest, Cass strode almost blindly to the desk; then, seeing Simon, he stopped and stared, suddenly reined in.

"Williams," Taylor began, but Cass said, "I know. I heard you downstairs."

Simon turned away, creaking the springs of the chair.

"You want to see the body?" Taylor asked.

"Why? Why should I see the body?"

Taylor shrugged.

Swiveling again, Simon said, "Why not?"

Cass gazed off toward the wall, saying without inflection, "The reason escapes me."

And Simon: "I would guess it does."

"Look," Cass said, then broke off. "Yes. Why not?"

Simon rose, the chair twanging, and moved toward the door. He said to Taylor, "You mind not coming with us?"

"Why?"

"Just like that."

"I mind, but all right."

Simon walked down the hall, hearing the almost drunken, unsyncopated thud of Cass's feet behind him. He opened the door to the small room where the body had been moved, and stepped aside, letting Cass precede him, watching him stop and stare at the heap of blankets on the floor. He shut the door and sat heavily on a crotchety chair, his eyes trained on Cass; somehow it seemed as if he could not understand that a corpse lay beneath the blankets. Then Cass narrowed his eyes as he might if he had been tricked, brought here by some ulterior, camouflaged reason.

Simon said, "He's there all right."

Cass turned and met his eyes.

"How it happened," Simon said, "was this. He was in the cave. His father went up and shot him. A simple end to a simple story."

"Why?"

"Why? I don't know why."

"Did Taylor ask him?"

"He won't speak. Or can't."

Cass nodded. Simon stared silently, and after a time Cass said irritably, "Now what is it I'm supposed to say?"

"Nothing."

"No, you want me to say something."

"Maybe I do."

"I feel no pity, if that's what you want. You won't see me beating my breast."

Simon shrugged, groaning the chair. Sneering, Cass said, "Well?"

"You know why he was up on that mountain?"

"Yes, I know."

"Alone."

"What is it you want? That Martha should have been with him? Die with him? I'd see him dead a hundred times over before I'd even allow myself that thought. What *is* it you want? For her to be dead too?"

"Don't be a fool. You know what I mean."

"Whatever you're saying, say it outright."

"You drove him up there."

"Him?"

230

"And her. You forced them; you made them sneak around like animals."

Cass snapped his head back violently and laughed, a shattering, mocking peal. Then, "They slept together. He and my daughter. You can't understand what that means, you can't get it through your head, can you? Why? Only God knows. You're a fool, but I never took you for corrupt."

"Can't you see? Before you even knew what they were doing, you made it out to be sinful, shameful, something you talk about in a saloon. And somehow she knew what was in your mind. If you used one minute of sense it wouldn't have happened. But you're what you are, no more. You didn't even give them the privilege of having a bed to decide *not* to sleep in."

"You're talking about my daughter."

"Yes, you mentioned her. The bitch in heat."

"That's enough from you."

"Enough? Shit. I haven't even begun. For months I've been sitting around here like a dummy, watching you tear their hearts to pieces."

"Then you acted properly. Because it was none of your business. But God knows, you blinded me for a long enough time."

Simon shook his head, Cass going on. "Frankly—and I say this with more conviction than I've ever said anything—frankly I'm glad he's dead. For what he did."

"They."

"She was an idiot. She didn't know what she was doing."

"My God! You can't make what's happened disappear by magic. His dying doesn't solve it. Nor does her not knowing."

"Be quiet with your hypocritical moralizing, goddamn you."

"God, God, God. Always God."

"Always."

"I'm sick of hearing that. Sick of you hiding behind it every time you can't control the part of you that hates, that wants to wreck everything in your life."

"Go to hell."

"Do you have the power to send me there? By Jesus, I guess you think you do. Sometimes you think you *are* God, don't you?

231

Made in His image, even when you're wrong. Years ago you pissed and moaned that you had the power to destroy Martha in some way, mark her forever, because she saw you smash up that boy's father," reflexively stabbing his thumb toward the blankets. "But you didn't just smash him up a little; you brought the whole thing to a finish. You wiped out the whole damned clan. Somehow. Some way. By default. Maybe you are God."

Cass's jaws mulched, the veins tumescent at his temples.

And Simon: "Why did you ever bring that boy to church? Where was it your business? What did you need to prove? You know something? Your failure with the boy, your hitting his old man—you never cared what effect Martha's seeing that would have on her. You wanted to tear somebody apart just for the joy of it, just to feel the bones break. And you kept on blaming the boy for it, for the whole thing, for your one irrational slip. You finally had to drive him up to some cave and make him an animal, so you could be sure he was one. Why didn't you just buy a gun and hunt him down?" He ran his tongue across his lips. "A few hours ago I said you were a sorry son-of-a-bitch. But you're the *sorriest* man I ever saw."

"You brought me here to tell me this. You didn't think I could resist you—because of that," indicating the blankets.

"I thought you might see something, that's all. Understand."

"That—whatever it is lying under that blanket—it raped my daughter."

Simon shook his head.

"Raped," Cass said, "because she couldn't help what she did."

"Why? Why do you have to believe that?"

"Because she's like her mother and she can't help that, and God willing she'll get over it."

"Do you *hear* what you're saying? Shitting on what you loved most in this stinking world. Just to prove you're right, to bail yourself out."

"To prove nothing."

"You're alone."

"Yes. So?"

"So the years of us talking together, of me somehow not want-

232

ing to tell you all about me—afraid to tell you what I really felt. But the things I *did* say, everything—you thought it was all bullshit, didn't you?"

"I listened."

"Only because you were alone."

"Maybe."

"And you came to hate me, didn't you? Because the doubts you told me about were too private to let go of; and when you let go, you had to hate me."

"I was a fool. I should have talked to a priest, not you. I had no right to show you my doubts. I ground God into the dirt."

"Stop, will you? God has nothing to do with this. It was you. You gave me some of yourself—the aloneness, the strength you felt you had. And you undermined it by giving it to me. You weren't so strong any more; and you hated me for seeing it, for seeing you were just a man who could suffer and maybe die. As if I took something away from you, as if I took it, not like you gave it to me. Is that why you hate me now? Because you can't talk to anyone without being superior, one up somehow?"

Cass doubled his fists, his body moving almost of itself toward the door, saying finally, "Yes, you took those things from me—my pride, my action, my understanding of what was right. Because you want to hypnotize people, you creep under their skins. You make them tell you things. I've spent years trying not to give in to you. Trying not to go your way, into a life without rules or ethics or meaning—the easy way."

"Easy? I have no family, no real friend—not any more. You have more than me, always have, so don't tell me easy. Tell me anything, but not that. The difference is that I don't know what's going to happen from one day to the next. But you need to be right; you need to think you know what will happen tomorrow. And all it does for you is to bring you down to your knees when the schedule's off.

"You're just as screwed up as me, but you won't admit it because it would make you less of a man. I *am* less of a man. I've known it for years. That's what the difference is." And then, almost a disconnected afterthought, as if it somehow summed up

233

all that he had said: "Do you always have to convert somebody? Get somebody on your side?"

"You talk about me? You should hear yourself—the insufferable pride in your wailing about your nothingness."

"Pride?"

"Pride. Even now, lording it over me. Lording it over me since I came into this room."

Simon stared, blinking, steadying his body in the chair. *Oh God*, he thought. *Yes, he's right. In some way he's right.* He bit his lip, then: "It's always been between us. Maybe that's what it's always been about. All right, then listen. The one thing I never told you. I wasn't just a preacher, I was a tub-thumper, a crook. I rode the circuits: a bum, a liar, the scum of the earth. I was afraid to tell you that, afraid you'd spit in my face. I didn't want that; I was afraid of being alone." His head drooped, his chins folding against his chest. "I guess I always envied your life, maybe even your God. Always wondering, thinking how good it would have been to believe like you. But I couldn't. I manipulated the whole idea of God right out of existence. Killed it forever. I *did* envy you. I guess if I can't pull the strings, run the show, I can't believe in anything." He looked up, saying, "I want to go down the stairs and preach to all those fools out there. Roll my dice. Shout and scream and watch them all puke in disgust. Lord it over them, just like you say. Lording it over them, pretending I'm some king whose word of God is too good for them. Just alone, pretending I'm right. I guess," he smiled painfully, "that's how we're alike."

"Alike."

"Yes. Alone, sitting and talking, all alone. Both afraid of really telling each other that we were just men, showing it. I used to think of it as needing to give you little pieces of myself, testing to see how far I could go before you'd reject me. And you the same, I guess. In a way, the same." He nodded reflectively, then, "There's one more piece, though. Just one."

"You don't have to tell me."

"I guess I do, Cass. I guess I just do. Years ago there was a boy in Fallsville who listened to me. Maybe the only human being who ever did listen—really. He went out to baptize himself and drowned. I never knew about it until recently; I quit the circuit long before I knew. I killed him, you know. Just as sure as if I'd tied him in a rock-filled sack and dropped him in the river." Then, pointing to the blankets, "Poor bastard. Born to be used—by you, by me. Just used, fodder for us to lord it over everybody. It's my guilt I'm putting on you, asking you to share."

"Yes. Your guilt."

"You didn't want me to tell you, did you? Because we have nothing any more, have we?"

"Because I knew. I've known for twenty-five years exactly what you were."

"You knew?"

"Did you really think you could hide? In a place like Southfield?"

"You knew about the boy in Fallsville?"

"You were *allowed* to hide."

Simon rose and walked heavily to the window, his eyes slitted, wet. And then the door opened; shut. After some time at the window, he went to the blankets, curled the upper one away, wincing as he looked at the mangled blackness, finally hiding the face again.

Adam Bratny entered. "Simon?"

"You'd best bring the body over to my place."

"I got to have some family come down here to say it's all right."

"There is no family, you know that as well as I do. I'll bury him."

"What for? I don't get it."

Looking at him, Simon thought: *Because I know what it is to drive a boy to death, and that makes me the proper judge and executor of his body. And that makes me his chief mourner.*

"Just like that," he said.

"Yes, well, you'd better come to the office first."

"Why?"

"We got Willy Kling in there."

Simon followed him down the hall.

But Simon did not enter Taylor's office, nor did he see Willy Kling. He stopped short, catching the office door as it swung sharply toward him. Cass walked out, his face set in a kind of strange paralysis, the lips drawn in and cemented together, drawing down the tip of the nose; his shoulders were humped. His arms, locked mechanically at the elbows, were extended away from his body. Striding clumsily toward the head of the stairs, his legs like pistons, unreal, mechanized, he plunged ahead down the stairs, his heels thumping; and Simon bent over the bannister watching him continue down. Finally, without warning or sense or explanation, his body unstiffening, unlocking as he slammed his knee into a stairpost—a cannonlike boom that shuddered the bannister under Simon's hands. He gripped the bannister tightly, curling his fingers around it as if to steady it, still watching Cass, seeing his body slither in pain, then relock, carrying him across the hall and through the door.

Behind him, someone was shouting: high, whining, fanatical.

Then the office door slammed shut, the bellowing ceased, and Taylor said, "This is some shit, Simon."

Turning, Simon said, "What? What's some shit?"

"That little moron in there," jerking his thumb toward the office, "has got the craziest goddamn story you ever heard."

"Talk straight."

"You know, Simon, you always talk like I was beneath you. Like you're way up there some place and nobody can touch you. I'm a little fed up on that shit."

"I had a hard night."

"Yeah, I suppose that must be it."

"Just what story did you hear?"

"Cass came in and Kling looks up at him and says, 'You're the one he was after, wasn't you?' And then he stuck his hand up in front of his eyes like he was about to be hit, and starts to scream, 'I never meant it to be you, I swear to Jesus.' And then he said he was trying to hang your ass. He told the old man you were shackin' up with his boy. You see what I mean? Crazy. I thought Cass was going to fall down; I never saw anybody look like that. And then Kling's eyeballs went up into his head and he started to shout and holler about how he saved the town. You know what this is all about?"

"We either go crazy or die. That's what it means." He turned back to look at the empty stairs and hall. "What's the difference? You send me over that boy, hear?"

He descended the stairs, following Cass's spoor, walking out to the portico heavily and intently, as if making his way resolutely through a crowd. Except that everyone had gone home.

# Nine

Matthew was buried two days later in the huge bronze coffin. Simon and Martha drove to the cemetery in the hearse, she dressed in dark green, because she had no black, he dressed as usual—black was all he had. They stood by the excavated rectangle, almost shuffle-footed, and Simon removed his hat and recited a string of words, the sense of which escaped him. He had not used them in years. The two gravediggers, mud-grimed and yawning, squatted back against a rounded ochre pyramid of freshly-turned earth.

No one else was there: no curiosity seekers, no mourners whose hobby it was to smell out funerals, no one, as if Matthew had never existed. Just Simon and Martha and the gravediggers—and then a scraggly bird that piloted down to a headstone with beating, balancing wings, not even looking their way.

Simon finished speaking, covered his head, and, touching Martha's elbow, guided her across the lawn and over the limp chain that ran along the path. She turned briefly as the shovels chomped; turned again and walked on.

She sat constricted and withdrawn in the corner of the seat as they drove to Southfield, her body pressed hard against the door. Finally she said, "I could never have seen him again, Simon. I could never have seen him anyway."

"Except he's dead. He didn't just go away."

"Don't be angry. I guess I sounded as if he—you know—got on a bus and left."

"I guess you did sound that way." He glanced at her, holding the wheel more tightly, then looked back at the road; thinking: *Somehow she feels important now.* More: *The resiliency of her age that lets her look ahead. That will cure her.* "I sounded angry?"

"Yes."

"I wanted to sound sad. Funny, because what I was thinking, it should have come out sad. I was thinking about burying little kids. Babies. They have these little caskets, like shoe boxes almost. Little boxes." He paused, then, "I'm sorry. Too long in this business. Too, too long. I've lost respect or consideration—whatever—for other people's feelings. Yours." He mumbled, almost to himself, "I'm getting out of this"; thinking: *With every burial I feel more dead.*

"You don't have to worry about my feelings. I don't have any. Never have. And I know I sounded as though he took some trip. But it's like your anger; it's not what I meant either."

"Maybe no matter what we mean, it comes out differently. Or opposite. Or whatever." He furrowed his forehead and sighed. "How old can you feel?"

They drove on in silence for some time, and finally Martha said, "What happened to me, Simon? Why did everything turn out this way?"

"I'm the last person in the world can give you the whys."

"Simon, I'm asking you for pity."

He nodded, but said nothing.

"I was a nice little Catholic girl—prim and proper—who loved her daddy and did everything he said, and worried about things like the state of grace and the purity of her soul, and sat straight in her chair with her legs closed tight . . ."

"Stop trying to sound like an old whore at a revival meeting. Just because you slept with him."

"Slept? That would have been nice. Anyway, I feel like a whore."

"Well, you have my pity now."

"It's the first word that occurs to me. Maybe because all I ever felt with him was numbness."

"It's none of my business."

"Stop it, Simon. Stop running away from me. Stop standing just out of reach—I can't stand that."

"I never ran far enough."

"Well then don't listen. Run."

"You're a spoiled brat. Sarcastic, too."

"I'll talk anyway. It doesn't matter what you do. Who ever listened to me anyway?"

"Look . . ."

"I felt nothing with him. Only once or twice—when you might as well have called it perverted."

"Who's fault was that? His? Do you want everything in this world without giving a dime in return?"

She thumped the seat with her fist. "Won't anyone, just once in my life, shut up and listen to me?"

"*He* did."

"Yes, every minute. He hung on my words. He looked at my stupid, ugly face, at my skinny and stiff dead body, and he listened to me. Without once ever saying anything. He hated himself so much that he had no idea of the hate I felt for myself. He treated me like a statue in a church, and inside me was the loneliest, emptiest, cryingest . . ." She turned to the window, pressing even deeper into the corner.

Simon said, "How in hell did you ever come to feel this way about yourself? Because you're not ugly. Nor dead."

"What's inside shows outside too."

"How? I asked how?"

"Because I had a mother I never saw. I had a legend instead. Like at Lourdes. Even if you leave there still crippled, you're supposed to believe anyway. Ever try to live up to a legend, a model without flesh and blood? Only knowing it—or her—through other people's stories and memories? And the stories were no good because my father had a wife he never really knew or understood as a woman. So he made her a saint, and I have her name. A saint's name." Jerking her head toward him, she said, "But I hear they were a pretty sexy pair, Simon—Mother and Father."

He shrugged.

"I read my father's diary."

"What diary?"

"I found it a few weeks ago, in among his ledger books at the store. They all look alike—accounts, sales, purchases. But two of them are filled with her—written in red ink. Why are they written in red, Simon? Like debits?"

"Ink is ink."

"If she was the way he says, if she was love incarnate, then how did I get this way? She didn't have the sixth commandment branded on her forehead. Why do I?"

"I guess maybe you don't."

She paused, reflective, then went on as if she hadn't heard him. "You know? My father thought I accused him of wanting me sexually."

"Poor bastard," he muttered, shaking his head.

"Maybe that's why I'm numb, Simon. Maybe that's just why he made me this way. So I wouldn't tempt him."

"You trying to make me vomit?"

"I believe what I said."

"You don't. You're kicking him when he's down. The man suffers enough, his thoughts are killing him. Look, he worked hard, gave up the use of a fine mind to run a rotten store because other things seemed more important to him. Like the love of a woman and a child born to that woman. Maybe you can't feel anything below your waist because you just can't feel anything at all. You're an eighteen-year-old infant, and I don't care if you slept with every man in Massachusetts. And the longer you need to blame him, the longer you'll stay an infant."

"Now you're really angry."

"Yes. You're damn straight. We finally managed to get the words and the feelings together."

"When Matthew was making love to me, know what I thought of? Those diaries—up there on the shelf as if she were a piece of property, a consignment. That's what I thought of, wishing I could be what those words said she was, and at the same time feeling like something owned, entered, and dated. In red ink. The dark, sexual beauty, and I used her as pornography, something to get me going. Well, that stopped me. If I ever had any life in me, the thought of her drove it away. I can't compete with the gods."

"Compete?"

"It seems that's what I have to do."

"What is it? You hate everybody now?"

"Maybe."

"Bullshit."

"You see?" she said, almost triumphantly, "you see, Simon. You're speaking to me as if I was a whore."

As he rammed the heel of his hand against the steering wheel, Simon almost impaled his lower lip on his eyetooth. He veered the hearse sharply to the side of the road. Turning to Martha he suddenly saw, past her, the Williams house extruding from its small hill. He glanced back at her almost furtively, but she did not seem to notice where they were; she was glaring at him, her eyes seething belligerence, waiting for his retort. But the sight of the house had in some way uncurled the hard fists of his anger. He crept the hearse along the side of the road for some distance before he braked, letting the engine idle.

He said, calmly, "What is it, Martha? What is it with all of you? Why do you go to bed and feel nothing, and still keep going on with it? What meaning does it have? What—if nobody feels anything? I had a dumb idea once. I thought when people loved each other, sex was just how they kept score. Now I don't know what to believe."

She had kept her eyes trained on him, then abruptly flicked them away. "Who did you have in mind, Simon?"

"You. I guess just you."

"Not Matthew?"

"No."

"Why not Matthew?" Her eyes glowed with belligerence again, waging some private war.

"Because it seems he felt something."

"Men always feel something, don't they, Simon?" Her voice quavered, edged with hysteria.

"No. Men don't always feel." Then, "Don't make a life's work of your numbness. Or turn your so-called deadness into a virtue."

"Stop spouting proverbs."

"You're like your father. Pig-headed, both of you. You get one idea in your head and ride it to death, and God help you if that idea is wrong—or leads no place. Because neither of you can ever see an alternative. The stuff martyrs are made of—a hairshirt where a heart should be."

"Maybe you're right," she said viciously, her eyes strangely accented by a bitter, animal smile. "I told him why Matthew was up on the mountain."

"You didn't think he knew?" He studied her face, the stubborn set of her determined mouth, the defiant thrust of her chin. And then the recrudescence of the child in her, or perhaps of the child that really lived so close to the surface; quickly raising her arms, she folded them obstinately across her breasts. "Whether he knew it or not," Simon said, "didn't matter. You just wanted to leave him with nothing. Bare to the bone and bleeding."

She tightened her arms, her breasts crushing together, tightening as if she desperately needed control. He said, "God knows why, but you got him. You set out to get him and you got him. Humiliated him. If that wasn't what you wanted, why didn't you go up to the cave that night? Because you solved something with

243

your father that never had anything to do with Matthew at all? Something happened; you got what you wanted; and you didn't need that boy any more?"

"My father got as good as he gave."

"Shut up. What I wanted to say was you castrated him, left him with nothing. Now what do you want him to do, kill himself? Who in hell did you really come to mourn today? Or why? Maybe just *why*?"

"Why are you defending him?" she shouted.

"Oh, you want an ally? My fight with him is mine and his— it's none of your business. I don't give you leave to use my fight in your cause." He paused, then, "And I defend him because you scare me, scare me down deep. You have too many possibilities; the whole world is a future for you. I'm an old man and all I have are memories—memories I need to preserve."

"He never loved me, Simon. Never. He trained me like a little dog, and there was no love in it. He had none left for me—and he knows it. You go and ask him and he'll admit it."

"He'll admit anything now—any crime, any sin, anything. Now he'll take the blame and the guilt of the whole world on his shoulders. And you know *that*. I won't make anybody a false Christ."

She laughed shrilly, digging her fingers into the soft flesh of her arms, and Simon said, "You couldn't even get him directly, could you?" She tried to speak, but he boomed over her "Could you?"

"No! No, no, no. How can you? How can anybody do anything to him directly? He doesn't let you. He never lets you."

"If truth be told, Martha, you never cared a tinker's damn for that boy. Not really. He just served a purpose."

"How can you say that? I let him make love to me . . ."

"The grand prize, the gift. The whole world spins in the space between a woman's legs, is that what you think? Is that all you think that boy died on that mountain for? You felt nothing because you gave him nothing. What are you going to be when you grow up, a man-eater? I'm sure they have good advanced courses for that in those fancy schools."

244

And suddenly he understood that he had accused her of killing Matthew, and his stomach seared with the hideous, annihilating feeling that he had exceeded a limit he had no right even to approach—an uncontrollable, nauseous swelling of guilt that left her oscillating before his eyes, that transformed her into the little girl he remembered, her face growing younger, childlike. He felt that he had violated her as surely as if he had knocked her to the floor and raped her. He half expected a blow, her slashing fingers across his face, half desired it. But the Nowells rarely hit; because when they did, they remembered it for a lifetime.

She said, "Whatever I did, whatever it really meant—it's better than you and my father sitting and rocking, rotting away without even trying to feel. Even if the try is no good, even if it comes out numb. When was the last time either of you tried to love anybody? Just *tried.*"

*The boy was born to be used.* The thought whirled through his mind, intersected itself, whirled again, jaggedly, like water clogged in the ventricle of an ear, pounding a hand frantically against the head to let it cascade warmly away. But it wouldn't. *Used.*

"No," he said finally, "he doesn't let you do anything directly."

"What?"

"Your father. I sit here and use that boy to get at him the same as you do." Then, dumbly, "Why?"

"It's not him, Simon, not Matthew. It's us. Maybe he came too close."

And Simon, before he even suspected that she was shuddering, before hearing the soft, broken, eerie wail her mouth was pouring into her hands, said, "And they brought Daniel, and cast him into the den of lions." Then, seeing her cry, he took her shoulders and turned her toward him, saying when she raised her face, "Forgive me. Because you did give him something. Don't you forget it."

"No."

"You let him love you. It's all he ever had. Maybe all he ever wanted."

Then she lowered her head to his shoulder and lay softly against him, and he held her gently for a long while before she spoke.

"I think I'm afraid to live without my father, to grow up without him. Without someone who knows everything. Simon—I once thought he knew everything."

"Maybe," he answered, "that's why people come to believe in God."

When she sat up and moved away, he drove off; they didn't speak again until he stopped in front of her house.

"Simon? Will you come in?"

He shook his head.

"Please?"

"No, I can't. I just can't."

"Please, Simon, make up for me. You used to do that when I was a child. Remember?"

"Too well. Anyway, we have a fight, I told you. I can't make up for you."

"Simon, I need him to love me."

"He loves you."

She said nothing, just left the hearse; and as she closed the door she began to speak, then snapped her mouth shut, nodded, and went up the path to the porch.

Simon drove to the service station, parked, then saw the attendant coming toward him, his eyes, under a grease-smeared cap, squinting in the sun.

"Wash it," Simon called.

"Smallest funeral you ever had, I bet. His old man couldn't afford a flower car?"

"Shut up, you beady-eyed bastard." He walked toward the square, slipping his pipe from a pocket, holding it in his hand, feeling it. He gazed up the street, suddenly recalling the state troopers' car that had spirited John Roger away the day before; watching from in front of the funeral chapel where the old man's son already lay, the old man himself appearing like an apparition at the rear window of the car. The head grinding around on the stalk of a neck, matted hair and features drained of life: eyes, a nose, the hint of a mouth—all suspended on a backdrop of badly molded paste. Where was he going? His face said that it didn't know, said that it didn't care. Perhaps he no longer knew who he was; perhaps he was dead. And then he vanished.

246

Laboring toward the square, Simon thought: *Came and gone.* His knees cried out as if bone grated against bone. And then he knew why he wouldn't see Cass, wouldn't see him even if he was wanted. Because Cass had always known the secret: of the dice, of Lucky, of Fallsville (and so knew more than Simon himself); knew and did not reveal his knowledge; deprived Simon of offering what he had always thought of as the last hidden piece of himself—to be told in the twilight of dotage, when each could accept the ravings of the other's senility without a qualm.

He had been upstaged. His fear had been a mask for the contempt that secret-bearers must necessarily have for the people to whom they refused to give. Had he been waiting to tell it all, surrender that last piece, only to exhibit the depth of his suffering, more suffering than even a martyr with mangled flesh? But it was as impossible to remember one's sufferings, as it was impossible to believe in the inevitability of one's own death.

He knew nothing now, but he could accuse himself of any conceit. He had no time to think; he stared ahead at the bank where he was no longer sure he kept his money; at the A&P where he could not remember shopping each week. Rage gouged his insides, burned him as if he had been plunged into hell, blurring the soldiers monument that hovered above him on the square. He stopped, engorged and paralyzed by the desire to murder, destroy, tear the world from the tendons which foolishly kept it from spinning insanely into the blackness of space, where it should immolate itself into a cinder.

*And the Lord said: "Art thou my servant?" And he said: "Verily," and went forth into the world. A black hat. Swallow-tailed coat. Tin Lizzie. Uncorked a bottle with one eye cocked at the sky and the hills or wherever God was or should have been, and preached and shot sacred craps and thumped a Bible and baptized and saved and carved a pew from any old ditch, bench, box, or running board; and almost ate a parrot and banged a wall-eyed farm girl whose perfume was sheepshit and sour milk, and was shotgunned for it. And ran. Uncorking more bottles and running, tipping them into his mouth on the run, scuttering through the asshole of America in the Lizzie and, looking up one day at the sky, couldn't even locate a strand of God's falling* hair. So he searched deeper in the bottle, in ditches brimming with rancid brackish hopes. Catching God in the thick concave bottom of an empty uptilted bottle, except that what he saw was a putrescent sun made gangrenous by the sickness of his drunkard's fragmented prism. Ran. Until he killed by proxy a boy in a river. And woke one morning not dead, and so just quit to commemorate the miracle. Found a town and ran into the profession of death so he could avoid life. Thereby becoming immortal. Found a friend. And he loved him. He did. He ran into himself. Corked the bottle and ran where he was definitely certain to be found: into himself.

With an agonizing wrench of his shoulder, he flailed out his arm and fired the pipe at the monument. A plonging echo of hollow metal and a sharp fine spray of briarwood shards, and then nothing but the slitted suspicious eyes of three old men sitting on a bench. He stared at the eyes, but they were not staring back; they were focused inward on another place, another time, expelling whatever memories they dredged up in globs of spit. And when the spit was dried up, when the river in their souls in which it was produced dried up, they would die.

Watching them, he trembled with loneliness and longing, then turned from the monument and the eyes and set off for Cass Nowell's house.

Thinking: Peace. Thinking: Amen.